"It's no good. We aren't going to pick up where we left off,"

Jordan said, shaking her head, her smile bitter.

Furious with her for sounding as if resisting their attraction was so easy, Stone challenged her. "Prove it. Make me believe you're not interested in what we had that night."

Then he locked his mouth to hers in a kiss that was as unapologetic as it was fierce.

Oh, yes. It was this that he'd been compelled—driven—to experience again. The flash of disbelief. That incredible heat. That searing sting of life. From the instant their lips connected, it was as if sunshine broke through the armor of night. Something unrepentant, free…and not quite controllable…took hold.

No, Stone's memory hadn't exaggerated.

It was exactly as it had been that shocking, anonymous night in Memphis….

Dear Reader,

What better cure for a hectic holiday season than settling in with romantic stories from Special Edition? And this month, we've got just what you've been searching for.

THE JONES GANG is back, with bestselling author Christine Rimmer's latest title, *Honeymoon Hotline*. Nevada Jones is November's THAT SPECIAL WOMAN!, and this adviser to the lovelorn is about to discover love firsthand!

Andrea Edwards's latest miniseries, GREAT EXPECTATIONS, continues this month with *One Big Happy Family*. If Big Sky Country is your kind of place, you won't want to miss *Montana Lovers*, the next book in Jackie Merritt's newest series, MADE IN MONTANA.

And the passion doesn't end there—for her first title in Special Edition, Helen R. Myers has a tantalizing tale of reunited lovers in *After That Night*.... Rounding out the month are a spellbinding amnesia story from Ann Howard White, *Making Memories*, and a second chance for two lovers in Kayla Daniels's heartwarming *Marriage Minded*.

I hope you enjoy all that we have in store for you this November. Happy Thanksgiving Day—all of us at Silhouette would like to wish you a happy holiday season!

Sincerely,

Tara Gavin
Senior Editor

Please address questions and book requests to:
Silhouette Reader Service
U.S.: 3010 Walden Ave., P.O. Box 1325, Buffalo, NY 14269
Canadian: P.O. Box 609, Fort Erie, Ont. L2A 5X3

HELEN R. MYERS

AFTER THAT NIGHT...

SPECIAL EDITION

Published by Silhouette Books
America's Publisher of Contemporary Romance

With special thanks to Merle Davis,
Texas Parks and Wildlife Department,
for her insight and generosity,
and
to B. J. Atkinson for research, advice
and, above all, true friendship.

 SILHOUETTE BOOKS

ISBN 0-373-24066-X

AFTER THAT NIGHT...

Books by Helen R. Myers

HELEN R. MYERS

satisfies her preference for a reclusive life-style by living deep in the Piney Woods of East Texas with her husband, Robert, and—because they were there first—the various species of four-legged and winged creatures that wander throughout their ranch. To write has been her lifelong dream, and to bring a slightly different flavor to each book is an ongoing ambition.

Admittedly restless, she says that it helps her writing, explaining, "It makes me reach for new territory and experiment with old boundaries." In 1993, the Romance Writers of America awarded *Navarrone* the prestigious RITA for Best Short Contemporary Novel of the Year.

Prologue

"**I** think the lady meant what she said." As he spoke, the stranger stepped between Jordan Mills and the two men who'd been persistent in their attempts to pick her up. "Take a walk, boys."

His gray sports jacket stretched across an impressive back, more than wide enough to block Jordan's view, so that when he shifted, she couldn't tell whether he intended to backhand one of them or was reaching into an inside pocket. Reaching for what? She suffered a moment's anxiety over not knowing what this human guard dog was up to. But apparently his presence was enough. No doubt the two men came to the conclusion that she was more trouble than she was worth and backed away.

Relieved, she murmured her thanks to her unsolicited protector and returned her attention to the snifter of brandy before her. Grateful though she was, she hoped he would go away, too. Surely he hadn't chased off those two hayseeds just to make room for himself?

"You shouldn't be here."

Once she realized he'd directed that comment at her, Jordan groaned to herself. Welcome back to the South, she thought with a newly honed cynicism. She could almost hear huge, rusty gates slamming shut back at the Mason-Dixon line—and on what had been her life. Maybe this stranger meant well, but his words only reminded her of what lay down the road: a gray, cheerless existence. That's why she'd been so impulsive about taking the extra day and stopping to spend the night in Memphis. It was also why she'd come into the hotel lounge before retiring to her room. She was trying to summon enough courage to face this new hand of cards that life had dealt her. Sir Galahad here wasn't helping in the least.

"And exactly which century do you come from?" she asked, making no attempt to hide her opinion of his statement. Although she didn't look up from her drink, she could feel his intense scrutiny.

"Listen, I'm only the messenger, okay?"

"Fine. But I'm over twenty-one, and last time I looked, this was still a free country."

"Point taken. Sorry to have bothered you."

Jordan expected him to leave at that moment. No man she knew would find any encouragement in such a rejection. But he didn't. To her surprise, he slid onto the bar stool beside hers.

"Scotch," he told the bartender. "On the rocks."

The man behind the counter nodded, expertly flipped over a tumbler and dipped it into a bin of ice cubes. Jordan watched as the guy's moussed hair wilted from the pace he'd been keeping in the dimly lit, busy lounge. Lovely, she thought with an inner sigh, apparently Sir Galahad intended to make certain she left sooner rather than later by making her as uncomfortable as possible.

Well, you deserve it, sweetie.

Her conscience was right. Just as it wasn't like her to frequent bars, she normally went out of her way to avoid being confrontational, not to mention being rude. She was a staunch advocate of honesty and succinctness, to be sure, but never impolite.

Terrific. She had only left Massachusetts two days ago and wouldn't reach Mount Liberty, Texas, until noon or so tomorrow, but between Brent and the Reverend, her personality was undergoing faster alterations than Dr. Jekyll had suffered from his fictional serum.

The bartender served the stranger his drink, and Jordan took a much-needed sip of hers. She knew she owed her rescuer an apology. The question was, would he understand that's all she was offering? She was too physically and emotionally tired for another major error in judgment; nevertheless, there was only one way to find out.

"I'm sorry for the way I reacted," she told the speckled marble between her elbow and his.

"No problem."

"It's just that I didn't come in here looking for company."

"Neither did I."

She nodded. That was good, as good as anything else he could have said. They could let things drop there...and did.

Several minutes later, Jordan swallowed the last trickle of brandy. After replacing the snifter onto the counter, she slipped her bag's strap over her shoulder and eased off the bar stool. The liquor warmed her stomach. The stranger remained silent. She felt ... almost human again, and less as if she were teetering on the edge of some abyss. She could go up to her room and get a few hours of real rest instead of lying there tense and stiff, full of worry and regrets. But before she could slip by him, the stranger turned his head and looked at her.

Jordan tried to convince herself that the punch she felt upon making eye contact had to do with their close proximity, not the dark-haired man's expression. Maybe his eyes were heart-clenching blue and, like his hard face, so stark with pain and grief that she had to will herself not to wince.

She had her own problems. She didn't have room or energy to hurt for someone else. And yet...she couldn't make herself move.

"Take care."

She read his lips more than heard him speak. "You, too."

Somehow she managed to tear her gaze from his, to put one foot before the other and step away from the bar. Stunned, she was at the elevator before she recovered her sense of control and spotted him walking toward her.

Her heart sank anew. Surely he didn't think...he wouldn't—

"Don't look at me that way," he muttered, more grim faced than before. "I'm trying to help. Didn't you see how those two guys watched you leave?"

"No." She'd been preoccupied with trying to deal with *his* attention.

"Check behind me. I'll bet you anything that they've come out into the lobby. They're probably waiting to see if you go up alone."

She did as he directed and saw that he was right. "Maybe I should notify the front desk. I could ask for a bellman to escort me to my room."

"From what I can tell, the average age of the staff around here is somewhere between pension and death. If you'll allow me, I'll be glad to do it, then take the elevator straight down to the garage. I'm not staying over. I only stopped long enough to get something to eat and have one drink before getting back on the road. As it is, it'll be past midnight before I get home."

Did he mean that? He seemed honest. At the same time, she found it unusual for a perfect stranger to offer to go that far out of his way to help someone. What stopped her from turning him down was that this was one of Memphis's older hotels, and while merely a modest five floors high, there were long hallways that weren't well lit. Since she'd previously concluded that many of the rooms on her floor seemed to be vacant, it might be smart to have an escort. Should it be him, though?

He turned out to be decent at the bar, didn't he?

True. But beneath that banker-neat hair—which was brown, not black, as she'd first guessed—was a face of someone not to be taken for granted, a face that looked as if it hadn't cracked a smile in ages. Good bones and attractive, she mused, interesting features, to be sure, but no less intimidating than a Marine drill instructor's. Or a murderer's?

It was the other two men who convinced her to take a chance. They continued to meander around the worn but antique-rich lobby, all the while covertly watching them. Jordan decided if she had to face trouble, she would prefer to do it in the company of this capable-looking stranger.

"All right. I would appreciate that," she told him just as the elevator groaned to a halt and ornate doors slid open.

She waited for him to follow her into the musty car before she pushed the button that would direct them toward the third floor. The doors rumbled closed. With a shudder, the elevator began a reluctant ascent.

On this ride, the noise level seemed worse than the first two times she'd used the car. She was about to warn her fellow passenger of the less-than-smooth stops when the elevator surprised them with a violent lurch. Wearing high heels designed for something far less physical than amusement-park rides, Jordan felt herself thrown off balance and grabbed for the first solid thing she could reach. To her chagrin, that turned out to be her companion.

"What the hell—?" The stranger used his entire body to keep her from toppling, but it was the electronic panel that earned a few more choice expletives from him. "We've stopped between the second and third floors!"

Embarrassed to have been reduced to grappling with the man, Jordan struggled to regain her footing. As soon as she succeeded, she stepped back to take a firm grip of the handrail.

"Are you okay?" He shot her a quick glance.

"Yes, but I'm so sorry to have gotten you into this mess." To think she'd chosen this landmark hotel for its quaintness. Now she had to wonder if her whimsical choice wasn't about to get them both injured, if not killed!

"Don't worry about it. Let's concentrate on getting out of here."

His tone, though gruff, held a soothing note. Grateful for it, and that he seemed more than willing to ignore their unexpected intimacy, Jordan watched as he experimented with several buttons on the panel. It took a few tries, but finally, as abruptly as before, the car jerked into motion.

"Thank heavens," she whispered, already altering her plans as to how she was going to get herself and her suitcase downstairs in the morning. No way would she be gambling her life in this contraption again!

They literally creaked the remaining distance to the third floor. If she wasn't so anxious, she might have found it funny that her companion edged toward the doors the instant she did. No tentativeness here—and for good reason, too, she realized seconds later, when the doors slid open and the car suddenly gave another horrifying jolt before slipping several inches.

"Move!" The stranger swept her out of the car and leapt himself.

She'd never been more terrified in her life! They went skidding across the hall and crashed in a tangled heap onto the hardwood floor. As the stranger crushed her flat, the force of their fall and weight of his large frame squooshed the air out of Jordan's lungs.

His groan came as a hot expulsion against her nape, followed by another when he swore again. To his credit, he did attempt to get off her without becoming more familiar with her anatomy than he already was. Inevitably, however, thighs rubbed against thighs, and groin nestled with shocking accuracy against derriere; Jordan stopped breathing completely when—in the process of trying to help her up—

the man inadvertently learned that her breast could fill his hand to perfection.

He quickly adjusted his hold and swung her to her feet.

"I'm really sorry about all that. Did I hurt you?"

Some part of her mind surmised that she would be lucky if she was merely black and blue by morning, but the rest of her concentration stayed elsewhere. On the hands that lingered at her waist, for example. She could also see awareness in his remarkable eyes and knew a similar sensitivity had to show in hers, as well.

"You couldn't help it. At any rate, I'm twice as embarrassed as bruised." And from the way her right heel wobbled, she knew she wouldn't be wearing her favorite slingback pumps again. Doubting she could even make it to her door, she took advantage of his protective hold and slipped off both shoes. Unfortunately that reduced her more confident five foot nine to where she barely reached his chin.

"You did fine. We should sue this place for negligence," he added with a renewed surge of temper. "That damned elevator is going to kill somebody if it isn't repaired."

"I—I'll notify the front desk as soon as I get to my room." She swallowed. Maybe it was aftershock or the depth of his anger, but her insides wouldn't stop quaking, and the way his thumbs kept stroking her sides didn't help. To make matters worse, her hair was tumbling loose from its neat chignon. With it flowing down to her breasts, she knew she resembled a lost flower child far more than a capable professional. The way the stranger stared at her only confirmed that.

"You're not going to faint on me, are you?"

"I've been rattled, I haven't had a lobotomy," she replied, annoyed that any weakness showed. But she had an awful feeling that if she didn't sit down soon, she might lose what little dinner she'd managed to eat.

With a softer "Damn," the stranger slipped a powerful arm around her waist. "Okay, tough guy, which way to your room?"

Too grateful to protest, Jordan pointed left, then she fumbled for the key in her blazer pocket.

They negotiated the shadowy corridor, and with each step she became increasingly conscious of being the only people around and how attentive he was to her every step. That reminded her of what she'd walked away from, memories of intimacy she didn't know if she ever wanted to experience again. Most of all, it made her think of the days, months...perhaps years of emptiness that lay like a gaping black hole before her. Small wonder that by the time they reached her door, she was shaking all the more, and her rescuer had to take the key from her trembling grasp to get the dead bolt unlocked.

"I'll make the call," he told her, his tone leaving no room for argument.

She didn't try. Again she thought it was crazy and completely unlike her, but she knew if left to her own devices, she would do something stupid during the call, like burst into tears...or worse yet, hysterics. Of course, she knew it wasn't just the mishap with the elevator or those creeps downstairs that was unraveling her. But her mystery rescuer needn't know any of that.

"Do you want me to ask them to get you a doctor? He could give you something to help you sleep."

She shook her head. "I'll be fine."

He was very good at taking control. Brisk without being rude, he left no doubt of the seriousness of their mishap and his displeasure with the condition of the elevator. Apparently satisfied with the response he was given, he hung up—and for the first time seemed to realize where he stood. His gaze slid from the turned-down bed to the lingerie that she'd set out on the nearby chair to wear tomorrow morning. All her best things because she knew she'd need all the courage she could get going into the dour environment that she was headed for. Clearing his throat, the stranger headed for her—or more accurately, the door.

"They assured me that someone will be on the job shortly to take care of the problem, but ring downstairs in the morning before you get into that thing, okay?"

"Of course. Thank you. For everything. I know I wasn't—"

Stopping before her, he waved away the rest of her rambling chatter. "I'm glad I was there to help."

"You're very kind."

That earned her a long appraising look. "No, I'm not. And you should know that you're not the tough cookie you pretended to be downstairs."

A smile was out of the question, but she managed a wry grimace and a weak shrug. "It's a new image. I guess it needs work."

"Yeah. Bunches." His eyes held hers captive. "I don't want to ask why you think it's necessary."

"Good."

His gaze began to roam over her face. "I don't want to know."

"I don't want to talk about it, either."

"Fine. Perfect."

Which meant there was nothing more to say. He would be leaving now...if she would just open the door. Instead, they continued to stand there, as still as the air around them, caught in some web of emotion that was as incredible as it was unbreakable.

She didn't mean to touch his arm.

He didn't look at all happy as he raised a hand to her hair. "My God, you're lovely."

Suddenly everything before her seemed to shift into slow motion. He lowered his head and touched his lips to hers, which ought to have triggered such a shock they should have jerked away from each other as if someone had ignited a Fourth of July firecracker between them. But it didn't. At least, the explosion didn't separate them.

His mouth shouldn't have felt so right against hers...not with the first kiss, or the second or third. Once again, she felt the power of him; it vibrated everywhere, even from the carpet beneath her feet. She curled her toes around the fibers just as she closed her fingers around the fabric of his jacket, wanting to draw closer to his strength and masculinity before he vanished like all the other good dreams she'd ever had.

With a groan, he tore his mouth free and stared down at her. "This is nuts."

"I know."

"Throw me out and lock the door."

She knew she should, but his arms were steel bands holding her tightly to him, defying her to try. "Why not just leave?"

"Because I'm not sure I can. Because I'm realizing how badly I want to stay. Only... there's no future in it."

"None." And that's what made this both so frightening and so right.

Uttering something unintelligible, he ducked his head again and sought her lips for a hungrier kiss. That one went on and on, until—from somewhere far beyond the rushing in her ears—she heard the lock on the door set.

The last rational thought Jordan had was the revelation that she had yet to ask him his name. But within the span of heartbeats, that, like everything else sane and logical, ceased to matter.

Chapter One

Six months later

Her feet ached. Her throat ached. In fact, Jordan thought as she drove out of the Mount Liberty High School parking lot, every inch of her hurt from the roots of her hair down. And worst of all was her throbbing head. If she survived the rest of the week as the supervisor of after-school detention without ripping up her teaching certificate, it would be a miracle.

Kids. They had never been as wild and uncontrollable when she'd been a student.

Now guess who you sound like?

How good it would be to get home. First she would draw a hot bath. Soak until her skin pruned thoroughly. No, first she would light some candles. And wasn't there at least one glass of wine left in that luscious bottle of chardonnay she'd splurged on during last month's drive to Dallas? Just imagining the medley of flavors romancing her palate and cooling her insides while the bathwater warmed her on the outside had her sighing in blissful anticipation.

At the Stop sign, a familiar ancient green-and-white pickup truck rambled by. Good old Mrs. Graves. As usual, the woman delivered a haughty stare that would have served the battle-ax better if she'd been in a limousine. In turn, Jordan did her best to pretend she didn't notice. After the wreck passed, though, she reached for her sunglasses—as much to shield her eyes against the late-afternoon sun as to avoid the world in general.

"Mean biddy." She turned onto Main Street but stayed well behind the smoking vehicle to avoid its fumes. "Where's the police when you need them?"

She didn't like the widow, and for more than personal or ecological reasons. The woman owned the farm adjacent to the school, and this year when the agriculture department asked to lease her pasture for their Future Farmers program, she hadn't batted an eye as she'd doubled her usual lease price. Adding insult to injury, she continually complained that the marching band played too loudly during field practice. It escaped Jordan how someone with such a greedy and sour disposition could also have been such a devoted member in her father's congregation. Then again, there was that "bird of a feather" adage, she thought with a mirthless smile; she supposed it could apply to hypocrites as easily as anyone else. In any case, at the Reverend's funeral, no one had cried harder or louder than Winifred Graves, and no one had been more judgmental of Jordan for not shedding a tear.

Well, old woman, I tried to tell you some things were just impossible.

Jordan had been back six months now, and the Reverend had been gone for four, but Mrs. Graves, among others, continued to make sure she felt like an outsider. It was a heck of a thing, considering that—except for being born in

Dallas—she'd grown up here. But far be it for her to expect logic from the good souls of Mount Liberty. Why, Rosemary Turner, who'd been buried a few days after the Reverend, had lived in the community for eighty-five of her ninety years, yet to her dying day she'd been considered a "transplant." It was only last week that Jordan heard someone finally refer to sweet Miss Turner as "a former local girl." If it took dying to achieve that nominal acceptance, Jordan figured she would remain an outcast. With pleasure.

Actually she found comfort in the solitude Mount Liberty clannishness provided. It was why she'd stayed on. She'd been seeking privacy, and since her father had kept his word about leaving her the deed to his house, once she heard that the high school had been in need of a new English teacher, it seemed the most reasonable thing in the world to get herself recertified to teach in Texas and apply for the job. New England had held nothing for her anymore, and one place seemed as good as another these days.

Jordan smiled to herself, pleased with her adaptability. Privacy-loving people could thrive where they were ignored or shunned. "So take that, Mrs. Graves," she said to the pickup as it turned in to Value Shop Grocery's parking lot.

As she approached downtown, traffic slowed to a Sunday-driver crawl. That gave her time to study the next clunker she found herself behind. The rusting sedan contained a Hispanic family of eight or ten—it was difficult to get an accurate count with so many small arms and legs flailing about. High-pitched screeches and loads of laughter poured out of the open windows. Between gaps in the writhing mass, Jordan occasionally glimpsed the mother clutching the steering wheel with such an intensity she looked as if she were navigating through a mine field, not the single-lane, farm-to-market road that ran straight through town. Small wonder, since none of the children appeared to be older than twelve or so.

"Shangri-la," Jordan murmured, watching the woman inch the relic with its wire-hanger antenna into a parking spot in front of Mount Liberty Drugs and Gifts. One of the little urchins probably had the sniffles or an earache, thanks to September's cooler nights.

To think she'd been grumbling over *her* challenging day. Shaking her head, she rolled to a stop behind the next vehicle waiting for the only traffic light in town to turn green. She used the opportunity to glance around a bit more.

A few dozen shoe-box-size stores made up the downtown. It hadn't changed much since she last left, almost nine years ago. One or two were minus their signs, thanks to the variety of storms that blew through East Texas. The owners' lack of anxiety about getting them rehung reflected just how well everyone knew everyone else around here.

Almost everyone, she amended as she finally settled her gaze on the gray four-wheel-drive truck ahead of her. From this angle, she couldn't see the doors to check for the blue, green and white state seal, but from the amount of mud on the back end and what she could see of the driver in the Western hat, she had a hunch this was one of the game-warden vehicles.

Where had he found mud in this weather? Usually Septembers were wet around here, but they had yet to receive a drop of rain, so the land—a combination of sandy loam and red clay—was parched. She supposed that meant the driver had spent his day at some marshy bottomland or at one of the countless area lakes. She'd only seen a truck like this a few times since returning to Wood County, and then from a distance. She wouldn't be able to describe the state official if it meant winning the lottery. What was his name? she mused, trying to remember one of the reports filed by the game warden in the local paper.

What she could see of the face in the outer rearview mirror was that he had a five-o'clock shadow and that, like her, he wore sunglasses. The whiskers emphasized a strong jaw, which was being worked hard at the moment.

Nice to see she wasn't the only one who got frustrated with that prolonged red light. "A person could drive the eighteen miles to Quitman before this thing turned green," she muttered. She'd come to the conclusion that this light and that tacky billboard outside of town were the extent of the chamber of commerce's creativity in devising a Shop Mount Liberty First advertising campaign.

Suddenly the man in front of her looked into the outside mirror, which made her uncomfortable. When he frowned and inched closer to it, discomfort turned to embarrassment. He couldn't have heard her; her windows were only open a few inches. Not that it would take a lip-reader to figure out what she'd been saying.

Her embarrassment grew into unease as she watched him reach up and draw down his glasses. Not completely. Just enough for him to see her without the filter...and for her to see him.

She wished he hadn't. With her mouth turning as dry as the sunbaked road, she lowered her glasses, too. Her heart lurched painfully in her chest.

It couldn't be!

Surely fate didn't have such a sick sense of humor! She all but touched her nose to the steering wheel in her attempt to get a better look at him. Oh, yes, she remembered those eyes...and now that she was paying attention, she recognized his arrow-sharp nose, too. As for his wide, sensual mouth...she would merely have to close her eyes to recall the feel of it against hers, against—

She could just die.

The car behind her honked, jarring them both out of their stupor. The man in the truck straightened, and the vehicle lurched forward through the intersection. Jordan didn't handle her car with any greater finesse, turning south onto Peach Road. Only when the truck was out of sight did she remember to breathe, and then she went straight into hyperventilating.

This couldn't be! She'd made a mistake—that's all. The driver had looked enough like him that her eyes and memory had played a trick on her.

You mean succumbed to wishful thinking?

Of course not! Besides, it had been dark most of the time they'd been together.

"Oh, Lord..." She didn't want to think about that!

No, she'd been right before...six months was a long time. Why, she could barely picture Brent's face, and she had loved him! Or thought she did. In the beginning.

By the time she passed the service station that marked the unofficial end of downtown, she almost had herself convinced. Her heart slowed to a near-regular beat, and invisible hands no longer threatened to twist her stomach into a pretzel. She was about to laugh at herself for being a silly ninny when a movement drew her gaze back to her rearview mirror.

His gray truck pulled in behind her. Dear heaven, he must have gone around the block and come out at Pine Street!

This was no mistake.

What was she going to do?

What was she going to do?

Stone watched the woman in the white car accelerate and adjusted his speed accordingly. Her response erased any doubts lingering in his mind. She was the one...his moment of lost sanity in Memphis.

What was she doing in Mount Liberty? How long had she been here? Most important of all, how long would she be staying?

"Come on," he urged under his breath, "pull over."

She didn't. Instead, she drove almost three more miles south before turning into a long residential driveway. Stone could only follow.

Did the modest wooden house belong to her? Nestled within the same dogwood, pine and hardwood trees for which East Texas was famous, the dove gray, chalet-style dwelling with the red shutters and flower boxes was attractive if somewhat small compared to what he would have expected to find her living in.

Expected? You never expected to see her again!

The name on the rural mailbox read J. L. Mills and listed the required route and box numbers. The name didn't begin to answer the dozens of questions racing through his mind. What it did do, however, was remind him that they'd never exchanged names...as if they'd been trying to protect themselves from such a moment. What a joke.

She stopped. He braked behind her and shut off his vehicle's engine. But he didn't climb out right away; he needed another few seconds to gather his wits. He'd already had a bad day, due to the new signs of poaching he'd come across over in the easternmost part of the county. It had left him feeling more edgy and combustible than usual, and was yet another of the reasons he would have preferred living a more solitary life. However, with Kristen so much a part of his world now, that was no longer possible.

But all of that had nothing to do with this. This strange, difficult-to-decipher reaction he was going through was entirely due to the woman in front of him.

Her door opened, and sexy high heels emerged, followed by trim ankles and shapely calves. Without conscious invitation, he remembered how he'd been drawn to explore the shape and sleekness of her legs again and again that night.

He felt a bead of sweat building on his forehead.

As before, she wore a suit, this one a conservative navy. But there was nothing modest about where the skirt inched to when she ducked back inside the vehicle to retrieve her purse. The view brought back the memory of walking into that hotel bar and seeing her cross her legs.

Once again Stone dealt with the guilt of having a strong sexual attraction for the woman who didn't bear even the faintest resemblance to his sweet Tracy. This woman was extremely fair, where Tracy had been dark. She had a dancer's lean tautness, slim hips and a girl's narrow waist. Tracy had been softer and rounder. The only part of this woman's anatomy that came close to deserving the term *lush* were her breasts, and he didn't want to think about them. But he did ... and as on that night months ago, there was no stopping his body from tightening with sheer, primitive lust.

Feeling more off balance than ever during these past two ungodly years, he shoved open his door. The professional in him noted there were no other vehicles around. Nevertheless, instinct cautioned him to be slow in stepping from behind the protection of the truck's door. A jealous husband or lover could be every bit as dangerous and unpredictable as a wanted felon. More. It was the woman's pale face and shell-shocked eyes that made him abandon his training and venture closer.

"Small world," he murmured, filing away the thought that in sunlight her wheat blond hair shimmered with as many shades of gold as of silver. In the faint bathroom light of her hotel room, it had seemed like pure silver thread...the spun moonbeams of fairy tales.

"Very."

"You seem a bit embarrassed."

"Aren't you?"

Of all the emotions playing havoc with his insides, embarrassment couldn't be counted among them. He might harbor some regrets, but he felt no shame. "Call it surprised. Have you been in town long?" Surely not. He would have seen her by now. Mount Liberty's population had yet to break eight hundred, and he moved through the county almost more than the sheriff and his deputies.

"Six months. I was on my way back here the night I...the night we ..."

"I understand." At least that part. But one thing she said had him frowning. "Wait. You said 'back.' "

"This is where I grew up. I was born in Dallas, but we moved here when I was a baby. After my mother died."

He hadn't believed she could stun him any more than she already had. This was one of the county's main thoroughfares. The road crossed the highway to Quitman, the county seat, and continued in a roundabout way to Tyler. So why hadn't their paths crossed sooner?

He shook his head at the irony of it all. "Why did you come back?"

"The— My... father asked me to. He was dying. Cancer."

There was quite a bit of that going around these days. Death. Dying. Heaven knows, he could vouch for that. And while they didn't know each other well enough to offer words of sympathy, Stone figured they knew too much not to say something.

"Don't grope for niceties," she said as he opened his mouth. "The Reverend and I weren't close. He considered his congregation his real family. He was pastor at First Fellowship Christian Church."

Stone thought of the austere chapel on the northeast side of town and wondered about the man whose daughter referred to him as "the Reverend." Did that explain why she'd looked so sad, so lost when they'd met? She seemed only slightly more at peace now, but he envied her even that achievement.

"What do you do?" he asked, steeling himself against his own pain all this reminiscing triggered.

"I teach English at the high school." Her gaze dropped to the gun on his right hip before eyeing his truck. "And you're... ?"

"The game warden. In Franklin County for several years, and Wood County for about twenty months."

"That explains a great deal. I left Texas for the last time just after I graduated from college and didn't return until the Reverend contacted me about his condition."

"Where was home until then?"

"New England."

Her decision not to be specific didn't pass unnoticed. Unable to resist, he asked, "You're not planning to go back?"

"No."

He waited for her to elaborate. There was a great deal going on behind those surprisingly dark, doe-like eyes that were at once vulnerable as they were wary. It had been their palpable melancholy that kept him from walking away from her in Memphis, and it was exactly what made him want to run now. But he didn't. Instead, he heard himself ask, "Is this going to present problems for you?"

"This?"

"Us. The fact that we know each other."

"Do we? I would hardly put it in those terms."

Hell. He could deal with her frankness—he even admired it—but this uppity attitude was something else. "All right. Is there a husband or someone who would be upset about what happened in Memphis?"

"Believe me, I wouldn't be standing here if there was." Her confidence slipped a notch or two. "You?"

"No." And that left them with nothing more to worry about. Despite the passion that had burned holes into every layer of his common sense six months ago, they'd practiced safe sex. He could get into his truck and go on with his life. She was okay. They both were. No enraged husband or lover would be hunting him to avenge an unwanted pregnancy or careless contamination.

He could make tracks. But before he took that step, he blurted out, "I never got to know your name."

"You didn't want to know it."

Had he labeled her "uppity"? She was a natural smart aleck. Worse than him.

He put his hands on his hips. "Well, I'm asking now."

Her gaze dropped to his badge and the gun again. "Jordan. Jordan Leslie Mills."

That explained the initials on the mailbox. The name suited her, at once denoting strength yet femininity, much like the woman did in the flesh. "I'm Stone Demarest." He watched for a reaction. When there failed to be one, he couldn't deny that her lack of interest stung.

She hid her soulful eyes with sable brown lashes. "I know," she said after several seconds. "I mean, I realize that now because I've seen your name in the newspaper."

She had to be referring to the weekly arrest reports in the *Mount Liberty Journal.* "That's not particularly interesting reading—unless you're looking for something or someone in particular."

"Is there anything wrong with being a compulsive reader?"

No, he supposed not, although she didn't resemble his idea of a bookworm. A model whose specialty was mattress ads maybe. It rattled him to realize that not much about her fit his preconceptions—outside of bed, that is. Growing warmer, he glanced around again. "Doesn't it bother you to live alone way out here by yourself?"

"I like being alone."

Great. The new Greta Garbo. "What I'm saying is that crime is on the increase everywhere these days. Rural areas aren't the safe havens they used to be."

"Then it doesn't matter where I live, does it?"

Stone dropped his gaze to the packed red clay between them. "I'm trying to do this without prying."

"Are you?"

"This is an awkward situation for both of us, and we'll be smart if we plan for the possibility of running into each other in the future. I'm simply trying to ensure that if and when it happens, it isn't the shock that it was today.''

"Do you live near here?"

"Not exactly. I'm west of town a few miles."

She lifted one shoulder. "Then I doubt we'll have a problem. Except for incidentals, I do most of my shopping in Tyler. Outside of school, I don't socialize. In other words, I meant what I said, I like my own company."

She couldn't have been more clear. Stone straightened and gave her a stiff nod. "That makes two of us. So I'll leave you to your life, and I'll get on with mine." Lord help him, he had enough worries without inviting more.

He returned to his truck and started the engine. Whatever had driven him to follow her was gone, frozen then pulverized by her rejection. By the time he had the truck turned and back on the farm-to-market road, one angry glance back told him that she'd retreated, too.

Didn't that figure? The first time he broke his own rule—in how long?—and had tried to be a little caring and considerate, look what it got him.

Well, Miss Jordan Leslie Mills could have her privacy. Absolutely. She couldn't know how relieved he was to accommodate her. What happened in Memphis had been a mistake, but it was over. She could play fantasy diva or turn into a sour-faced old prune with his blessings. His duty was done!

The moment Jordan closed and locked the door behind her, she slumped against the smooth wood and began shaking all over. She hadn't meant to sound like such a cold-hearted witch, but his unexpected appearance had rattled her so. This wasn't supposed to have happened!

Stone Demarest. The county game warden was Stone Demarest! Of all the scenarios she'd considered since that night last April, when—despite her attempts not to—thoughts of him flooded her mind, none could match this!

During the last few weeks of the Reverend's life, while sitting with him those long days and nights, she'd had no defense against the wistful images triggered by her imagination. She'd guessed the stranger must have been a cattle rancher or oilman...someone involved in an occupation that required physical work and hours outdoors to give him those callused hands, that permanent tan and weather-roughened skin. She shivered anew as she remembered the feel of those masculine hands exploring her. Not in her wildest dreams would she have pictured him as a state official...and why did he have to be a game warden for Wood County of all places?

She groaned and let her purse and briefcase drop to the floor. She needed that wine. Now.

On numb legs, she went straight to the kitchen, grateful that the refrigerator stood in line with the doorway. At the moment, she didn't know if she could handle anything requiring coordination.

A cool blast of air hit her once she opened the door, providing twofold relief. Not only did the chilled air soothe her feverish skin, but it helped clear her befuddled mind somewhat. She did, however, have to admit the heat wasn't all due to the room's temperature, and that had her snatching up the wine even as she wrestled with the buttons of her suit jacket. Left in her camisole, she was again grateful to be able to afford not having a roommate, and what a relief not to have a neighbor's house ten feet outside her kitchen window! At least she could walk around this way—or naked if it suited her—and she didn't have to worry about Peeping Toms or offending anyone.

After nudging the refrigerator door closed with her hip, she hooked her jacket over the back of the nearest dinette chair and reached for a wineglass from the open cupboard. Then she poured, and brooded on.

When she'd first noticed Stone Demarest's name in the paper, she'd thought it intriguing, perfect for a novel's protagonist. The strong name had her concluding that he must be one tough customer, considering how the paper repeatedly reported his relentless pursuit of those who violated the law. Then one day while getting gas, she overheard someone refer to him as "the Stone Man."

He was that, she thought as she sipped her drink and thought of the man in the straw hat and khaki uniform she'd just faced. He'd looked every bit capable of using that handgun in that holster. But how did she reconcile that persona with the man she'd slept with in Memphis? It wasn't the Stone Man who'd broken through her defenses and tapped into a depth of passion and desperation she hadn't known she'd possessed—was it?

Why not? He just used a secret weapon most of the men you've known didn't have a clue about, you fool. He used sensitivity!

Jordan promptly choked on the wine. With tears blurring her vision, she lowered herself to a chair and set the wobbling crystal onto the elegant smoky-glass table. Oh, yes, she remembered that skill very well. He'd made her feel as if she was... if not the first woman he'd had in a long time, at least that she mattered, that she was special, maybe even rare. He'd made her believe that her pleasure was as important to him as his own.

"It's not fair!" she cried to the empty room.

First to have to face Brent's lies, then to endure the Reverend again and now to be taunted with a living reminder of her one weak moment? What had she done to deserve this? Despite what the Reverend had claimed, she'd been a good daughter. And she would never have had that long affair with Brent if she'd known the truth about him. Once she realized what he had done—which ironically happened only days before she got that equally unforgettable call from her father—hadn't she made the right decision to call it quits?

That was why her reaction to Stone just now had been as abrupt as it was. She had no intention of having him or that night of sweet madness hanging over her head for the rest of her life. But heaven help her, help them both, if she'd failed to chase him off for good.

Jordan didn't sleep well that night; however, that came as no surprise. Between the coyotes, owls and her dreams, it would have been more odd not to keep waking every hour or so. By three in the morning, she gave up and made herself a cup of instant coffee, then another and another, while reading through her first-period junior class's compositions, which she hadn't expected to get to until the weekend.

By the time she arrived at school, she felt as if she'd already put in a full day. Her students picked up on it, too, as if through osmosis. Both the junior and senior groups behaved more like six- and seven-year-olds instead of teenagers on the brink of adulthood.

By the end of the day, she could happily have fed her diploma into a paper shredder. Unfortunately the only one available was in the main office, and she tried to avoid that place whenever possible. But regretting the day she'd decided she would like to spend her life helping young people expand their minds and hardly ready to cope with yet another blow, she drove toward home—and did a double take when she spotted Stone Demarest's truck once again in her rearview mirror.

The entire trip from the traffic light onward, she hoped against hope that it was a fluke . . . and watched in disbelief as he followed her into her driveway. With her heart bruising her ribs, she got out of her car to face heaven knew what.

He wasted no time getting to the point. Heading straight for her, he boxed her in the triangle of door and car and his chest.

"We need to talk," he announced, not looking any happier than she felt.

Chapter Two

Caught by the blue fire in Stone's eyes, Jordan almost missed seeing the parcel-post delivery truck that drove by. Only the reminder of what a conduit of information and misinformation delivery people could provide in rural areas had her rallying somewhat.

"Please." Trying to avoid too much contact, she gently pushed against Stone's chest, hoping he would get the hint. "Could we continue whatever you wanted to say inside? We're in full view of the street out here, and I don't think either one of us needs the gossip that could come from being seen together."

He glanced over his shoulder, spotting the infamous truck just before it disappeared down the hill. "You're right. I should have thought of that myself."

With a nod of agreement as much as gratitude, Jordan retrieved her things from her car and led the way. She could feel his gaze following her every step and had to concentrate not to stumble or drop her keys as she unlocked the front door. She also felt self-conscious about her home; the renovations were by no means completed. Would he get the wrong impression that she was a terrible housekeeper?

Very good, worrywart. Nothing like shirking off those old psychological chains.

All right, so she was making more progress in some areas than in others. If Madonna could have time off to reinvent herself, so could she.

As she opened the door, a barren, L-shaped living room—save a ladder, small mountain of sheets and several cans of eggshell white paint—greeted them, along with warm, stuffy air. Sighing because it was worse than she'd thought, Jordan made a beeline toward the base of the steps on the right side of the room to adjust the thermostat.

"As you can see, I'm still working on the place," she said, crossing back to see him.

"You did a good job with the kitchen."

She followed his nod toward the room she'd recently completed. The contrast from this austere room did draw the eye with the clean simplicity of white walls and the matching cabinets with their smoky glass doors. To add color and character, she'd added many touches of brass, ceramic molds and plants. The results were a stark but welcome change from the dreary tones of neglected wood still apparent throughout the rest of the house.

"Thank you. We'll be more comfortable in there," she said, leading the way. Of course, she'd lied. She wouldn't feel comfortable until he was gone! "Can I offer you something?" Realizing how suggestive that sounded, she quickly added, "Coffee? Iced tea? I don't have beer, but—"

"This isn't really a social call."

"Believe it or not, I would offer anyone something to drink when it's as warm as it is." For her part, she yearned to shed the jacket of her gray-and-black suit. Already she could feel the tendrils at the base of her chignon getting damp.

"Summer is hanging on. All right," he said, removing his hat. "Iced tea sounds good, thanks."

Glad for something to do to burn off some nervous energy, Jordan busied herself with taking out glasses and then the pitcher of tea from the refrigerator. She nodded to the small round table and two chairs by the windowed corner next to the refrigerator. "Have a seat."

He hesitated, eyeing the glass-and-chrome set with its tan suede seats. "I spent a good part of the day in the woods. Are you sure you want me on your furniture?"

"The fabric's treated...and sturdy." Even though his khaki shirt and pants didn't look as dirty as he'd suggested, Jordan could understand how her rather airy and feminine furniture would give pause to a man built like Stone Demarest. Wondering if there would be room for her to sit down once he got his long, muscular legs under her table, she added ice to the glasses, poured the tea and went to find out.

Even though he had only one leg under the table, and used the other to rest his hat on, Jordan had to settle for sitting sideways. "Which woods?" she asked, automatically crossing her legs.

It was a mistake. His gaze locked on her legs as if he'd just emerged from a year-long stay in solitary confinement. Not wanting to draw additional attention by uncrossing them and tugging at her skirt, she tried clearing her throat instead.

He snapped to attention. "Pardon?"

"You said you'd been in the woods. Is there a problem around here? Is that why you came back again?"

He looked out the window. She was glad she'd at least mowed the lawn last Sunday, but the yard remained essentially barren because her father had not believed in spending money on frivolous things like shrubs and trees. Because she was concentrating on the inside of the house, she hadn't yet had a chance to do much outside. Beyond the birdbath and ring of rosebushes were the dense woods that once belonged to the vast commercial timber industry in the forties, and were close to reaching their maximum size again.

The woods could hide many crimes. Poaching went on year-round, but more prevalent these days were the drug labs popping up on rarely inspected land. Surely he wouldn't be involved with any burglary investigation, although that, too, was common in rural areas where so many houses were left empty during the day while residents commuted to larger cities like Tyler and Longview. Sometimes after reading the local paper, particularly the arrest reports, she concluded that things hadn't changed much from the days when East Texas had been a haven for desperadoes, renegades and a variety of types who used the Pineywoods to protect them from the law and each other.

"No," Stone said, "you don't have to worry about anything like that."

He could have looked more convincing. Did that mean whatever he did have to say was even worse? As he rotated his glass between his hands, Jordan waited, noting again that he wore no rings, not even a watch. Was he going to tell her that he hadn't been entirely truthful yesterday, that he was in fact engaged? Or... heaven forbid, maybe he had discovered he had some communicable disease!

Lord, you're getting morbid.

"Look, I don't mean to be rude," she said, deciding she'd waited long enough, "but would you please tell me what's going on? I don't deal well with suspense. I can't even appreciate it as an entertainment form in film or fiction. It's an old childhood thing," she said, dismissing his quizzical look.

"I didn't mean to do that. It's just that I found out something last night that I thought we needed to discuss."

He looked so uncomfortable, so embarrassed, that she couldn't repress her dry wit. "Really? Well, if you're here to tell me that you're pregnant, forget it. The kid can't possibly be mine."

Few people, including the Reverend or Brent, had ever appreciated her rather droll sense of humor, and they certainly never understood that it was a survival mechanism. As a result, when a slow, sheepish smile tugged at one corner of Stone's firm mouth, Jordan wasn't quite sure that her eyes weren't playing tricks on her.

"I am being a jerk about this. Let me just get it out." He shifted in his seat and looked directly into her eyes. "The thing is that I have a niece who lives with me. We're not doing very well, although to be fair it's only been a few months since her father died. Lung cancer."

"He smoked?"

"Three packs a day."

"Incredible. He was your brother?"

"Brother-in-law. It hasn't been easy, and my niece and I are still trying to deal with our personal losses, let alone get used to each other."

That she could understand. It had only been four and a half months since the Reverend succumbed to his own bout with cancer. They had never been anywhere near close; even so, sometimes she still had bad moments with the hole now in her life. Of course, that hole was deep and wide because it had been growing since she'd been a child and realized he would never be the parent she'd wanted and needed. Phantom grief for the father who'd never existed, was how she described it.

"Where's her mother?" Jordan asked, repressing an impulse to reach over and squeeze his hand. Heaven knows where that impulse came from.

"Janine's been gone for years. She was killed by a drunk driver."

Despite her policy not to get involved with other people's problems, Jordan wasn't able to squelch completely a pang of compassion for the child. No wonder Stone's eyes continued to look as if he'd had a head-on collision himself. "That must have been rough . . . on everyone."

"Don't get me wrong, Kristen's a super kid, and I'm glad to be here for her, but my work intrudes. Usually when she needs to talk. Worse yet, I'll be the first to admit that I'm not at all clued in to what's going on in kids' heads these days."

What on earth was he driving at? What did any of this have to do with her? "From what I've heard and seen in my classrooms, I don't suppose a person who's never been a parent is any more disadvantaged than a person who's had children. We're all equally suspect in their eyes, and at a loss as to how to get through to them."

"But I had a child. A baby and a wife. Our house burned to the ground less than two years before Jackson died."

Jordan grappled with the perspiring glass slipping through her fingers; nevertheless, the tea spilled over the table and herself.

With a gasp, she sprang to her feet. "Of all the clumsy things!" She rushed to the counter for the dish towel. "Did I get any on you?"

"I'm fine. But your suit isn't."

"That's no problem. It's headed for the cleaners anyway." She made a quick wipe or two at the worst of the stain spreading across her lap before concentrating on the puddle on the table. The fussing gave her an opportunity to recover from his unexpected announcement. No wonder he'd looked so stricken in Memphis. Bad enough to lose one member of your family, but both, and in such a terrible way? And anyone would be a wreck at the prospect of being responsible for another person's child. She couldn't imagine herself in such a predicament as he'd found himself in so soon after his own family loss.

"I don't know what to say," she murmured once she finally sat down again. "All the clichéd responses feel inadequate to me."

"Don't worry about it. That's not why I told you, anyway."

Something about his glance from beneath his straight, stark eyebrows had her stomach twisting into a familiar knot. "Is—Kristen, right?—is Kristen close in age to what your daughter had been? Is that the problem?"

"Hardly. Billie Ann was three. Kristen's almost eighteen. What's troubling me is that you have her in your class."

It all came together at once. "Kristen Thomas is your niece?" A person would need a microscope to find any physical resemblance. Kristen was fair, closer to Jordan's coloring than his and built like a dancer. With Stone darker and clearly a throwback to more-rugged stock...well, the girl could more easily be mistaken for *her* kin than his. "Small world."

"Then you didn't know?"

"How could I?"

"That's good. I was concerned that somehow you might have heard something or figured it out. At any rate, I wanted to ask you to be easy with her if at all possible. Don't let what happened between us make you resent having her in your class."

Indignation came fast and without mercy. "Please tell me I misunderstood what you just said."

"Look, Kristen's talked about you before, only I didn't know who you were at the time. She admires you. She says you're exactly the kind of woman she wants to be—confident, thoughtful and independent. Considering what she's already been through in her young life, I don't know that she would recover if you were the cause for breaking her heart yet again."

A quiet fury seethed inside Jordan. "You have the audacity to believe that I would hurt a child because I did something stupid with her guardian?"

"I didn't say— What do you mean 'stupid'?"

"Don't change the subject."

"I said—" He almost knocked over his chair as he rose and paced across the kitchen. "All I was asking is for you to forget she's my niece."

Oh, he was digging himself a nice, deep hole. "I have a better idea. Why don't I forget you're her uncle?"

A faint flush darkened his bronzed face until he looked ready to explode. "How did I suddenly turn into the bad guy here?"

"By spouting ridiculous accusations, that's how!"

"What accusations? I was merely sharing a concern, voicing a rhetorical concept I thought we could discuss like mature adults."

"For your information, I have the mayor's son, the sheriff's nephew, the postmaster's daughter and the children of assorted businesspeople in my classes. That's what you face with teaching in a small town, and believe me, whatever their genealogy, all I care about is that they follow the curriculum I'm presenting in class."

He stood there looking as stiff and angry as she felt. "I didn't mean to offend you or to jump to the wrong conclusions."

"You forgot to add 'again.'"

Suddenly she had firsthand proof of why people called him the Stone Man. The planes of his face grew flinty, each feature almost taking on a razor's edge. The flint in his cool blue eyes could have sparked an inferno. No matter how she tried, Jordan knew she would never forget his touch, but right now she was grateful she had the length of the kitchen between them.

"Again," he replied, his voice low and lethal. "Unfortunately, since I only have intimate knowledge of your body, and I'm not a mind reader, and because I've been making nothing but one mistake after another with Kristen, I took a gamble and thought I'd try speaking from the heart. How was I to know that's the least accessible part of you?"

* * *

A half hour later, as Stone stopped downtown to top off his truck's gas tank, he continued to mentally kick himself. Any way he tried to look at it, he kept coming to the conclusion that he'd behaved like a gorilla at a tea party. Damn it, he should never have gone back to see her and left things to fate. Chances were things would have turned out far better.

By the time he reached home, he was thoroughly disgusted with himself. So much so that even the term *home* had him snorting in disdain.

Jackson's ranch house no more felt like his home than he felt comfortable in parental shoes. Besides his truck, the boxy three-bedroom dwelling with the yellow-gray brick and cracking concrete foundation had been the sum total of his brother-in-law's assets. Jackson had never worried about the future much, even after Janine's death. Stone supposed Kristen was lucky her father had purchased the house beforehand, or the poor kid wouldn't even have had that much of an inheritance. Her daddy sure hadn't made an effort to add anything to the place, either. The property remained as it was bought, with almost-empty flower boxes and no trees. An eyesore in a cluster of five houses that were manicured to perfection and had trees a timber company would drool at.

With a sigh, Stone parked beside Kristen's weeks-old red compact. He'd traded Jackson's pickup for it after Kristen begged to use her father's souped-up vehicle because her cheerleader-squad responsibilities taxed his own schedule beyond endurance. Not about to tempt fate by giving one emotion-driven young girl so much machine, he'd taken her straight to town for something with the smallest engine he could find. Thank goodness she'd fallen in love with the cherry color and sporty style on sight. Now, if only he could change her taste in boys.

Drained, he let his head fall back to the headrest. As expected, his churning thoughts continued, with disgust's only competition for space in his mind coming from shame.

When was he going to stop feeling as if every step forward cost him three steps back? Heaven knows he'd had justification for behaving like a bastard during those first weeks after the fire. Back then, it was understandable to strike out at anyone and everyone like some injured beast. And even when Jackson lost his fight with cancer, Stone didn't blame himself for the fear and fury that left him with a teenage girl to finish raising. But how did he justify being so quick on the verbal trigger with Jordan just because she'd proved to be a pretty closed book herself.

No doubt about it—life was taking its toll on him. Thirty-five wasn't old for traipsing through the woods, putting in sixteen-plus-hour days and taking calls around the clock, but it was near ancient for someone going from diapers straight to boyfriends with no training in between. And forget about dealing with the so-called weaker sex. If he hadn't known it before, Jordan Mills had set him straight: he didn't have a clue as to how to communicate with a woman.

Tracy had spoiled him. Sheltered him. With her sweet temperament and her "whatever you want, dear" attitude, he'd gone through his early adulthood like a new car getting a grace period on its inspection. How ill prepared that left him for the women of today, especially someone carrying as much emotional baggage as he did. Particularly when confronted with a complex puzzle like Jordan Mills.

Well, resolving that might be a lost cause, but at least she'd seemed sincere when she'd said that she wouldn't take out her regrets on Kristen. He should be grateful for that . . . even while the word *stupid* stuck in his mind.

She needn't know, but he'd often been thinking about the night they'd shared, and since their reunion, the memory had become a constant preoccupation. How could it not?

She'd not only taken away his breath, but she'd made him forget his emptiness. For a few precious hours, she'd re-awakened his sexuality and ever since left him uninterested in finding her equal.

How did you share that with a woman who treated you like something she couldn't get off the bottom of her shoe?

"Uncle Stone?"

At the sound of his name, he sat up and found Kristen standing between his truck and the garage, her purse under her arm as if she was ready to go somewhere. Frowning, he reached for the watch he kept on the gearshift column. It was almost six. Where on earth was she going now?

"Did I forget an appointment or something?" he asked as he eased his tired body out of the truck.

"Um, Terry, Michelle and I thought we'd grab a burger and then do some brainstorming on new cheers."

In that getup? She was wearing a half T-shirt and shorts that looked spread on like liquid deodorant. Did she have any clue as to what little it took to incite a teenage boy's hormones?

He took a deep breath. "But I thought we were going to spend the evening looking through more of your family things, boxing what you'll want to keep after you leave for college and phoning some charity to give away what you don't want."

"Not tonight. It's too depressing."

"But, Kris, the sooner we get it over with, the sooner you can get on with your life." For once, he was going to try to remember not to throw in that he didn't have all the time in the world to donate to this project.

"Uncle Stone, it's Thursday night. Tomorrow's our first game. If I don't stay loose and limber, I'm not going to be able to do those jumps and splits in the routines."

Who was she trying to kid? The only difference between her and a rubber band was that she had corkscrew curls that were tied in an adorable golden ponytail.

"Honey, come on...you're terrific." As he reached the front of the truck, she backed up to her car's front end to avoid his "hello" kiss on her cheek. Since he was used to that, too, it only hurt a little. "You, er, don't want to risk overpracticing, do you?"

"I won't. You go on in. Mrs. Tucker brought over a casserole for you, and it's on the stove. Just pop it in the microwave for a few minutes, and you'll be set."

She was too eager to get rid of him. He eyed her with new suspicion as she stayed rooted before the front end of the car and tried to usher him by. Pretty, with her father's sunny coloring and her mother's soft features, but guilty.

"Okay," he sighed. "If you promise..." His gaze fell on the awkward way she held her purse. She'd dropped it to her side and held it out sideways from her body. As if she was trying to create a wall. As if she wanted to hide something.

Giving her no warning, Stone nudged her out of the way. Only then did he see the shattered left headlight on her car.

"It's not what you think!" she cried, her expression anxious. "I didn't have an accident, and Jack's going to fix it tonight. He's getting a replacement over in Mineola right now. He promised!"

"John Nolan, Jr., never volunteers for anything resembling work."

"Well, he did, so that just goes to show you that you can be wrong."

Maybe, but he doubted it. "How did it happen?" The body looked intact, which told him that she hadn't had a collision with another car.

"Jack tripped and accidentally hit it."

"With what? That thick head of his?"

Of course, it was the wrong thing to say, as wrong as her deceit had been. Stone knew it before seeing the rebellious glint return to her eyes and the petulant thrust of her lips. Ironically it reminded him of Jordan's expression when he'd put his foot in his mouth over at her place. Could he do nothing right?

Nevertheless, when she spun around and headed for the driver's door, he caught her arm. "Whoa. That car's not leaving this driveway until it's repaired."

"That's what I'm trying to do, if you'll let me."

"What I mean is, let Mr. Big-Time Quarterback come here and do it. I can't wait for him to explain this. Something tells me the story's a whopper."

Jack Nolan, Jr., had a temper and acted as if he owned Kristen. Because he also happened to be the mayor's eldest son and quarterback of Mount Liberty's winningest football team in history, he'd achieved a popularity in the community that awarded him a certain privilege or protection that Stone didn't approve of one bit.

"Please, Uncle Stone! He doesn't want to come out here. He knows you're going to be all over him for this."

"If he deserves it, he'll be right. All the more reason for him to come and take it like a man."

"But he has curfew, remember? There's a game tomorrow night. The first one of the regular season, not just a scrimmage."

Just once he would like for life in Texas not to revolve wholly around sports. "Here's a news flash. You have a curfew, too."

"Since when?" Kristen cried, aghast.

"Since you tried to lie to me."

He didn't raise his voice, and he was proud of that. In fact, he actually regretted having to take this position at all. But she'd forced him into it as a matter of principle. If she'd told him about the accident outright, he wouldn't have been pleased, but he would have repaired the thing himself this evening, and to hell with the paperwork he was always behind on. Now, unless young Jack came out here eating humble pie, that car was going to sit in the driveway if it took slicing a tire with his own pocketknife.

Although her lower lip trembled, Kristen raised her chin. Without another word, she stormed back into the house, slamming the door behind her.

"Welcome home, Uncle Stone," Stone muttered under his breath as he followed. "How was your day, Uncle Stone?"

Fatigue plagued him. If he'd thought he'd reached his limit before, he knew better now, and his step showed it. Fortunately Kristen wasn't anywhere around when he entered the house, so he didn't have to worry that she thought she could still wear him down.

He heard her using the phone in the kitchen. No doubt she was calling Jack. That canceled any plans for warming his dinner now, although he wasn't really hungry anyway. A shower would be great after the day's tour of the flora and fauna. Only his concern that his niece would sneak out behind his back made him detour to his office-away-from-the-office to check his answering machine. But the moment he sat down, his gaze fell on a photograph of Tracy and Billie Ann.

It was the sole reminder he had left of them, a copy he'd had made from the picture he carried in his billfold. As he looked at their smiling faces, he knew the sharpest pangs of grief and loss had eased, but the loneliness proved as tough to deal with as ever.

All the more reason to hate having to discipline Kristen. He knew exactly what she must be going through, how her judgments in people and on issues still weren't well thought out. What's more, with her loss being relatively new, anything he said to her had to hurt twice as much. And, of course, she conveniently forgot how Jackson hadn't been the most responsible father on the planet, and that she and her father had experienced their share of conflict.

He looked out the window at the fenced backyard, where—like the front yard—hardly a shrub broke the monotony of the wood fence. What a difference this place was to Jordan's. At least she had huge trees framing the house and the woods in back. Damn it, he needed to get out of this blue funk and get motivated. Maybe Kristen would be out of college and working in Walla Walla by the time anything grew to a decent size, but this was her property. He owed her the attention and improvements it needed to yield a good sale price, in case she decided to become a doctor or something and tuition became a problem. He also owed Mrs. Tucker and their other neighbors something better than this eyesore. But unlike Jordan, he didn't have the luxury of focusing all of his free time on a house.

Thoughts of the comely Ms. Mills had him remembering how she'd looked in her gray suit. The style had proclaimed her as a professional, while at the same time the jacket's narrow waist and the skirt's pencil thinness reminded him of her alluring assets. To the point of distraction.

When his business line rang, he was almost relieved. But as he grabbed for the receiver, he did pray it wasn't an emergency that would take him right out again. Granted, he'd been expecting the sheriff to phone, asking for help on a case, but he would tell Ralph to call the Marines or Mounties if need be—anyone but him tonight. No way could he leave with Kristen itching to let him know she didn't give a nickel for his authority.

"Demarest," he snapped into the mouthpiece. The stretch of silence that followed made him think someone wasn't sure whether to identify himself or not. "Hello? Speak now or talk to the dial tone."

"It's me." The reply came with considerable hesitation. "Jordan Mills."

He would have bet it was anyone but her, even John Marshall Nolan, Sr., since Jack's father had a reputation for calling people at any hour to get his son out of hot water.

Stone settled back in his swivel chair. "It may be a cliché, but this is a surprise."

"I wouldn't blame you for hanging up, but I hope you won't. At least, not before I have a chance to apologize."

Not a chance. This was too intriguing. "Where'd you get my number? The phone book?"

"Yes. Once you have a name, it's ridiculously simple. If I'd known who you were before, maybe this call wouldn't be necessary."

"What's that supposed to mean?"

"That I wouldn't have stayed on here."

"Thanks," Stone replied, a bit peeved by how honest she could be. "I think that's the most polite kick in the teeth I've ever received."

"You know what I mean. I did call to apologize. I was rude, and I truly regret it."

"Consider it forgotten . . . if you'll answer one question. Why were you?"

She remained silent a good while. He found himself enjoying that, found himself intrigued with the internal battle he could feel going on inside her, and that he'd caused it.

"You know why," she said at last. "You make me nervous."

Sitting forward, Stone stared at the county map on the wall before him and zeroed in on the location of her place. "You could have fooled me."

"I did my best. But when you followed me home again, I thought . . ."

"The worst."

"I can't afford trouble. I'm just starting my first year at the school, and gaining tenure isn't a guaranteed thing."

"I'm not looking for trouble, either."

"Then let's put Memphis behind us."

The entreaty in her voice had him gripping the receiver tighter. He meant to give her the answer she wanted, only the words wouldn't come. Instead, he found himself asking, "Who hurt you so badly that you're not going to risk letting your guard down again? Besides your father, that is."

"He would be enough, believe me."

"But he's not the only one."

Again there was a telling silence. This one lingered until she cleared her throat. "About Kristen . . . I want you to know that I don't encourage my students to get close to me, but . . . you don't have to worry that I'll be less than compassionate or unfair to her, either. She's a good student, and she's one of a handful who don't approach my class as if it were a death sentence."

He decided to let her get away with dodging his question. "I'm glad to hear that . . . although I think you're missing out on a great deal using that philosophy with your students. The kids are poorer for it, too."

"No one can be all things to all people. You know that better than most."

True, but their intimacy had reminded him of more than the pleasures life could bring. It had also exposed things about her that she didn't realize he'd seen. He had a hunch she needed those kids as much as they needed her. But this might not be the time to bring up any of that.

"And if we cross paths somewhere?" he asked, hoping to keep her talking. "Do you still want me to pretend I've never seen you before?"

"It would be wise."

"I don't know about that."

"We can only try. That's all I ask. Thank you . . . Stone."

She hung up before he could respond, and he had to ask himself why what she'd asked didn't feel right, why putting her behind him seemed so impossible. Playing devil's advocate had never appealed to him.

How about the simple fact that she once saved your sanity? Maybe it's your turn to save hers.

Chapter Three

"All right, everyone," Jordan said, crossing her arms as she leaned against the front of her desk. "Since it's not only Friday, but the last class of the day, I know your minds are on tonight's opening game of the football season, so I'm going to let you all off easy."

"You mean we can duck out of here, Ms. Mills?"

She eyed a hopeful Bo Spradlin, the nephew of Wood County's sheriff, sitting nearest to the door. With his yolk-wide shoulders and bulky thighs, it remained a moot point whether he dragged his chair there to give himself plenty of room or the hastiest exit. However, today there was no contest, for even as he voiced his question, he was raising his considerable bulk out of his seat.

Jordan put up a hand to caution him, then pointed to the chair he'd abandoned. "Put it down, Mr. Spradlin. Obviously I need to add that 'off the hook' will mean more to some of you than others."

"Oh, man," Bo groaned as he slumped back into the combination desk-chair that really was too small for his giant's frame. "Are we going to read more of that sissy stuff?"

"If you're referring to poetry, Mr. Spradlin, specifically the work of Emily Dickinson and Elizabeth Barrett Browning, you're right, we're not. What we're going to do is write some verse of our own."

If she thought Bo's groan had been loud, virtually every male voice rose in despair and protest against her announcement. A few girls complained, too. Jordan lifted both eyebrows. "Calm down, people. I'm not talking about rewriting *The Iliad* and *The Odyssey* here. A minimum of four lines on any topic, more if you're feeling expansive. How difficult can that be?"

She heard a few opinions from other members of the football team sitting in the back of the room. None of them was encouraging, and one bordered on rude. While none of this surprised her, it did have her once again doubting the wisdom of resigning from her junior college post in Massachusetts instead of asking for a leave of absence as Brent had wanted her to do. What on earth made her think she could deal with the status quo mind-set going on in this community? This is what she got for wanting to get as far away from Brent as possible.

She focused on identifying the person she thought had voiced the inappropriate comment. Because she'd seen Kristen's eyes grow wide when it had happened, she had a good idea who the guilty party was. "Jack Nolan, do you have a particular grievance you'd like to share with the class?"

The bronzed teen heartthrob responded with a typical "who me?" look that on anyone else would have appeared goofy. "Er, no, ma'am."

"I'm glad. I'd hate for the quarterback of our football team to set a poor example off the playing field."

"Ms. Mills?" Kristen raised her hand. "Do the poems have to rhyme?"

"Not necessarily." She spread her arms wide in appeal. "Come on, people. Let your creativity flow. Remember I told you at the start of this semester when I outlined this year's course of study for you, poetry isn't necessarily about flowers or romance. It's about how you feel . . . right now. It's about honesty. What is your truth today?"

She let them chew that over as she circled to her seat. This wasn't anything new, but the students' ongoing resistance and negativity continued to bother her. During lunch, she'd begun grading the papers collected from her third-period junior class. They'd had all week to write a composition entitled "My Life." She'd used the assignment not only to judge where the students were in their language skills, but to get a feel for who was in her class. Unfortunately she only read the first four before she realized that she was doomed to end up as shocked as she would be disappointed.

The worst so far were submissions from the athletes, and it boggled her mind how—with the skills they were exhibiting—they could be allowed to participate in sports. They couldn't possibly have been getting passing grades up until now. That some had made it as far as their junior year without being left back had her wondering.

From the looks of things as she watched these seniors squirm, frown and openly resent her for what they appeared to view as punishment, this class would yield some disturbing revelations, as well. She had long since abandoned her idealistic notion that she alone could make a difference in the system, but there was something about this growing pattern in her classes that stirred old passions.

Deciding she'd better deal with the compositions at home, she checked her watch. The class had been working for ten minutes. Long enough. She resumed her perch on the front edge of her desk.

"Okay, who wants to go first?" A roomwide gasp was followed by twenty-seven heads snapping up and eyes popping wide open. Jordan crossed her arms and eyed them mildly. "Why the surprise? What good is poetry if it's not read?"

"What good is it at all?" Jack Nolan replied, his handsome blond features contorted by a sneer.

Jordan saw that question in many eyes and addressed the room as a whole. "Poetry is a communicator. Through it, the reader learns to hear. He discovers someone has put into words thoughts and emotions that perfectly mirror his confusion, his pride and his pain, his concerns... and suddenly he feels less alone. He says to himself, 'If this person knows how I feel, maybe there's someone else out there who understands me. Maybe the situation isn't hopeless.' Certainly the world is no longer the huge sea of strangers we thought it was before."

A few of the students looked as if they liked that idea, including Kristen. One or two more seemed at least intrigued. But no one volunteered to go first—not surprising, and that confirmed several articles she'd read, where studies reported that people listed public speaking as their greatest fear.

"So be it." She scanned the room as if making a decision, although she already had. "We'll start on the left side of the room and go up and down the aisles. Mr. Spradlin."

"Why me?" His voice broke, he reacted with such surprise.

"Because you're as far left as someone can get without sitting in the hall."

"I could move."

"You're fine where you are."

He squirmed. He slouched deeper, almost sliding off the chair. He glared across the room at his cohorts, who made a number of guttural, farmyard noises. "It doesn't rhyme good," he said at last.

"That doesn't matter, and this isn't a test. Relax. Try to enjoy what you're doing."

"I'd rather be giving blood."

If the boy couldn't write poetry, he surely had a future in stand-up comedy. "Look at it this way, you'll be done first. Once you're through, you can sit back and enjoy everyone else writhing as they await their turn."

That seemed to appease him somewhat. He sat up and hunkered over his loose-leaf notebook. "Okay... it kinda goes like this. 'The field is green. Our uniforms are white. We're not backing down. We're here to fight.'"

A combination of groans and giggles followed. Looking disgusted, Bo ripped the sheet out of the notebook, crushed the paper into a tight ball and threw it across the room.

"That's enough," Jordan said even as the ball came flying back at him. She motioned to the embarrassed boy to hold on to the missile. "That's exactly what I wanted, Bo. You told me what was on your mind, and you were honest. You did fine."

She signaled the next student. Some of the poems were funny, some were such a jumble of barely connected thoughts that they more resembled abstract art, but several were quite impressive. The most surprising came from Ridge Biggs, a tall, brooding boy who so reminded her of a young Heathcliff that she'd spotted him as another loner the first day of school.

"'You don't know me, but you want to,'" he began, his unruly black hair falling over his forehead. His voice was mature, if not quite steady. "'You don't speak, but you look. I can't touch you, but I dream of you. Shouldn't life be more than this?'"

For several seconds, the room stayed spellbound, then Jack drawled, "Sounds like a smart girl to me."

He earned a snicker from the boys around him. Several girls shot him resentful looks, including Kristen. For her part, Jordan had just about had it with the boy.

"One more outburst like that, Mr. Nolan, and you'll be reading your poem to your fellow inmates in detention." She didn't care if he was the son of the mayor and a sports star in Mount Liberty. "Ridge, that was sensitive and profound. Thank you."

They made it through two-thirds of the students before the end-of-school bell sounded, stopping just before Kristen. It surprised Jordan to see that the girl looked disappointed, but then everyone started rising and heading for the exit, forcing her attention elsewhere.

"Don't forget your short stories are due a week from Monday, people!" she called after the escaping mob.

When the last person had rushed out the door, it felt as if every ounce of her energy had gone with them. Suddenly even the air hovering around her shoulders weighed too much; however, she still had to get through detention. She shook her head and began collecting her things.

"Ms. Mills?"

Jordan glanced up to see Kristen hesitating in the doorway, her pretty face flushed, her expression hopeful and guileless, hinting at an unexpected shyness. No matter how she tried, she couldn't look at the girl without feeling a little jolt, without thinking of Stone.

"What's up?" she asked, trying for casual. "Did you forget something?"

"No, I..." The teen glanced over her shoulder. "Could I speak to you?"

"Sure. But I was about to go to my car to put away this briefcase before I head over to the cafeteria to supervise detention. You're welcome to walk with me if you like."

"That would be great, thanks."

The girl hugged her books to her small breasts. Dressed in jeans and a red-and-white Mount Liberty Lions T-shirt, on first glance she looked like any of the girls Jordan had in her classes. But when one looked closer, there was something about Kristen Thomas that made her stand out like a weeping willow tree stood out amid the sturdy oaks and sweet gums around East Texas stock ponds. The sadness in her blue gray eyes made her more mature somehow. While Jordan felt an inevitable pang of empathy with the girl because of the parallels in their backgrounds, she knew better than to leave herself too open.

"I wanted you to know I really like the things you're focusing on this year," Kristen said as they exited the building.

The parking lot had emptied quickly—an expected condition considering tonight's event. Virtually the only vehicles left belonged to staff. Jordan didn't notice the cute red compact she'd seen Kristen drive before.

"Good. Trying to satisfy, let alone inspire everyone is virtually impossible, so it's nice to hear when something's well received. Of course, you know you're in the minority about that?"

"Yeah . . . to a degree, I suppose. But Ridge seemed to— His poem was pretty good, wasn't it?"

"Very."

"He, um, didn't strike me as the type to like that sort of thing."

"And what type is that?"

"You know, a guy who's sensitive and poetic."

Jordan pursed her lips as she unlocked the passenger side of her car. "Take it from me, looks can be deceiving. Even when you've known someone for years, you can be shocked at how far off base you were about them." She set her briefcase on the passenger seat and relocked the door. "Was Ridge's poem about you?"

The question was meant to startle, and it did.

"No! I'm . . . Jack Nolan and I are going together." But even as she said that, Kristen averted her gaze. "I thought you knew."

Jordan knew, and a dozen things—protests and warnings, for the most part—came to mind regarding *that* combination, but she had no intention of playing Good Samaritan or attempting any facsimile thereof. She believed in the theory that people enjoyed shooting the messenger of bad news. So, ignoring the hinted question, she countered with, "What exactly did you want to talk to me about?"

"I was wondering if you would read my poem. You've taught in college, you know about writing and I was hoping you could tell me if I have any talent. If my work is at least as interesting as Ridge's."

Sensing a deeper appeal beneath the question, Jordan grew ever more uneasy. "You should never compare your work against someone else's."

"But what he read was so... real."

Inevitably Jordan recalled a line from Shaw: "Do you think that the things people make fools of themselves about are any less real and true than the things they behave sensibly about?"

"It's all real, Kristen," Jordan said despite herself. "When it's happening to you. And of course I'm going to read your work. That's my job."

"No, you don't understand. Ms. Mills, I think... No, I *know* I want to be a writer. Maybe a journalist or a novelist, I'm not sure which yet, but that doesn't matter, does it? What I was wondering is if you could help. Not only me," the girl added, barely taking time to breathe at this point. "We could use a writing club. You probably know I'm on the yearbook staff already, but that's different. Besides, Mr. Ethridge is more of a security guard to make sure we don't mess up the building than an adviser or teacher. You would be so much better. I've already learned tons from your classes, and I'm sure a number of other people would be interested in joining."

Like Ridge? Panic waged war on Jordan's insides. This was exactly what she'd told Principal Fields she wanted to avoid when she applied for this job. All she'd agreed to was to teach her classes. All she wanted was to live in peace. Live with the freedom of space, choices and time! Why did fate seem determined to make that an ongoing trial for her?

She moistened her lips. "That's a flattering request, but I'm afraid it's not possible, Kristen. I'd be happy to take your poem and recommend some books—"

Her face flushed, the girl made a sound of helplessness and disbelief. "I can get books, Ms. Mills. That's not enough."

This time, Jordan was the one who couldn't bring herself to meet the girl's gaze. She knew the hurt that would show there, but she couldn't let it matter. "It's all that I can offer."

"What about what you said during class when you spoke of what poetry meant? That wasn't from a textbook. You spoke from the heart!"

Before Jordan could think of a reply, a gray vehicle pulled into the parking lot...a vehicle with a too-familiar emblem on the door. All she needed now was the ground to split open and a wicked belly laugh to spew forth along with fire and snakes to make her humiliation complete.

"We're going to have to postpone this conversation until another time," she told the girl, her survival instincts going full throttle. "I really have to get to the cafeteria."

"I have to go, too. That's my uncle."

Her dejected expression had Jordan hesitating in spite of herself. "Kristen..." The truck stopped beside them. The passenger window began easing down. "I'm sorry."

"It doesn't matter. Forget it."

"Forget what?"

Although Stone's question was posed to Kristen, Jordan could feel the touch of his gaze, despite his eyes being hidden behind the mirror lenses of his sunglasses. Having lost the opportunity to make a quick escape without appearing rude, all she could do was stand there and endure the inevitable.

"Nothing." As the girl opened the passenger door, she must have spotted Stone's slow nod to Jordan. She glanced back and made a face. "Ms. Mills, this is my uncle. He's the game warden." To him, she added, "This is my English teacher, Ms. Mills."

"Ma'am. Is there a problem? I could be wrong, but you two seemed to be in the middle of a serious conversation."

She would bet the man could spot a tick on a deer at a hundred yards without binoculars or a rifle scope. "No, Mr. Demarest. Kristen and I were just discussing this afternoon's class."

The teen gaped. "How did you know his name?"

Too late, Jordan realized her blunder. "Well, I . . . I must have . . ."

"It's in the paper all the time, Kris." Stone eased off his sunglasses, exposing eyes as bloodshot as they were mocking. "And I'm sure being an English teacher, Ms. Mills is an avid reader who's interested in anything and everything."

Jordan tried not to bristle as he used her own words against her. What's more, he made her all the more disgusted with herself for regretting that she hadn't touched up her lipstick or checked her hair since lunch. At least her newest suit was also her most flattering, a bold orange that added warmth to her cool coloring, and wasn't bad for her figure.

Lord, Mills, you need your head examined. You're off men, remember?

Tearing her gaze from his sun-bronzed face and taunting eyes, she said to Kristen, "That must be it. The newspaper. Now I really have to get back. Good luck tonight. Mr. Demarest."

She hurried away and refused to look back, despite the temptation. Not even when she heard the truck pull away. But nothing had ever sounded better.

* * *

"Teachers look a sight better than when I went to school."

"I thought she was different, but she's not."

Intrigued, Stone glanced at his niece as they approached the intersection where he'd had his fateful reunion with Jordan. "What do you mean?" Not only did he want a clarification, but it was a relief to have this respite from Kristen's silent treatment. After Jack's failure to pick up the correct headlight yesterday, Stone had forbidden the young man from driving Kristen to school this morning. He'd insisted on taking her and picking her up, and as a result, she'd been making him feel like the worst kind of ghoul.

"It's hard to explain," she replied, staring sullenly at the traffic light. "There's something about her when she's teaching class. She comes alive. She's passionate. Even fun, though I doubt anyone else would think so. It's obvious she cares about what she's teaching. But when you get her one-on-one, all that vanishes. It's as if you're talking to an entirely different person."

"Could you give me an example?"

"I just asked her to sponsor a writers' club, and she turned me down cold."

Although he knew exactly how chilly Jordan Mills could get with him, Stone didn't find it easy to accept she would treat her students the same way. Especially not after their last discussion. "Maybe she's carrying a full schedule."

"She's single and she teaches eleventh- and twelfth-grade English. How busy can she be?" With a sigh, Kristen hugged her books closer to herself. "I thought teachers were supposed to care."

Having no clue as to how to respond to that, Stone chose a different focus. "You never said you were interested in writing."

"You never asked."

He grunted. "Unfair."

"Okay," she sighed. "So you do ask. But in the old days, Dad and I didn't see much of you, which made you something of a stranger to me. And you have to admit, you're not the easiest guy to talk to. On top of that, there've been other things on my mind."

Same with him. Too often, he let himself get caught up in his own dark memories. "I should notice more, be there for you."

"As I said to her, it's no big deal."

He didn't believe her. "Do you plan on focusing on writing in college?"

"I don't know. Maybe. I'm not sure anymore."

"But you've already begun applying to schools, right?"

"Can this wait? I have to get myself up for the game tonight, and that's not going to happen if I have to worry about what's nearly a whole year away."

It was on the tip of his tongue to tell her that the year would fly by faster than a brushfire eating up East Texas timberland and pasture, but as the light turned green, Stone knew he should count himself fortunate that they'd discussed as much as they had. Besides, he had plenty of other things to think about.

Now more than ever, he resented the strong emotions he'd experienced toward Jordan back at the school. Dread and desire had intertwined, making a mockery of the agreement that if they ran into each other, they would pretend they'd never met before. Hell, just seeing her had made his body react as if he'd touched jumper cables to the wrong terminals on a car battery. And now to find out that she was going to hurt Kristen, after she'd been so adamant that she wouldn't!

She was as much a liar as she was a temptation. Well, he might have to work on his lust, but he knew exactly how to deal with someone who lied to him.

"I'm going to have to go out again for a bit," he told Kristen as he pulled into their driveway. He made an excuse about having to drop some report off at the sheriff's department, but he had every intention of going back to the school and having a few words with the devious Ms. Mills.

"When will you be back?"

"An hour or so."

"You always say that, and then I don't see you until I'm about to go to bed. I'll bet you've already forgotten that I have to be back at school this evening."

"I haven't—"

"Thanks for nothing!"

As she thrust open her door, Stone grabbed hold of her arm. "I said I'll be back and I will."

"I'll believe that when I see it. Or maybe I'll just have Michelle come get me," she added, shrugging off his hand.

He massaged his neck as he watched her storm into the house, wondering how a near-perfect ride home could disintegrate so quickly. Damn, but he hated this mess. And thanks to Jordan, the situation was worse than ever!

Jordan wasn't among the spectators at the game that night.

After halftime, Stone eased away from the crowded stands to head for the main gate. The Lions were comfortably ahead, and although she had ignored him, Kristen knew he'd been there to watch her cheer on the team. Knowing her friend would also bring her home later, he intended to check Jordan's house once more to see if she was home yet.

Nothing had gone as planned this evening. Earlier, with every intention of returning to the school to talk to Jordan, he'd barely left the driveway when he had indeed been paged by the sheriff. By the time he returned to Mount Liberty, the only vehicles in the school parking lot were those of concession attendants and others affiliated with the game.

Jordan hadn't been at home, either, and Stone had ultimately concluded the woman must have ESP to elude him so well.

He was thinking that again as he passed through the gates, leaving much of the noise and lights behind him. Which was also why he didn't immediately recognize the person standing by the massive oak that offered the only shade to athletes during summer practices.

There was enough of a chill in the air for him to wish he had slipped on his windbreaker. She'd been the wise one, having changed into a heavy sweater and jeans. It was the ivory sweater that caught his eye and made him take a second look. That and her hair, loose and flowing to her breasts.

His step faltered.

The effect was a far cry from the ice queen he'd been tracking. In the glow of the distant stadium lights, she could have been mistaken for a student herself.

"What brings you out to mingle with the masses?" he asked once he got within speaking distance.

"Who's mingling?"

He didn't want her to make him smile; he wanted to stay angry with her. "I've been looking for you."

A couple carrying the colors of the opposing team strolled past them. Although they barely cast them a glance, Jordan's wary expression had Stone nodding toward the parking lot. "Where's your car—that is, if you're about ready to head out of here? Traffic will get impossible well before the fourth quarter is over."

"I'm ready. I only stopped for the lights and music anyway."

She'd parked on the far left side of the lot—about as far away from where he'd left his vehicle to make him decide to believe that was intentional, too.

You need a vacation, Demarest.

Upon reaching her sedan, she unlocked the driver's door before facing him. "You're angry about something. What is it now?"

The unnatural lighting created a nimbus around her pale hair. He resented the aura of fragility it lent her. He didn't want anything, especially her femininity, to interfere with what he had to say.

"You have to ask? You gave me your word about Kristen."

Her frown was in her eyes and barely marred her model-perfect skin. "And I've kept it."

"No, not even one day. She asked you for help. You turned her down."

"I turned down part of her request. She was asking for a great deal. Did she tell you that?"

"An extra hour or so after school to help kids achieve their dreams is asking too much?"

Jordan lifted one finely arched eyebrow. "It's the 'or so' that gets costly. Do you really think it would stop there?"

"You're a teacher. Either you're helping or you're not."

Confusion flared into temper, turning her dark eyes into piercing darts. "I see. You're going to set my schedule and dictate my life choices now? Unless someone's forgotten to tell me about something, I don't think your jurisdiction stretches quite as far as this school."

He knew he was beginning to step way out of bounds, but he couldn't stop. Whether she was angry at him or not, Kristen was his flesh and blood. "This is a kid who's been dealt more blows in a handful of years than most people experience in an entire lifetime."

"Her situation is sad, yes, but unfortunately not unique."

As she reached for the door handle, Stone covered her hand with his, unwilling to take that as an answer. Startled, she stared at their joined hands a moment before shooting him a warning look.

"Let go."

"Jordan . . . this isn't fair."

"That's not my problem."

"Even though I'm the one doing the asking?"

Memory flickered in her eyes before she hid them with her long lashes. The fight seemed to drain out of her. "Why can't you leave me alone?" she asked softly, wearily.

"I wish I could, believe me. But you're Kristen's teacher. The one who's most important to her. Her decision, not mine."

She shook her head, her smile bitter. "This isn't about her. It's the rest. You can't forget."

As soon as she said it, he knew she'd hit on the truth he'd been too stubborn to admit. "All right. What if I can't?"

"It's no good. Just because we both live here doesn't mean I'm willing to act like the local convenience store. We aren't going to pick up where we left off."

But that's exactly what had been playing in the back of his mind, exactly what he'd been trying not to fantasize. Furious with her for sounding as if it was so easy, he challenged her. "Prove it. Make me believe you're not interested."

He didn't give her a chance. Blocking her against the car with his hands, he kept her there by pressing the lower half of his body against hers. Then he locked his mouth to hers in a kiss that was as unapologetic as it was fierce.

Oh, yes, it was this that he'd been compelled, driven, to experience again. The flash of surprise and disbelief, followed by that incredible heat, that searing sting of life. From the instant their lips connected, it was as if sunshine broke the armor of night. Something unrepentant, free and not quite controllable took hold.

It was exactly as it had been the first time. He pressed closer to her, and she tried to arch nearer to him. His memory hadn't exaggerated.

"Stone!"

He let her break the kiss only so he could suck some much-needed air into his lungs. And if it wasn't for the dread suffocating the passion in her eyes, he would have kissed her again. She might as well have been a card-carrying witch; she'd cast that much of a spell on him. But she was clearly no more pleased about this revelation than he was.

"So you proved your point. Now will you let me go?" she whispered, staring hard at his Adam's apple.

"I'm not sure I can."

Her gaze shot up to his. "What's it going to take for you to believe that regardless of our chemistry, I don't want this?"

"Do you think it's easy for me? I loved my wife. She meant everything to me. I haven't been with anyone else until . . . until you. And not since then, either."

Even though she looked stunned for a moment, the effect didn't last long. "Is that supposed to be a compliment or an indictment?"

"I don't know what it is, only that it hasn't gone away, and I know now it isn't going to until we deal with it."

Chapter Four

Jordan knew what Stone meant, and it made her lose track of the night, the time, their conspicuous location, the roar of the crowd way behind them...everything. Unless cars suddenly grew ears, there wasn't even anyone to eavesdrop at the moment—and that left her far more vulnerable than she wanted to be. It wasn't the first time she'd known such a devastating feeling; the Reverend and Brent had been experts at knowing which buttons to press and when. But this had nothing to do with their kind of intellectual sabotage. At the same time, this man was all but a stranger.

An intimate stranger.

"You can't be serious," she whispered once she realized he was waiting for her reply.

"I wish I wasn't. But can you say in all honesty that you've had a moment's peace since we saw each other at that signal light?"

"That doesn't mean we should act like..."

"Animals responding to their physical cravings?" Stone exhaled as if relieved the obvious had been voiced. "I agree. But it is the physical that's creating the problem. Look, I've had some counseling. My doctor told me there would come a time when my body made demands that my brain wouldn't be ready to accept."

"Well, mine hasn't!"

"Liar. If that's true, Memphis would never have happened."

She shut her eyes tight. "You're wrong. That was an exception. Circumstances—"

"Life," he interjected gruffly. "Life intrudes. It always does. What makes what I say true is the kiss we just shared."

She glared at him. "There was nothing sharing about that." She wouldn't let him get away with making her an equal partner. He'd forced the issue, and she'd been trying to push him away. Despite a considerable strength she'd gained from trying to keep physically toned, he'd treated her like a gnat trying to wrestle a bear.

"You're lying again." He framed her face with his hands. "Just once admit that you're as messed up about this as I am."

Jordan took hold of his wrists, intent on pushing him away for good this time. But to her dismay, his close proximity let her see too much of his own conflict, the shadows of fatigue and lingering grief that she'd been trying to ignore.

Before she knew it, he was lowering his head again. "Oh, Stone, no. Please..." she whispered.

This kiss was slower, but no less overwhelming. His lips melted into hers, and his tongue immediately sought and won union, stroked, consumed. He triggered so much...and at the same time not enough. Not nearly enough...because she already knew how he undressed a woman, his large hands—which nerves could make unsteady and passion made unsteadier—moving over her with a hunger she'd learned wasn't easily sated. She knew he didn't so much linger, but possessed what he uncovered. And even after he moved on, a woman would continue to feel his touch molding, exploring, devouring.

He was a man with an appetite as great as his size and strength. He'd proved it again and again that night in Memphis. Consequently, regardless of what her mind screamed at her to do, her body wanted to experience that, *him*, again, which was why when he moved and pressed himself deeper into the juncture of her thighs, she could no more resist drawing him closer than she could have stopped breathing.

With a groan, he pressed his mouth to the side of her neck. "Jordan...Jordan..."

She could feel herself melting inside.

"Let me follow you to your place. Just for a little while."

His brutal honesty snapped her out of her sensual stupor. With all her might, she shoved hard at his chest. "That's enough. Stop it!"

He stopped, but his breathing sounded like a freight train and the skin on his face looked stretched to the point of painfulness. "What's wrong now?"

"If you can't think of a half-dozen answers to that yourself, then nothing I could say will make any difference to you. Please let me go."

The lack of emotion in her voice even surprised her. No wonder he finally released her and backed away.

Uttering a sound of frustration, he swept off his hat and combed his hand over his hair. "I won't apologize."

"I didn't ask you to. But I do want you to stay away from me."

"We're over twenty-one, Jordan. Who the devil would we be hurting?"

"Will you listen to yourself? It's...disgusting!"

She might as well have accused him of something perverse. No man ever recovered from passion faster. For another moment, he stood there glaring at her, and then he strode away as if someone had a gun at his back. Jordan didn't watch for long, though; too weak-kneed and feeling physically ill, she poured herself into her car and raced home.

Only after she had her front door safely locked behind her did she succumb to the tidal wave of shame and humiliation that was as much a part of her memories as Stone was. Stumbling a few steps farther, she let her purse drop to the floor and flung her keys in the direction of the bowl of loose change and odds and ends on the entryway table. But she avoided looking at her reflection in the wood-and-wrought-iron mirror above it. She hated that all she ever saw in there was herself years younger, as she'd been the time the Reverend had intruded on her first kiss with Marty Lake behind the church. The scene after they got home, the cruelty and punishment. The way Brent made her feel outside of bed.

Racing to the bathroom, she turned on the shower and began ripping off her clothes. She couldn't scrub all the visions and memories out of her brain, but she could scrub Stone's touch off her body. Once and for all. "And then never, never again," she whispered, reaching for the huge natural sponge from a basket beside the shower stall.

Forgetting was easier said than done, especially since the first few days of the following week seemed born out of a nightmare designed by Stone himself. Besides having to deal with incriminating looks from Kristen, she found her seventh period class growing rowdier than ever. And as if that wasn't enough, Jordan kept crossing paths with Stone.

At first, she tried to ignore him, but that was like trying to ignore a tornado in a wind tunnel. His flinty stares made it impossible not to meet his gaze, and when she did she felt physically and emotionally naked. Most of the time, even the choice to walk away wasn't hers to make. That was the most jarring because control was of the utmost importance to her at this stage of her life. Every man she'd ever known had battled her for it, leaving her scarred and wary. Stone didn't have to fight her; his mere presence was enough to usurp her will.

Initially they met at the market. Monday she rushed in to pick up some vegetables for a dinner salad. He was in the produce aisle, too, inspecting melons. He had two in his hands when he happened to glance over the display and see her. Well, saw her back, actually. She'd already spotted him in the mirror and had frozen. They stood there like the only two people on earth, as if it were her body his big hands cupped, his thumbs caressed...until the melons slipped out of his grasp and fell onto the plateau of fruit and he walked away.

On Tuesday at school, she was heading to the office when he suddenly came out. He had to grab her to avoid a full-body collision. Even so, she dropped a file full of papers.

Swearing under his breath, he crouched to collect them. "My fault."

"No kidding." She crouched, too, her skirt riding higher. She sensed it the instant he noticed how, with every move she made, her hose whispered.

"Will you stop that?" he muttered under his breath.

"I'm not doing anything but trying to get my things, do you mind? If I'm annoying you, leave!"

He left.

Two days of blissful noncontact followed. Not that she felt very peaceful. The moment she closed her eyes or looked at Kristen or saw a truck like Stone's somewhere, it began all over again—the inner upheaval, the flashbacks, the what-ifs. Blast it, she hated the what-ifs most of all. They intruded so much that when Paul Nash, the new history teacher who turned every female head in the hallways, invited her to dinner, she never considered saying anything besides no.

And then on Friday just after lunch, the principal, Morris Fields, stopped her between classes. Beside him stood Stone.

"Ms. Mills. Just the person I wanted to see. Have you had an opportunity to meet our game warden since your return to Mount Liberty?"

"I . . . we've . . ."

"Stone Demarest, meet Jordan Mills."

"We've crossed paths once or twice," Stone said, finishing for her.

"Good, good." The man bobbed his head up and down, though perhaps it was to see through his new trifocals rather than to indicate his approval. "Stone's making the rounds to all the schools this week prior to career day to remind everyone about game laws and licenses. He's also helping out the fire department by warning of the forest and brush-fire hazards we'll be facing until we get some rain again. Will it be all right if he comes to speak to your seventh-period class for the last ten or fifteen minutes of the day?"

Jordan stared at the wiry administrator who was every bit as tall as Stone, but seemed shorter. What choice did she have? Morris Fields had the ultimate power to decide; asking her approval didn't fool anyone. Nevertheless, she nodded her acceptance. At least it saved her from having to speak.

Under different circumstances, the visit might have been entertaining, maybe even amusing, since it appeared the game warden had a strong effect on more than just her. He was dressed in his cool-weather uniform, which included long sleeves, a tie and a felt hat instead of the straw one. Girls devoured him with their eyes, boys squirmed under his relentless gaze and looked as if they would prefer detention to staying in class. Poor Kristen, however, was the one female besides her who looked as if she agreed with the male members of the class.

"Now, most of you have lived around here, or at least in Texas, all of your lives, so I'll only touch briefly on the license rules," Stone said after a brief explanation of why he'd come. After he was through, he crossed his arms over his chest. "Suffice it to say every year I come across a few locations where poaching's been a problem. Remember that if I catch you, I'll see you're prosecuted to the full extent of the law. It won't matter who your daddy is."

"That means you, Nolan," one of Jack's buddies declared.

Jack rocked on the back legs of his chair. "Well, it sure doesn't mean Biggs, does it?" He glanced over at the teen who sat rigid but still, staring at the pen he held between his hands. "Your daddy doesn't stay sober enough to shoot anything, unless you stuffed it first and planted it outside your front door."

"Mr. Nolan!" Jordan snapped. Her look held even more warning.

Jack's expression reflected sheer innocence. "What did I say that wasn't the truth?"

"For crying out loud, Jack. Will you grow up!" Kristen swept up her books and stormed out of the room.

Had it been anyone else, Jordan would have ordered the girl back to her seat, but she'd seen the tears of embarrassment and frustration in Kristen's eyes. Knowing full well what that was like, Jordan felt there was no way she could add to the girl's misery. Fortunately the bell sounded soon afterward.

"Don't forget—no throwing cigarette butts out the windows of cars or trucks, and make sure you put out camp fires completely," Stone added as the class began rising and heading for the door. "We're in a drought situation, and unless you want to play football on black soot, be careful out there."

At the door, someone called out something about Smokey the Bear. Someone else shouted they could smell smoke in the hall. That was followed by boos and hisses as the rest of the class pushed to gain their freedom.

Stone watched them, shaking his head, his hands on his hips. But only after they were all gone did he face her. It was then that she noticed how tired and defeated he looked. She supposed he'd put in a long day going from class to class, school to school, and she had a hunch that the responses from the other students hadn't been all that different from hers. She had a strong urge to reach out and smooth his furrowed brow, touch his cheek.

Crazy.

"You could have warned her that I was coming."

It took Jordan a second to grasp what he was driving at, but that was all the time she needed for her sympathy to metamorphose into indignation. How could he suddenly turn what happened into her fault? Tempted to swing her briefcase at him, she concentrated on packing it instead. "If you have problems communicating with your niece, that's your problem. Leave me out of it."

"I'd be happy to, but the only times she deigns to speak to me, it's about you!"

"Believe me, I'm not encouraging her."

"Right. Like you didn't encourage me?"

The blood had to have drained from her face, she felt that empty and cold. "Get out," she whispered, her voice hoarse from having to force out the words.

A recklessness flared in his eyes. Rather than leave, he stepped closer, leaned his hands on her desk, which brought them almost nose to nose. "How much longer, Jordan? Do you need a man to beg? Is that it?"

Jordan clenched her hands into fists. "I've never struck anyone in my life. Worse than hypocrisy, I hate violence. But if I were you, I'd get out before you make a liar out of me."

"With pleasure."

* * *

Stone was glad he'd given Kristen permission to sleep at a friend's that night. Considering his foul mood, he knew forbidding her request would only have added to the damage in the cold war that had become their relationship. And because there was no one at the house, he avoided going there at the end of his day, too. It didn't feel like home anyway. He hated its artificial silence, which was so different than the woods, where silence was better understood as an absence of man and one could always be serenaded by a bird or some animal, or at least be soothed by the whisper of wind in the trees.

He drove around Lake Fork, checking the boat landings, inspecting a few fishing boats late to come in. But he took no satisfaction for citing one man for not having a license, or another for keeping bass under legal size. Around eight, he stopped by a nearby café, but he only picked at the catfish dinner he ordered. Jess Nugent and Stu Wiggins spotted him from the pool room and invited him for a game. When he turned that down, the two fishing guides suggested a game of cards at Stu's cabin, but he declined again. He wasn't in the mood for tall tales, and he didn't need a hangover from drinking beer half the night. So he drove some more—and thought of *her*.

She was driving him out of his mind. He'd tried to deal with it, lose himself in his work, but besides ending up more exhausted than ever, he was as sexually frustrated as a man could get this side of solitary confinement. There were options for that, of course. But he didn't want any other woman; he wanted her. He wanted Memphis again. The memory of that night was like a disease growing in his blood. How long before it affected his job? How long before he wiped out every tender memory of the way lovemaking had been with Tracy?

It shocked him when he discovered he'd driven for hours—worse, that he was coming upon the entrance to her driveway. The decision to turn hardly felt like his.

More outside lights turned on after his second series of knocks, then he saw her lift the blinds at the living-room window and peek out to see who was there. Recognizing him had her bowing her head—in defeat or prayer, he couldn't tell which. It certainly didn't make her open the door any faster.

When she did open up, he saw she was dressed in a fluffy white robe, and her hair, loose and silky, competed for the light's shine, as did her freshly scrubbed face. She looked ready for bed, far younger and vulnerable than the artfully made-up schoolgirls she taught. But it wouldn't matter if she had a halo glowing over her head tonight. He knew the body that deceptively modest robe hid, the passion that simmered behind those wide, wary eyes, and he wanted it all.

She knew. There was an awareness about her that almost carried a scent—although he couldn't have described it if his life depended on it. Blended with the almond and vanilla of her bath soap or shampoo, it intoxicated and seduced as he passed her and stepped farther into the room. Then triumph left him dizzy because he'd achieved the impossible; he'd breached her outermost defenses, and they both understood what that meant.

"Do you need a drink?" she asked, her voice devoid of any emotion except resignation.

Hardly. Already inebriated by his imagination, he couldn't quite convince himself he was even here. So he shook his head and continued to stare at her, wondering if this, she, could be a figment.

"This will only cause more trouble, you know."

Undoubtedly, but he didn't see any need to respond to the obvious. She had opened the door. That said everything to him that mattered tonight.

She waited, standing in the middle of that grim, empty room, digging her hands deep into her pockets with an intensity that tested the threading of the robe and deepened the V of her neckline. His guess was that she wore very little if anything under the robe.

"I don't know what to do."

The catch in her voice, the surrender beneath it, motivated him into action. One unhurried stride closed the distance between them, and then he took hold of her shoulders. "I remember."

She lifted her hands to his chest. To push him away? Relief rushed through him when he felt her fingers grip handfuls of material; he didn't even mind the slight pinch when she caught flesh, too.

"I remember," he said again just before claiming her mouth.

Some resilient part of her didn't want to kiss him. He understood that by the lingering rigidity in her spine, the way she tried to keep her mouth impassive beneath his, although he could already feel her trembling. Because he had seduction on his mind, though, nothing less than her full complicity would be enough for him.

He deepened and intensified the kiss. When her hands began to push instead of grasp, he wrapped one arm around her waist and buried the other into the cool silk of her hair to keep her close. He could have absorbed her into him, his hunger was that great—all the more reason to convince her that this was necessary if not sane.

A low, pleading sound rose from inside her. "I'll want to hate you afterward," she moaned when he relinquished her mouth for a moment to taste the creamy expanse of her neck.

"You'll have to stand in line. I'm disturbed by this, too. Nothing this consuming has happened to me before. The difference is, I'm willing to accept that and the guilt that may follow."

"Excuse me if I'm not flattered."

He raised his head to meet her indignant gaze. "At least I'm honest. You're too hung up with being a minister's daughter and living by pretense."

"I'm not! I've fought that—any hypocrisy—my entire life, which just goes to show that you don't know or care anything about me!"

"I know I want you. I know you want me. That's all we have to know tonight."

And with that, he took possession of her mouth again. Expecting anything—including violence—in response, he was stunned when she responded to that kiss. More than responded.

She came alive. Suddenly, instead of waging a war with herself and him, she began straining to get closer, closer. Her arms went around his neck, her hands gripped at his hair; she matched the provocative thrust of his hips with an erotic dance of her own, until a fever spread through him that demanded more.

With his mouth locked to hers, he reached for the knot at her waist. The anticipation of touching her skin again, that sleek, hot flesh that he'd tried and failed to forget, left his hands shaking like a drug addict's. He almost had to tear at the knot, but when he succeeded in parting the robe, the first instant of experiencing her heat and womanly softness again dragged a groan from deep inside him that sounded like someone being tortured.

He took an excruciatingly slow survey of her exquisite breasts, which had haunted his dreams, the nipples that were already taut before he even got near them with his mouth. She stirred hot, delicious sensations that fed his need to reexplore…to close his hands over her bottom that, though small, was wickedly saucy.

Intent on infecting her with the same fever consuming him, he trailed a line of scorching kisses down her neck and beyond.

She shuddered as he moved beyond her collarbone, dug her short fingernails into his shoulders, arched back against his arm that braced her. Wanting to give her more, he sank to his knees and continued, refusing to stop until he won a choked cry from her.

Rising, he didn't have to ask her to unbutton his shirt or beg her to shove it and his jacket off. By the end of their next kiss, she had him naked from the waist up, and he had her totally nude. He already knew he could forget any attempt to make it to the stairs, let alone a bedroom.

Relying more on memory than vision, he backed her to the pile of sheets she'd been using to protect the floor during painting. Neither one of them was being very careful with the other at that point. Had her nails been longer, their kisses any wilder, they would be leaving marks that only full attire could hide.

Once at the mountain of linens, it was a rhetorical question as to who drew whom down. Only when Jordan lay beneath him did she open her eyes, finally meeting what he knew was his feverish gaze.

"Okay?" he breathed.

"Don't talk."

That was fine with him. They only got into trouble when they tried anyway. He much preferred the rest—touching, exploring, possessing.

She had no right to look so good, like a dream, an angel on clouds. But there was nothing angelic about what he wanted from her, and as she reached for his belt buckle, it was clear she felt the same. They kissed again, and there was as much fierceness as provocation. Near-anger. Neither would relent to the other until they were jointly fumbling with his jeans.

The touch of slender fingers on him was too much. Afraid he would explode there and then, he grabbed her wrists, pressed them into the sheets and at the same instant thrust himself deep inside her. He swallowed her throaty moan just as the rest of his body absorbed the vibrations of shock and desire that quaked through hers. But it was when she wrapped her legs around him that he felt that last link with control sever.

Then madness reigned, passion commanded. He began pumping himself into her, and Jordan dug her nails into his hips, urging him on.

They never said a word, but sounds roared in his head—music, curses, prayers. And yet their moment came too quickly to finesse any of it. In a rush of fiery heat and sharp cries, it was over. Then there was only their shallow gasps...and beyond that, a strange, shaky silence that promised too much time to remember.

Nothing in Stone's memory came close to resembling this.

Jordan never wanted to open her eyes again. For a small eternity, Stone continued to pulsate inside her, and she couldn't believe the pleasure she drew even from that. But already her mind was racing, and she knew she would rather die than have to face the humiliation of seeing a smug smile or hearing him say, *I told you so.*

It was a childish, coward's fantasy, but a part of her wished she could abruptly waken, discover she was really in her bed and that she could keep the best parts as a dream.

As if sensing the doubt in her, Stone raised himself on his forearms. She held her breath as sweat trickled from his body to hers, the liquid caress seductive and infuriating at the same time.

"No...don't tell me you want me to go?"

She forced herself to open her eyes, but she only met his gaze for a fraction of a moment. "That might be best."

"You're already regretting this."

"I didn't say that."

"But you're thinking it."

She turned her head to the dark, dull wall. "Look, you got what you wanted. What difference does it make what I'm thinking?"

Although he reared back a bit more, she could feel muscles twitch inside her.

"We both got what we wanted," he said with a deceptive softness.

She couldn't blame him for being angry with her, because he was right; nevertheless, as soon as he rose, she curled onto her side and dragged a sheet over herself. She stayed in that fetal position, staring at the wall, but she listened carefully to every sound as he adjusted his clothing.

Finally he swept back her hair from her face, his touch so gentle it belied the frantic, almost animalistic emotions they'd indulged in a short while ago.

"You're not going to say anything?"

"There's no need."

"Jordan—"

"I really need to be alone right now."

He exhaled. "It's not right to leave it this way."

"I don't care, don't you understand? Just leave me alone!"

He rose. "You've got it."

At least he didn't slam the door behind himself. But even so, Jordan sat up the instant she heard the sound of him leaving. With an anguished moan, she pressed her forehead against her raised knees.

"Stupid . . . stupid . . . stupid!"

Chapter Five

"**S**tupid . . . stupid . . . stupid."

Stone shook his head as he stood beside Sheriff Ralph Spradlin and watched the tow-truck driver use the mechanical winch as several deputies and passersby helped roll the overturned pickup right side up. When he'd come upon the accident scene, he'd pulled over, having every intention of offering help. But Ralph had plenty of his people on-site to get the job done, and the big, burly sheriff enjoyed delegating and bossing everyone around.

"That guy could have killed who knows how many people along with himself," Stone added with a shake of his head.

"You know it." The burly lawman chomped his toothpick into a smaller stump. "Me 'n' my people are forever telling kids to watch this hill because of that unexpected curve in the road right after the crest. But how do you convince a full-grown man to behave himself and not drive like some grand-prix racer?"

Stone nodded as medics lifted the driver on the stretcher into the ambulance. "Ticket him until he gets it, I guess."

"That goes without saying. Not that any of that will pay for my time or my deputies', not to mention those ambulance folks'. You know that's Riley Biggs, don't you? I'm not even sure yet if he has proper insurance to get his vehicle repaired."

"Now that you mention it, that blue-and-white truck does look familiar." Stone ran the name through his memory. "Do you know I fined him for fishing without a license only a month ago?"

"Sounds like Riley. He wouldn't have a current inspection sticker on that pickup's window if I hadn't made him a solemn promise that I'd stalk him like an old bloodhound if he let the thing expire. Figured it was the least I could do for his wife and the boys. That truck's the only transportation his family has, and it's mostly Georgia's income from working at the school cafeteria that keeps a roof over her and the three kids' heads. Such as it is." The gray-haired man sighed. "Bet you a six-pack he doesn't have any medical insurance to cover that broken arm and concussion, either."

"I'll take your word for it." But Stone was impressed with Ralph's knowledge of the locals. Of course, the older man had been sheriff of the county for fifteen years, which gave him something of an edge in knowing the people he was supposed to protect and serve. Stone didn't figure he would know many more people by the time he retired than he did now. He and Tracy used to socialize quite a bit, and like Ralph's, his job demanded a personable attitude, but all the rest had changed after the fire. He still did what he had to do regarding his job, and at Jackson's place, he knew Mrs. Tucker, who lived on their west side; however, he only forced himself to talk to her because she would watch Kristen if he had to be gone overnight, and she did a bit of housekeeping for them, too. Otherwise, he preferred to keep to himself...that is, except for when Jordan messed with his mind.

The deputy a few dozen yards away waved on traffic, and the cars that had been waiting down the hill began to ease through the scene. Stone was more than a little surprised when Jordan appeared leading the short convoy.

It had been a week since she'd told him to leave her house, and he couldn't deny that she'd been on his mind. The moment their eyes met and held, it was obvious that this was a shaky moment for her, too. Only when oncoming traffic forced her to focus on the road did he realize he needed to breathe.

"You been holding out on me, old son?"

"Say what?"

Ralph pointed at him with the toothpick. "Don't try that on me. I've seen you walk past some knockout ladies since you've been working in this county. This is the first time you acted as if you're in some kind of coma *because* you noticed one."

He tried to think of some safe response. "She's my niece's English teacher."

"That so? Well, I'd let a lady like that tutor me any day."

"And what would Roseanne say about that?"

"Who?"

"Your wife."

"Ah. She'd probably be grateful if someone would take the time to give me some culture."

"Uh-huh."

"Listen, as long as I don't touch, Rosie lets me look to my heart's content." He nodded toward the white sedan as it disappeared from view. "Now her, I could look at for a long time. Come to think of it, she's too classy for the likes of you. Don't think she's a local girl, either."

"You might remember her from the old days. Her father was a preacher here. The last name was Mills."

"The Reverend Charles Franklin. Oh, yeah."

Stone's attention intensified tenfold at the way Ralph responded. "What's that supposed to mean?"

"Nothing. Nothing. Fine man from what I heard. Real fiery speaker."

"But . . . ?"

"If that's his daughter, being away from papa did her a world of good. She was one puny little thing from what I remember."

"'Puny' as in 'sickly' or 'small'?"

"Both. Cute little chicken but quiet. Real quiet. I always had the feeling . . . But the Reverend Mills was well loved. Impeccable reputation." Ralph cast him a curious, slightly amused look. "So she's the one, huh?"

The one what? Stone stiffened at the thought that rumors might get started. "Don't let your imagination run loose. She's as cool as they come. She even turned down Kristen for some after-school help."

"You sound a little bent out of shape about that."

"I guess I am. I don't know. What gets me is that she won't argue a point. She just tells you the way things are, and that's that."

"That would be a problem for me. I have to have someone around who'll keep my mouth company." Chuckling, the sheriff slapped Stone on the back. "Go on and get back to tracking down renegade alligators and illegal fishermen. And don't forget our little outing tomorrow."

The sheriff's department had gotten good information on yet another drug lab deep in the woods. Since Stone knew the area better than anyone, he had agreed to go along. "I'll be there. Call me if something changes."

Once Stone returned to his truck, however, it wasn't tomorrow that preoccupied his mind. As he headed back toward Mount Liberty and the house to check on Kristen and what her plans were for dinner, his thoughts went back to Jordan.

Despite his remarks to Ralph, he did care, and it concerned him that she'd appeared less confident somehow. Almost . . . troubled?

Considering what you pulled on her, you're lucky she didn't try to run you down.

What he pulled—now, there was a good one. What happened had been consensual.

Emotionally she hadn't been in good shape when you left that night. You could have called since then and asked if she was okay.

No, he couldn't. If he'd called, he would have asked if he could come back again. If there was one truth in all this, that was it. No, as screwy as he seemed to be acting lately, he wasn't yet completely nuts. He needed to stay away from her, which was exactly what she'd said she wanted.

At least he was trying to turn over a new leaf. He'd been trying to spend a good deal more time with Kristen, to draw her into making household decisions, like where to put the pines and dogwood he'd bought for the empty backyard. The experience hadn't been totally successful, but she liked the dogwood he planted near her bedroom window. Yet while he'd been busting his back, he hadn't been thinking of what else he could do to improve his relationship with his niece, he was brooding about Jordan . . . and, yes, aching.

So he was human.

"Sue me," he muttered, turning into his driveway.

"Jordan . . . ? Can I speak to you for a moment? You don't mind me calling you by your first name, do you? I must admit, I tend to be somewhat irreverent when it comes to protocol and formality."

Jordan glanced longingly toward the resource center where she'd been hoping to pick up a book on tape that she could listen to this weekend while painting the bathroom, but then gave the petite woman with the shaggy but flattering hairdo and huge hoop earrings a polite nod. "I don't mind. You're...Barbara Flynn, right?"

"Bess. Drama and sophomore English." The perky blonde wrinkled a puckish nose, which did nothing to mar her stunning features. "If I had my way, only drama, but this is, after all, only Mount Liberty and not Dallas or Houston."

She looked perfect for the stage. Laughter lit her hazel eyes, but it was balanced by intelligence, too. They'd met during the opening get-together that the school had put on for the faculty, but Jordan had said just enough to everyone to make her way around the room and clear out.

"Larger schools do have their benefits," Jordan murmured, wondering what the woman wanted.

"But the good thing about small schools is that they give you a chance to get to know people better. Everyone, that is, except you. What's it been, six weeks since school started? And I swear you've been short of impossible to corner again for a chat."

"They gave me the honor of supervising detention right off the bat." Not the strongest of excuses, but Jordan used it anyway.

"Exactly where I'm headed in a minute, since it's my turn. But I swore to myself that I didn't care if the not-so-little varmints tore down the place or covered the walls with graffiti, I was going to talk to you before another day passed. You weren't at the party they threw for the coaches at the Fieldses' place after the opening game."

"Parties aren't my favorite thing."

"Neither is the faculty lounge."

"I'm usually in the resource center if I have a spare minute."

Bess Flynn nibbled at a full lower lip that men would probably call pouty, but it was the twinkle in her eyes that held Jordan's attention. "You are a loner, just as they said."

Jordan supposed "they" included every other member of the faculty, since she hadn't felt a need to develop more than a passing-nod relationship with any of them. She had a feeling, however, that this shapely bundle of energy might be a bit tougher to shake loose.

"Don't worry," she drawled, a faint smile tugging at one side of her mouth. "It's not catching."

"Oh, I'm not worried. You're looking at someone who could never pull off being by herself for long, even if she wanted to try it as an experiment. I'm too curious about life."

"I have nothing against life, it's the people who mess it up that bother me."

Bess laughed. "You've got something there. And you know what? I don't think you're half the sourpuss you pretend to be."

The comment reminded her of what Stone had said to her on the night they met. Jordan couldn't help but chuckle. "Back to the drawing board."

"Oh, just call me resilient . . . and persistent."

Jordan liked the woman's spunk and admired her openness; however, she also suspected Bess had experienced a vastly different life than she had. And Bess was still young, hardly more than twenty-five. At thirty, Jordan knew firsthand how life experiences affected one's personality.

"What did you really want to talk to me about?" she asked, using her own persistence to move their odd conversation toward some conclusion.

"The writing club in general. Kristen Thomas in particular. She's a former student of mine and she asked me to sponsor it . . . after you turned her down."

"Why do I get the feeling that I'm not going to be thrilled with what you're going to say next?"

"Because as the cliché goes, you're more than a pretty face. The problem is I'm already advising the drama club and helping out with the majorettes and color guard while

Marge Harding, one of the gym teachers, is on maternity leave. Besides, from what I hear, you'd be more qualified."

"Hardly."

"You're published!"

Jordan winced at the loud declaration. Fortunately the hallway was virtually empty. "A few poems in magazines and one very slim volume." So much for trusting that information on a résumé was kept confidential. She was going to have a few words with the secretaries in the office.

"It received respectable reviews in some noted trade magazines. That's saying a great deal for poetry. Morris Fields called your publisher to get copies of the book. Did you think telling him that you didn't have any extras would stop him? Small towns like to have their celebrities, too."

Good grief, this was turning into a bad dream. Mr. Fields was less easy to complain to than a gossipy secretary. "Surely he's not planning to put it in the school library? It's not written for students."

"No, it's quite sensual, isn't it? Thought provoking, too." When Jordan lifted both eyebrows, Bess shrugged. "I've had my own copy since it came out. A friend gave it to me for my twenty-first birthday. Maybe I'll bring it in and you can autograph it for me. In the meantime, I want you to reconsider being adviser. There are a few kids here who really do crave help with their writing."

"A handful of poems doesn't make me an expert. Besides, they were...therapy."

"Whatever works. Don't you think Kristen has talent?"

As promised, Jordan had studied the girl's work carefully and saw more than a glimmer of ability. "Yes, but—"

"She was my favorite student during her sophomore year. Poor kid. You know she lost her dad this summer? It was tough enough getting past the death of her mother. She could use a woman's influence in her life."

"That leaves me out," Jordan replied, holding up her hand to stop Bess from saying any more. "Any maternal instincts I may have had didn't survive my own teen years."

"She would settle for what she could get. Her daddy wasn't any prize. A typical good old boy, who had to be reminded by everyone that he had a kid at home. Just tell me you'll think about it?"

Clearly there would be no getting rid of the woman unless she said something that at least suggested she might. "I can't promise anything."

"Fair enough. Sleep on it. We're not talking about a big group by any means. If you get five kids, I'll be surprised. But Kristen said she knew Ridge Biggs would be interested, too, and you must have noticed how gifted he is."

"It would be hard to miss, although he doesn't advertise it. He's extremely aware of how being different provokes his peers."

"So you have noticed that some of our athletes don't behave in a manner befitting their heroic stature in the town."

"Noticed? I can't believe some of them are seniors!" This time, Jordan didn't bother hiding her indignation. "I've tried to set up a meeting to talk to Mr. Fields about it, but he keeps putting me off."

"And he'll continue to until you get the message. Listen, I did the same thing when I first started here, but you might as well know the parents wouldn't hear of their darlings getting left back. All they see is sports scholarships and big professional contracts. When I threatened to flunk the kids anyway, I was told it would guarantee me not being invited back the following year."

"Under those circumstances, would it matter?"

"I was just starting out. I didn't need the stain of being a troublemaker following me without having a good reputation to offset that. But maybe if there are two of us..."

"Great." Jordan sighed at the ceiling. "First you want me to become a foster parent and guardian angel all in one, and now you want me to charge at windmills with you."

Bess's grin was nothing short of unabashed. "Let's get together and talk more soon. No pressure—I'm not clingy! Bye!"

As the blonde dashed away, her A-line skirt teasing athletic legs, Jordan fumed. "It wouldn't do you any good if you were!" she called after her. "I wear an invisible layer of Teflon!"

When Bess only waved and disappeared into the cafeteria, Jordan uttered a wholly unladylike word under her breath. While she couldn't help but admire the younger woman for her tenacity, she despised being pushed, particularly into doing something she knew would create problems for her. Problems she could do without.

And just what would Stone say if she did turn around and help out his niece? He had to be so disgusted with her at this point that he might not want her anywhere near Kristen now.

Thinking of him had her sighing anew. She hadn't seen Stone since that wreck on the farm-to-market road the other day, but he'd been on her mind. And how. About as welcome as a flea on a dog, too. There she would be, happily involved with some project or other at the house, and suddenly a comment he'd made or the way he'd touched her would shoot to the front of her thoughts and leave her hot and restless. Or she would be reading some passage out of a wholly engrossing book, and a character's expression or behavior conjured Stone's face in her mind's eye. It was frustrating...and nerve-racking. There had been times during her childhood when resentment or near-hatred for the Reverend had all but ruled her daily life. In the end, her feelings for Brent hadn't been much better. But not even they had had the ability to consume her thoughts the way Stone did. Why?

He's your first big mistake since Brent, and your reactions with him proved you haven't learned nearly as much as you thought you had about men.

She took a deep breath, knowing this wasn't the time to lose herself in that ongoing internal battle. She would get the tape she'd come for, and come Monday, she would tell Bess Flynn she was sorry but she couldn't take on advising the writing club, and that would be that.

As for Stone... practice made perfect. She would clear him out of her mind if it took saying a mantra ten times a day to do it!

"Hells bells, will you look at that boy run!"

Not only did Stone look, but he took off after the second man Ralph pointed out to him. He figured Ralph could take care of the one who'd dropped his hunting knife and was raising his hands above his head.

When he had gotten the call to meet the sheriff outside the dirt road west of the Upshur county line, he knew Ralph had come upon a situation requiring backup. A mere mile away at the time while on his Saturday-afternoon rounds, Stone had driven over immediately. Apparently Ralph had received a tip about some poaching going on, and that the guilty party was still down in the woods dressing his kill.

It turned out there were two men and they had taken a total of three doe out of season. Typical of such incidents, they were planning to leave considerable evidence behind— a waste, as well as a tragedy, but in this case a move that when described to a judge would get them the maximum fine.

As he chased the man in camouflage coveralls through the thick woods, Stone hoped for the guy to get his boot stuck in a tree root or clump of vines to put a quick end to this. Why on earth was the fool running anyway? How tight-lipped did he think that guy back at the campsite would be when tempted with a chance to plea-bargain down his sentence for identifying his friend?

He caught up with the man at a rusty barbed-wire fence at a property line. But even then, the guy wasn't planning to come in peacefully. Snatching up a big pine knot from the leaf-strewed ground, he came at Stone snarling.

"What the hell's wrong with you, mister?" he yelled, ducking as the man took a swipe at him. "Don't you see I'm wearing a gun?"

"I ain't going in!"

The .357 Magnum would have taken care of the situation with no problem, but Stone had long ago promised Tracy that he would never pull it from his holster unless he absolutely had to. As a result, he deflected a second attack with his right forearm, which hurt enough to make him too slow to miss a third strike. That one caught him on the right side of his head. Swearing and blinded by pain, he abandoned reason for brawn.

Plowing into the man's midsection, he knocked him to the ground and fell on him. He was landing blow after blow when he felt a pair of hands grab hold of the back of his down vest and yank him off the guy.

"Cripes! Don't kill him, son. Stone! Save something for the judge to sentence! Danged fools," Ralph growled at the dazed man. "You guys couldn't wait three more weeks until deer season opened?"

It was Ralph's second hard shake rather than his gruff, concerned voice that finally got through to Stone. While Ralph handcuffed their second prisoner, Stone took stock of the situation, finally realizing how out of control he'd been.

"Damn..." he muttered, touching his forehead for the first time. When he noticed the blood on his fingertips, he stared in amazement.

"Don't you pass out on me, Stone Man. Between this turkey and the one I left cuffed back yonder, I have enough on my hands. I don't want to carry you to the truck, too."

The friendly taunting was all Stone needed to clear his head. "I'm all right. Just winded."

"And bleeding like a stuck hog." Ralph dragged the prisoner to his feet and pushed him toward the campsite. "Let's get to Quitman. You need a doctor. And after I unload Speedo and his buddy at the jail, you and I need to talk."

An hour later, Stone walked out of the hospital, which was barely more than two blocks away from the courthouse. Ralph was outside, smoking the remains of the one-per-day fat cigar he allowed himself. He lifted his silver eyebrows as he eyed the gauze bandage on Stone's forehead.

"They didn't take out any brains before they sewed you back up, did they?"

"Wouldn't make much difference if they did. It's obvious I'm already lacking any common sense."

The sheriff waved away the remark with his cigar. "Aw, don't be so hard on yourself. Mistakes happen."

"That wasn't a mistake."

"You've been under a great deal of stress."

"That's no excuse."

Ralph pushed his tan felt hat farther back on his head. "Stone, damn it. You're making me sorry for saying what I did back there."

"You did everything right. I'm the one who was way off base. Lately it seems everything I do or say is wrong, and it's time I took responsibility for that."

An ambulance pulled up under the portico of the Emergency entrance. Ralph put his arm around Stone's shoulder and ushered him in the direction of their vehicles. "What I think is that you should go home and lie down."

"And pretend this didn't happen? Even if I could, Ralph, do you think that guy I almost beat to a pulp will?"

"Shoot. He's drunker than a buck in love. He isn't gonna remember why he was arrested, let alone that he provoked you into fighting back. You were defending yourself, son. You could have, and damn well should have, used that gun, as far as I'm concerned. There isn't anything you have to apologize for or feel guilty about."

Wasn't there? As they reached his truck, Stone leaned back against the fender. Although it was cloudy enough to add a bite to the autumn breeze, he didn't bother putting on his jacket because it was stained with his blood. What's more, the hazy sky hurt his eyes, and he shut them to alleviate the throbbing in his head. In the background, life continued to go on around them: traffic on the roads, visitors and staff coming into and going out of the hospital....

"Too many familiar faces," Ralph muttered.

When Stone opened his eyes again, he saw Ralph turn his back on a couple who eyed them with curiosity. Ralph reached for the driver's door and directed him behind it.

"Do you want to come to the station? We could sit in my office and talk."

"Thanks, but... I need to be alone for a while."

"You've been alone too much lately, son."

"I know."

"You need to get on with your life."

Inevitably Jordan's face appeared in his mind. "I've tried. I keep... running into roadblocks. I guess some of us only get one chance at doing things right and being happy."

"Bull. That blow to your head did more damage than I thought. But no way are you gonna make me believe you mean that garbage."

He meant every word. But it was nothing compared to what was going on in his mind. God, he needed to be alone... needed to sleep so he could stop thinking—and wanting.

"I'll call you," he said, climbing into his truck.

"You'd better. Or I'll be calling you."

"Why are you calling me?"

"I miss hearing your voice. I miss you."

About to sweep her hair back from her face—at least the tendrils that had crept free from her ponytail—Jordan spotted her palm. It was covered with white paint. She'd been working in the bathroom, but had come down for something cool to drink when the phone had begun to ring. With a grimace for both the mess and who was calling, she rubbed her hand against her black oversize T-shirt.

"We have nothing more to say to each other."

"Don't hang up, Jordan. I'll just call back."

"I can fix that."

She hung up and, right afterward, she pulled the phone plug out of the wall. Then she hurried to the living room and pulled out the phone jack from that phone, too. There was a last one upstairs, but she would deal with that in a minute. First . . .

She went to the sink and ran the cold water, pumped some liquid soap into her paint-covered hand and began rubbing. The milky liquid ran down the drain. Watching it made her wish she could wash away her troubles just as easily, wash away her memories as thoroughly.

It came as no surprise when the phone upstairs began to ring. No surprise, but a decided annoyance. "How dare you!" she said, rubbing harder at her stained hand, particularly the fate line running deep across her palm. "How dare you try to do this to me. It won't work." Once . . . maybe. But no more. Never again.

After all these months, she'd come to believe that Brent had gotten the message and was out of her life forever. Nothing he could do or say could change her mind.

"Leave me alone!" she shouted up at the ceiling.

The ringing stopped.

Surprised, she uttered a brief laugh. "Thank you."

Maybe an angel or two existed who had a soft spot toward her after all. But as quickly as the whimsical thought came, it passed, leaving her feeling depressed.

She'd been working so hard to change the house, fulfill its potential, fulfill hers. All she wanted was time, a chance to be her own person, whoever that was. Why was it that everyone who came into her life kept wanting to turn her into something else?

Particularly every man.

Jordan meant Brent, but the image that appeared before her eyes was Stone. She groaned. The last thing she wanted was to be reminded of him. So he'd been different in a way. But he'd wanted something, too. Too much. At least, more than she felt comfortable with giving.

Passion.

His brand scared her. *He* scared her. He made her yearn for things she'd dreamed about when she'd been younger and naive. Stronger. Now not even in her most reckless, rebellious moments would she be fool enough to ignore what a mistake it would be to go from someone like the Reverend or Brent to someone like Stone. She needed nourishing and pampering herself, not to get lost and ultimately drown in someone else's emotional storm.

Turning off the water, she wiped her hands on a clean part of the T-shirt. She might be a novice at male-female relationships compared to some women, but suicidal she wasn't. No one would ever turn her heart into Swiss cheese again.

She was about to reach for the refrigerator door when a noise out front caught her attention. Frowning, she went to the front window.

Peering through the miniblinds, she sucked in a quick breath, then expelled it in a noisy sigh. "I don't believe this."

Maybe if she stayed very still and didn't answer the door, he would go away.

Your car's outside, Ms. Brilliant.

And her stereo was playing.

Not loud.

Who was she kidding? The man was the game warden! He could probably hear a flea belch.

He knocked.

She bit her thumbnail and debated with herself some more.

The phone began to ring upstairs again.

"Collusion," she muttered, deciding for the lesser of two evils. She reached for the knob and dead bolt.

Good Lord, he looked like hell, even with the sinking sun silhouetting him. She stared at the bandage, at his pale face, at his slightly glazed eyes, at the blood on his khaki shirt and tie.... "What on earth happened to you?" she finally asked, the cooler, early-October air reminding her that she wore no bra beneath the T-shirt and no shoes or socks.

"I tried to beat a man to pulp today because I don't like my life."

She nodded, trying to gauge what was going on. "And I suppose he hit you back because he resents having to pay taxes?"

He blinked. A touch of humor replaced some of the misery and exhaustion in his eyes and relaxed the tightness around his darkly whiskered mouth. "I knew there was a reason to come here. Who else could I rely on to refuse to let me feel sorry for myself?"

"Next you're going to tell me that if I don't let you in, you'll stand there until you pass out?"

"Actually I was going to say something like 'Don't make me use force.'"

Chapter Six

"For an injured man, you have one warped sense of humor," Jordan muttered, reaching out to grab Stone as he wobbled. She wasn't sure why she bothered, though; if he did topple, she doubted she had the strength to stop him. He would simply take her with him. She'd also thought she'd gotten rid of any residual caretaker instincts inside her; as thorough as she'd been to pluck those characteristics out of her personality, finger roots appeared to be growing back. Well, forewarned was forearmed.

"Uh-oh."

As Stone stopped midway into the room, staring, Jordan eyed the place as he must see it. She'd been working extra-hard since she'd seen him last. Gone were the dreary, dark walls and the threadbare furniture that the Reverend had accepted as donations over the years. Everything was ivory now. Everything from the couch facing the fireplace; the cushioned rocking chair, which sat at an angle to the left; the high-backed chair to the right; and the chaise longue by the window where she liked to read. Only the desk by the front window and the occasional tables scattered about and accented in brass, pottery lamps with hunter green shades and a number of different-sized plants added color.

"Jordan...am I dead?"

Looking at things the way he must see them, Jordan allowed a slight smile. To her, this wasn't an overly luxurious room, although her choices certainly weren't sensible if she changed her mind and decided to get a dog or cat; however, it would probably appear dreamlike to someone with a head injury.

"No," she replied tongue in cheek, "but this may be as close to heaven as *you'll* ever get."

He might be feeling faint, but that hadn't slowed his mind much. With a sidelong look, he countered, "How about spreading some newspapers on the floor or something? I don't want to add dirtying your furniture to my mother lode of sins."

Jordan took another brief inventory of Stone's blood-and-dirt-smeared uniform and snatched up an ivory throw from the rocking chair. She spread it on the couch and gestured to him. "Try that. Yes, I know what you're thinking, this looks new, too. But at least it can be washed."

"I promise not to homestead. Just need to sit down for a minute."

She stayed close in case he was underestimating his condition big time. The couch wasn't big enough for him to stretch out—it was actually more of a love seat, because that suited the size of the house better—but he looked relieved to get something solid beneath him. Under that perennial tan, he did look paler than she'd ever seen him.

"Are there stitches under that bandage?"

"Seven. My new lucky number."

"You look as if there's seventy."

"Feel it, too."

"Did the doctor give you anything to take for the pain?"

"A prescription. I knew I wouldn't make it to town to have it filled."

"I have aspirin."

"Anything stronger?"

She lifted an eyebrow. "Are you sure you should be drinking if you're already having problems driving?"

"The way I feel right now, it can only improve things."

"Brandy or Scotch?"

"Great."

"Which?"

"Either. Both. It doesn't matter as long as there's enough of it to take the edge off the chisel trying to turn me into the fifth face on Mount Rushmore."

Jordan was glad she'd made that impulsive detour on her way home from Tyler the other day and stopped by the liquor store in Big Sandy. She rarely drank anything stronger than wine, but Brent had introduced her to occasionally taking brandy with her coffee when the weather cooled. She didn't mind giving up Brent, but she wanted to keep the ritual.

"I'll be right back," she said, heading for the kitchen.

As she reached for one of the two snifters that had come with the boxed French cognac, she caught sight of her reflection in the cabinet glass. Rolling her eyes at the messy image that greeted her, she snatched up the other snifter, poured two drinks and returned to her guest.

"So, am I allowed to ask what really happened?"

Stone accepted the snifter with a murmur of thanks. Jordan noticed his hands were filthy and bruised and not quite steady.

"Ralph and I arrested a couple of poachers on a back road near Rhonesboro."

"Ralph . . . Sheriff Spradlin?"

"Mmm-hmm. And one didn't want to come quietly." Stone took a swallow of the liquor—and shuddered.

Jordan seated herself on the coffee table between his legs. "Excuse me. I don't mean to sound like a snob, but that's French and very old. You're supposed to sip, not guzzle as if it was beer."

"Sweetheart, I don't want to seduce the pain, I want to knock it unconscious."

She didn't know which word sent a warmer rush of emotions through her, *sweetheart* or *seduce*. They must have had a strong impact on Stone, too, because he suddenly averted his gaze and took another swallow. Unsure whether to be flattered or worried, Jordan chose her next words carefully.

"Because you don't like your life?"

He leaned back, and the upholstery sighed under his weight. "I could have destroyed that man, and if you asked me now what he looks like, I'm not sure I could tell you. I wanted to—" he held up his hands, the glass becoming the poacher "—crush him. Beat him into the ground with my fists."

"You were angry."

"Don't defend me."

His eyes were instantly clear; his look held warning. Oddly enough, Jordan knew no fear. Confusion, yes. But she understood that at the moment, Stone's self-loathing made him the safest man to be around.

"Then why did you come to me?"

He took forever to answer. At first, she thought he might ignore the question. If he did, she didn't know what she would do. Talk about the weather? Ask him to leave? If he continued to drink that brandy the way he was, he would be in no shape to drive, but she didn't want to think of him passing out in her house. However, she also didn't want to call Sheriff Spradlin. It was enough that Stone's truck was parked in her driveway and visible from the road. At least it was growing dark....

"You make me forget."

Lost in her own thoughts, she thought she'd misunderstood. "Pardon?"

"You make me forget."

Swallowing against her dry throat, Jordan knew she needed a sip of her cognac, too, but she wouldn't bring the glass to her lips, afraid it would rattle against her teeth. "You mean your wife ... and baby?"

"Everything."

"And that's good? But when you come here, we do nothing but argue, and ..."

Muscles around his mouth twitched, lending it a wry twist. "I was referring mostly to the 'and,' although I have to admit just being around you has a strong effect on me."

The quiet declaration made goose bumps rise on her arms. "This is crazy. That injury to your head must have—"

"If you don't mind, I've already heard a variation of that theme once too often today."

Jordan stared at him as he leaned his head against the back of the couch and shut his eyes. After waiting almost a full minute, she began to believe—albeit incredulously—that he'd gone to sleep, he was so still. Tempted to reach for his glass before he did ruin her couch, she leaned forward.

He opened his eyes. "I'm all right."

"You could have fooled me."

"I was thinking. Remembering. Jordan...it bothered me to leave you the way I did last time."

When he looked at her with his gem-bright eyes so full of anguish and more, he tied every one of her ribs into a knot. "Forget it. I'm the one who asked you to leave."

"Before that. I was selfish. I should have given you more. Pleasure, I mean."

If he had, she wouldn't have been able to stand it. She'd been too vulnerable that night.

"Jordan?"

"You gave enough."

Slowly, ever so slowly, he sat forward. He set his glass on the coffee table and began to frame her face. It was at that moment he focused on his hands.

"Damn. Look at me." He sat back slightly and grimaced as he inspected himself. "Can I use your bathroom?"

"Stone." Jordan shook her head, even if she was grateful for the reprieve. "If you're capable of getting up those stairs, you're capable of getting home. Besides, it's getting late. Isn't Kristen waiting for you?"

"Unless I'm wrong and this isn't still Saturday, she's with a friend and the friend's family in Dallas for a concert. They're staying overnight."

That was twice in a row that he'd told her she'd gone off with friends. "She's out a great deal."

"I told you. She does her best to avoid me."

He waited. For criticism? Good grief, she wasn't about to judge him because of Kristen, not when she was still only beginning to test the solutions to her own problems.

"I'm painting up there." She nodded toward the stairs. "Be careful what you touch."

She watched him. His step was steady enough, but slowed by a definite fatigue that tempted her to go after him. Instead, she made herself carry their snifters to the kitchen, deciding that neither one of them needed more alcohol. She also detoured into the utility room to make sure she didn't have any paint smudges on her face. As for the hair—it was hopeless without a brush, so she pulled off the band and combed her hands through the mess. With a shrug, she decided to settle for the windblown look.

By the time she returned to the living room, she expected to hear Stone coming back downstairs. The room was definitely darkening, and she turned on both lamps at either window and fluffed up the sofa pillows.

When he still didn't return, she grew concerned. All she heard from upstairs was her stereo playing softly. It was on an easy-listening station; a bluesy number was just starting. But there wasn't a peep out of Stone.

Beginning to worry that his injury might be worse than she'd guessed, she went upstairs. The paint fumes from the bathroom were potent at the top of the stairs, despite her having left open the window a split. But not strong enough to make him pass out, she thought, heading for the bedroom.

And there she found him . . . on her bed.

She couldn't believe his nerve. Her new Battenburg lace bedspread!

With every intention of giving him a piece of her mind, she entered the room . . . only to realize he was asleep. Dead to the world, she amended as she bent over him. So far gone, he didn't even seem to mind that he lay crosswise and that his feet were still on the floor.

"Stone? This isn't amusing," she murmured, gazing down at him. His face in the dim light from the hallway bore the signs of emotional, as well as physical, exhaustion. And yet his five-o'clock shadow accented the rougher, masculine side of him, the same way each deep breath emphasized the impressive span of his chest.

The dark splotches of blood running down the length of his shirt made her shudder. She despised violence; at the same time, she couldn't deny she was glad that he hadn't been hurt worse.

The corners of her mouth tugged upward again. At least he'd had the courtesy to keep those filthy boots off her spread.

What harm would come from letting him have a few minutes of peace? After all, if he was sleeping, he wasn't trying to get under her defenses the way he had been downstairs!

Over an hour later, she started to rethink that logic. She'd checked on him twice, and he hadn't so much as budged.

What if he did have a concussion? Could he have slipped into a coma?

She'd been keeping herself busy. She'd closed up the paint, cleaned up the brush and roller...she even had some homemade vegetable soup she'd made with local-grown produce warming in the oven along with her own honey-nut bread. And she'd just finished washing up and changed into a clean T-shirt and jeans. It was as she stood in the bathroom brushing her hair that she'd come to the conclusion she needed to wake him to make sure he was all right.

On her way to the bedroom, the phone rang. She swore softly. Stone had arrived, and she'd forgotten all about unplugging the one up here!

She snatched the receiver, aware of Stone out of the corner of her eye. He stirred. "Hello?" she said into the mouthpiece, but keeping her voice low.

"Jordan. If you've gotten over your little temper tantrum, will you please listen to me?"

Brent. She'd been hoping her hunch would be wrong. "No," she replied, furious with that cool arrogance he was back to using now. So much for the humble, romantic tone in his earlier call. Oh, yes, she'd come to know him very well indeed. "We have nothing more to say to each other. It's over. Please stop calling!"

She didn't want to slam down the phone, but as soon as she disconnected, she did stoop to yank the jack out of the wall in case Brent was too thickheaded to realize she meant business.

When she straightened, she found Stone had risen on one elbow and was watching her.

"You sounded as if you meant that," he said, glancing from the loose wire on the floor to her.

"I did."

"Is he anyone I know?"

"No. From Massachusetts."

"Ah. The mysterious past life."

"Not mysterious. Just over. He's married." The words still left a bitter taste in her mouth. "Unfortunately I only learned that the week before the Reverend contacted me about his illness."

"A wife is a pretty difficult thing to keep secret."

His expression remained impassive, which she interpreted as skeptical. She couldn't blame him; had their situation been reversed, she doubted that she would believe such a pronouncement, either. That allowed her to break her own new rule and explain a bit more.

"It's not too difficult if the wife's in a private mental institution. No one knew, not even the faculty at the college where he teaches. For that matter, I doubt they do even now. Brent is as meticulous as he is convincing."

"There's a great deal of anger in your voice." Stone sat up. "That might suggest you're not over him."

"Well, *Dr.* Demarest, don't quit your day job. I was over him the moment I learned the truth." Before, now that she had the benefit of hindsight. Only she'd been too much of a coward to end it. "I'm the last person to resent someone their privacy, but I foam at the mouth when fed a steady diet of lies."

"Even if he told them because he was afraid of losing you?"

She set her hands on her hips to keep from making fists. "Dr. Brent Hilliard is a selfish, egotistical snob who has never been afraid of anything because he thinks he's superior to everything! And this conversation is over," she added, tilting her head toward the door. "I'm warming some soup if you're hungry."

"Very."

Assuming he would follow her downstairs, Jordan started for the door, only to find herself caught and pulled back, then down onto him as he rolled onto the bed. "Stone! What are you—?"

"The thing is, there are all kinds of hunger."

From the way he slid his hands over her hips and bottom and rocked her against his growing arousal, she got an instant education. But before she could tell him that they weren't about to finish what he'd started earlier, his hands had made it under her T-shirt. Drawing it up, he then lifted her to his mouth.

The shock of having first cool air then the hot moistness of his mouth on her breast drew a gasp from her and an inevitable shiver of pleasure. But her rational mind didn't shut off completely.

"Stone...you don't mean this."

"Yes, I do."

Oh, yes, he did. For no sooner did he speak than he laved her beading nipple, only to suckle it deep into his mouth again. At the same time, he used his hands to counter her attempts to wriggle off him, while still exploring the rest of her bared body. The combination of eager exploration and the masculinity of his callused hands played devil's advocate on her determination.

"What about your head?" she demanded, grasping at logic like a person in quicksand would grab at any line.

"I'm not planning to do any algebra tonight."

"You should be at home, resting in your own—ah! Mmm..."

He'd moved on to her other breast, his caresses a bit more hungry. Closing her eyes because it felt too good not to, Jordan pressed closer to the heat of his mouth.

He proved relentless, tasting and teasing, inciting her to join him in a place where thought held no value...except to feel. She wanted to. It had nothing to do with Brent's call or loneliness or repressed anger turned into revenge. From the moment Stone had entered her house, she'd been bombarded with reaction and memory. Her reaction to who he was physically, and the strange, inexplicable history they'd been building regardless. A history formed on ashes, to be sure, but a structure to be reckoned with.

Crazy or not, no one made her feel more real and, heaven help her, alive! Who had a right to begrudge her that?

"Stone...? Wait a minute. Wait!"

He stopped. But he didn't look too happy about it.

"I have to run downstairs and turn off the oven."

He tightened his arms around her. "You're just trying to get away from me."

"I'm trying not to ruin some damned good soup and bread. And this bedspread. While I'm downstairs, you can turn down the covers," she said more softly.

For an instant, he searched her face, as if he was trying to see any trace of deceit. She met his dubious gaze with an honesty that surprised even her, letting him see her acceptance, even her desire.

"You mean it," he said at last. He sounded almost boyish, but there was nothing inexperienced about the possessive way he swept his hands over her.

"Unless you're sleeping again when I get back up here."

He didn't smile, but satisfaction, and, yes, relief warmed his gaze. "Fat chance."

Although she didn't run, she didn't stop to water any plants, either. Leaving the soup and foil-wrapped bread in the oven, concluding they could eat it later, she returned upstairs, just as Stone was arranging the pillows against the solid walnut headboard. She was glad she hadn't turned off the light in the hallway, for while it only silhouetted her, she could appreciate how it let her see the defined ripples of muscles on his arms, across his chest and abdomen, and the dark hair that arrowed intriguingly beyond the sheet at his waist.

"I should have asked if you were thirsty," she said, hesitating as she unsnapped her jeans.

"If I was walking out of Death Valley, I wouldn't let you leave again." He did, however, nod toward the hallway. "Will the light bother you?"

"No."

"Good. Because touching isn't enough."

For a quiet man, he could say the most provocative things. Even before the words stopped vibrating in her mind, Jordan felt the soft cotton of her T-shirt against her aroused nipples as if he were already caressing her.

Being shy never entered her thoughts. Desire obliterated that emotion, despite a background wherein she'd been raised to hide herself, as if exposing any amount of skin beyond her wrists or knees was sinful. But as she reached for the hem of her T-shirt, lifted the material over her head, she thought only of how good it would feel to be free of the top's cumbersome weight. Free to experience the kiss of air on her skin, the caress of the sheets, but most of all, the incredible, sensual power and heat his body generated when it came in contact with hers.

Stone's breath came out as a rasp as she tossed the top to the chair in the corner. "I keep telling myself you can't have breasts like that on such a small body."

"I'm not small, I'm simply not proportioned well."

"You're just fine."

At first, she hadn't believed he thought so. Oh, he'd called her "lovely" that night in Memphis, but she'd doubted he'd really seen her that night. She'd thought he'd been too wrapped up in the purging of pain and loneliness. Now, as she slipped off the rest of her clothes, she noted the change in his breathing, the tension grow in his face and the way he rubbed his hands against his thighs, and knew he'd meant what he said. He looked . . . almost as if he couldn't wait to get his hands on her. But she wouldn't be merely a body to him; she was the woman he wanted, in the same way he—whether she liked it or not—had become the man she wanted.

This was a dangerous thing they were doing. Thank goodness they were both mature adults. No one need get hurt if they were careful not to let their hearts get involved.

"Do you ever stop thinking?" he asked as she drew back the sheet to join him.

She hesitated. "It shows?"

"If you were a telegraph machine, we would be suffocating in ticker tape. Fortunately," he said, wrapping an arm around her waist and drawing her across his chest, "you're no machine."

It was surprising whimsy coming from him, but it ended the instant their bodies touched. Then silence reigned, and with her heart pounding as hard as his, she lifted her mouth to meet his kiss.

As with almost every kiss they'd shared so far, he didn't waste time on coaxing. No gentle brush strokes for him, no teasing nibbles. When she opened to him, he drove into her with a groan of relief and pleasure. Then their tongues tangled and mated, and tangled some more. His arm around her waist became a band of steel, the hand he drove into her hair became a vise on her skull guaranteeing the kiss would go on and on. And it did.

It didn't take long for the room, comfortable before, to suddenly turn into a furnace. Stone was the first to kick at the sheet—but he countered the move by rubbing her against him as if she were the only thing keeping him from freezing to death. But she reveled in the sensations he inspired in her. She was too honest not to admit she'd been aching to feel this alive again. Already she sensed his patience slipping and knew he wanted badly to find his place inside her, and so it was with some surprise that she felt him shift his leg between hers, urging her to ride him, to find the rhythm that matched their erotic kiss.

His coarse hair teased her thighs. His powerful muscles offered the perfect seat as she clasped him more tightly and followed his lead. And as he spread a searing path of open-mouthed kisses over her face and down her neck, she understood what his generosity was costing him.

"Ah, damn." He stiffened as a shudder ran through him. "Why does it always have to feel so urgent with you?"

"It's all right. I—ah!"

He'd shifted, and now his hand had control. "Let me. Let me take care of you first this time."

She wanted to repeat that she understood, to explain how it was enough, almost too much, just having him inside her; as he delved into her moist heat, it was all she could do to catch her breath. Forget about thinking or voicing any gratitude. Impossible, when the only sounds coming out of her were whimpers of pleasure and entreaties for more...more. So she let him give her what he wanted, and it was as terrifying as it was special. What else could she have expected from someone who was as much a stranger to her as a consummate lover?

Stone held her close afterward. Close and still, with her face buried against his shoulder, even though he was giving off enough body heat to start his own inferno. He needed this interim moment, because she was something when she came apart in his arms, and experiencing that had nearly ended things for him, too.

"And you were complaining about your endurance?"

The subtle self-deprecation in her voice had him shifting slightly to see her face. "You're not embarrassed, are you?"

"I deserve to be. All you had to do was touch me and it was over."

Another provocative comment. "Is that unique for you?"

She sat up and swept her hair back from her face. He noted a bit of tension returning in her body.

"You want a comparison report?"

When she raised her eyebrow, she looked like a queen contemplating a beheading. "I want to know you enjoyed it."

"I did...very much."

He liked hearing that. Very much. "Then stop worrying about what only means that you're a normal woman who enjoys a healthy sexual appetite. Especially since you turn me on just as fast."

"Do I?"

"I told you," he murmured, stroking his thumb across her lower lip. "You make me forget."

That caress initiated another kiss, ever more familiar and daring because of their growing knowledge of each other. She inspired such complex impulses and reactions in him, but no matter what he did, where he touched or how, she was there with him, riding the same emotional wave.

"I hate to bring this up so late in the program, but you'd better tell me you have something to protect us," she said, her breathing growing as shallow as before. "We can't afford to take the risk we did last time."

He reached over for the packet he'd placed on the nightstand. "Believe it or not, I had this with me then, too. But..."

Whatever else he'd meant to say was forgotten once she took the foil from him and opened it with her teeth. The instant she touched him, his mind went into a white zone. In fact, when she lowered herself onto him, he couldn't see anything, only feel... feel.

Gripping her hips, he pressed a kiss between her breasts, wanting to feel the vibration of her pounding heart. "See what I mean?"

She made a sound that might have been agreement or denial. Only when he raised his head and saw that her eyes were closed, her expression remote, did he understand that she was slipping away from him again, losing herself in her own pleasure.

Wanting her with him, to be a part of her, just as he wanted her to be a part of him, he took her mouth with his. Within moments, the phantoms that had begun to taunt him again, slipped back into the darkness. There was only now, this exquisite woman. He stroked his hands up and down her elegant length because he loved the feel of her—and it assured him that she was real and not a dream that might vanish.

When he finally fell back against the pillows, he took her with him. Her hair framed them like a gossamer veil. Once again, almonds and vanilla embalmed him in an intoxicating, sweet madness. Her body ignited cravings he couldn't hope to quench in one quick race toward bliss.

It didn't.

What all that meant didn't escape him. He was healing. Moving on. His mind might not ever want to forget totally, but like his body, it desired life. Craved it.

It's not just your body I want, Jordan. But I know you need time to get used to that idea. I can be patient.

Considering his options, he could be damned patient.

When Jordan opened her eyes, he was waiting. "Again," he murmured, rolling her beneath him.

Chapter Seven

On Monday afternoon as Jordan entered the tension-filled room, she immediately took in the situation and knew she had no idea how to resolve it. And yet she had to. This was her classroom. These were her students.

"Jack...Ridge...back off from each other and sit down. Now!"

"I'm not turning my back on that field rat," Jack replied, not taking his eyes off the slimmer boy confronting him in the narrow aisle between the two rows of abandoned seats. His expression was sneering as he held some paper crushed in his fist—and a knife in his other hand.

Trying to determine why and how things had deteriorated so badly and so quickly, Jordan scanned the room, took in the mocking, gleeful glances of Jack's teammates and admirers, the disgust of several other students and the apathy of most of the rest of the class. The only person to look really concerned for Ridge was Kristen, and yet she stood beside Jack, while Ridge faced them holding a chair as if Jack were a wild animal needing taming.

Making her decision, Jordan shut the door with a definite but careful thud. "Okay, everyone except Jack and Ridge, back off to the far side of the room. Jack...close the knife. Ridge put down the chair."

A few people on the periphery murmured in relief. Jack and Ridge stayed poised like a wax-museum display for *West Side Story.*

"Down, gentlemen," she said with more force, "or I swear by all that's holy I'll physically haul both of you by the scruff of the neck to Principal Fields's office and have you both expelled!"

"I hear you, Ms. Mills, but I can't put down this chair until he puts down the knife," Ridge told her without taking his eyes off Jack.

"And that's not gonna happen," Jack all but snarled, "because of this note you were passing to my girl."

Jordan drew a deep breath as she finally had a grasp of the situation. Not that the scenario needed much interpretation, and from the beseeching look Kristen shot her, she was now expected to perform a miracle. "I should have become a nun," she muttered under her breath.

"Ms. Mills?" Kristen whispered, looking as if she might burst into tears at any moment.

Wholly disgusted with the position these boys had placed her and their classmates in, she crossed the room and stepped between them. Facing Jack, she held out her hand. "Knife. Now."

He looked at her palm. "You're kidding."

"Try me."

Catcalls behind him egged him on. Thank goodness one or two sane friends reminded him of the next football game, which was only four days away. That made the greatest impression on him, and he finally folded the knife and passed it over.

As soon as she had it, she gestured to his fist. "And the note."

"It's private business."

"There are no notes passed around in my class. That is now my property, Mr. Nolan, and you will hand it over or the same threat applies."

"Do I get both back at the end of class?"

"No."

"Then forget it. And by the way, that knife was a gift."

"Then you should use some discretion about how you use it. Stop disrupting this class, and perhaps I'll reconsider toward the end of the week."

He glared at her, but she could tell he was trying to gauge if she was lying or not. After several more seconds, he uttered a crude expletive and thrust it at her.

Jordan immediately turned to Ridge. "Put down the chair and take a seat at the far side of the room."

Ridge hesitated, but after a glance toward Kristen, he did as directed. Once he was across the room, Jack and his pals began a barrage of chiding remarks and insults.

"Enough!" Jordan snapped. After pointing for them to sit, she went to her desk and set her briefcase on top with an angry thud. "I did not become a teacher so I could play prison guard!" With her hands on her hips, she glared at everyone in the room. "Are you people proud of this kind of behavior? Is this the way you plan to resolve conflict through the rest of your lives? If it is, I'd really like to know so I can change professions, because frankly they don't pay me enough to justify the increase in insurance premiums I'm sure will be forthcoming, thanks to you!"

They thought her a comedian. She could see it in their smirks and smiles, hear it in the guffaws and murmurs that spread throughout the room. At that instant, she could have happily walked out of there and turned her back on the lot of them and teaching. They had driven her as close to despising her profession as she could get. She resented the administration for having lost control of the school well before she joined the faculty. Resented the fact that only two days after thinking her personal life had taken some new, pleasant turn, her professional life was being wrenched inside out.

She could have wept at the waste and injustice. She *wanted* to scream until the windows shook.

Suppressing both impulses, she stiffened her spine. "You want to behave like infants?" she said so quietly, some students leaned forward to hear her. "We'll hold a class for infants. No need to burden your overtaxed minds with ideals and art. That's for intelligent people who care about their future. Everyone, put your heads down on your desks and remain silent for the duration of the class."

"But, Ms. Mills," Andy Beckman said, raising a tentative hand. "Some of us had no part of this."

"Mr. Beckman, put your head down and consider this lesson. Apathy is a form of complicity." However, even as she all but growled those words at the pale youth, she cringed inwardly, because she knew that made her guilty, too.

Damn, damn, damn!

"Uh, Ms. Mills?" Bo raised his muscular arm. Although it was barely sixty degrees this afternoon, he was still wearing his short-sleeved football jersey. "Do you want our desks cleared first or can we—?"

"Mr. Spradlin," she interjected, not quite sure she believed what she was hearing, "do you have a problem with the English language, as well? Put your head down and be silent." She continued scanning the room. "And if anyone is doubting whether I mean this or not, I invite you to challenge me. You'll find you'll not only earn yourself a failing mark regardless of how well you do on your next test, but you'll also get a free, week-long invitation to detention."

Warming to her fury, she strode around the room. "I've had it with the lot of you, so now hear this. You *will* become your brothers' keepers. In the future, if someone in this class does something intentionally disruptive or mean spirited, you will all see the effects of that on your semester grades."

"You can't do that!"

"We didn't do anything!"

"That's not fair!"

The protests came fast and in predictable whines. Jordan was ready for them.

"Fair?" She punctuated that with a brief, mocking laugh. "Since when do you know anything about fairness? Is it fair to subject me to this kind of... nonsense when I'm only trying to do my job? Is it fair to steal the opportunities of fellow classmates, who might like to learn something this year? Is it *fair* to waste the tax dollars paid by your parents so that you could get a decent education in a decent environment?" She shook her head in disgust. "Down. And no more interruptions."

She was still seething when the bell rang signaling the end of the class. As several students began to rise, Jordan gave them dark looks. "Did you hear me dismiss you? Sit and wait until I do. Besides, you haven't received your homework assignments yet."

"But, Ms. Mills, some of us already got swamped in algebra and history!" one student cried.

Jordan was determined to teach them a strong lesson. "My heart's breaking. By tomorrow, I want a five-hundred-word composition on what education means to you."

A louder groan spread throughout the room. She ignored it.

"Class dismissed."

An interesting thing happened when the room began clearing. As Jack rose and waited beside Kristen, she slipped off his school ring and handed it back to him. Jordan had never seen such an expression; Jack's eyes grew so wide, if he'd been wearing contacts, they would have popped half-way to Dallas.

"Is this a joke?" he asked, his voice lifting into the tenor range.

"Hardly. We're through, Jack."

"You're dumping me for him?"

"I'm not dumping you for anyone. I'm breaking up with you because you're an embarrassment to be around, and I'm sick and tired of having to pretend that I don't notice how crude, rude and selfish you are."

"Well, pardon me all to hell," he shot back, snatching the big silver ring with the red stone. "No problem, babe. There are plenty waiting to take your place."

"They have my sympathies," Kristen replied, staring down at her books.

Jack stalked out of the room, followed by his entourage. Ridge held back. At first, it appeared as if he intended to go over and talk to Kristen. But when she failed to acknowledge his intent gaze, he gave up and left, too.

With a sigh that sounded more relieved than sad, Kristen rose, collected her books and approached Jordan's desk. "I'm sorry, Ms. Mills. This was all my fault. If you flunk anyone, it should be me."

Although sick at heart for having done what she had, Jordan sat back in her chair and considered the stricken girl. "Really? So you're to blame for males and snails and puppy-dog tails?"

It took Kristen a moment to catch on, but then she burst into spontaneous if brief laughter. "Are you kidding? I can't even get a ship launched for me."

"Don't underrate yourself too much. At least you've had poetry written for you." She nodded to the crunched paper visible in her briefcase. "And from the looks of things, maybe more than once."

The girl couldn't hide her pleasure, but at the same time, she nervously tugged at her curls. "Ridge isn't to blame for any of this, Ms. Mills. All he did was write that note. But if you report this to Mr. Fields, he'll punish Ridge, while Jack will get away with little more than a chewing out by his coach. If that."

"Because his father is the mayor?"

"This is a small town. There are more cliques than those we develop in school."

Jordan didn't like having her worst theories confirmed. "Well, Mr. Nolan isn't the mayor of this school."

Kristen's expression grew panicked. "Ms. Mills, I told you all that in confidence. Please don't—"

"Relax, Kristen. I appreciate what you told me, but Jack's actions today are inexcusable. Besides, don't think that giving him his ring back will suddenly make him behave himself. Especially not if you and Ridge become closer."

The girl's winsome features grew aggrieved. "That's not likely to happen. I know he likes me, but... his life is complicated, Ms. Mills. His father drinks and can't keep a steady job. Mrs. Biggs supports the family for the most part on what she can bring in working in the school cafeteria. When Ridge isn't watching his younger brothers, he takes odd jobs to bring in what he can, but it never seems quite enough." Kristen bit at her lower lip. "He's not going to get to go to college, Ms. Mills. There's no way his family can afford it, and he's had to take business and mechanical courses to give him whatever skills might be marketable around here to help his mom make ends meet. If he was an only child... maybe. But he has two younger brothers."

Jordan remembered her own worries when she was Ridge's age. The Reverend hadn't seen a reason for her to go to college, either. He'd argued there was no sense in throwing out good money on someone who would end up getting pregnant—and he'd done his best to avoid that by forbidding her to date until she was eighteen!

Determined to gain her freedom, she'd applied for every scholarship she could find and had been awarded two. They hadn't been much, but they had gotten her through her first year, and she'd shared expenses with another student at a horrific hole-in-the-wall apartment to cut costs even more. What kept her afloat was landing a job at an exclusive restaurant where the tips were as opulent as the atmosphere. It wasn't a history she enjoyed recalling, except that she'd learned a great deal from it—particularly how to survive.

"It seems you know more about Ridge than you've suggested," Jordan said, not wanting to get lost in the past.

"I—we've talked during his breaks at the supermarket, where he's a bagger and stock boy. And . . . we've run into each other a few times at other places."

"So Jack's concern wasn't without merit?"

Something stronger and rebellious flared in the teen's clear blue gray eyes. "Jack has a temper to match his ego. Ridge saw it well before I did. He was only trying to warn me."

It sounded innocent, and maybe at one time it was; however, Jordan had seen the way Ridge looked at Stone's pretty niece. He, at least, was well past the good-shepherd role and was well into that of heartsick lover.

"Kristen." She leaned forward to rest her elbows on the desk. Clasping her hands, she eyed the girl clutching her books so hard it was a wonder she could breathe. "You've been indulging in emotional deception."

"Wh— No, I haven't."

"I think so," Jordan replied gently. "And while you're not the first, nor will you be the last, you have to understand that it can turn dangerous. Think about what could have happened if I hadn't arrived an hour ago when Jack pulled that knife."

"He was only trying to scare off Ridge. He wouldn't have actually used the thing."

"Wouldn't he? Didn't you just tell me that he has a temper?"

She could see by Kristen's expression that her words had some impact. She also knew she would have to mention this episode to Stone in case there were repercussions.

Getting deeper into this by the minute, aren't you?

A slight uneasiness in her stomach had her pressing a hand there.

"I only wanted you to see that Ridge can't afford more trouble. To ask you not to report him to Mr. Fields. To ask you again to help us with the writing club."

She should have known there would be a whopper tied to the bottom of all this. Young Kristen might have a talent for getting herself into trouble with the men in her life, but she also knew how to work a situation to her own advantage. Fortunately Jordan had met the girl's equal many times in her years of teaching.

"An after-school club isn't going to help Ridge, Kristen. Especially this late. Besides, you yourself said he's terribly busy."

"How do you know unless you try?"

"Even if I had the time to invest, you don't merely announce there's going to be a club and start having meetings. I would have to present the idea to Mr. Fields, and he would have to decide if there was a room available in the building. We're also talking about insurance, security—"

"Excuses."

No wonder Stone was almost pulling out his hair by the roots over this girl. "For your information, young lady, these days even leaving the lights on in a room after class can get you into trouble because of skyrocketing expenditures."

Kristen scowled. "I wish they'd be as tightfisted with the boys' sports programs."

"I couldn't agree more," Jordan replied, knowing it was time to head the girl toward home. She rose. "Unfortunately our opinion doesn't hold much weight, because history proves the *T* in *Texas* also tends to stand for *testosterone.*"

Although she smiled, Kristen didn't give up. "You're a teacher. This is your job."

Good grief. "Yes, I teach. Or, at least, I try to. But that doesn't mean I've taken a vow to dedicate every waking hour of my life to sacrificing all of my brain cells and energy to you people. I take your papers home to be graded. I work weekends to develop tests, through holidays to create fair and interesting assignments. Not that anyone should care, but I'm entitled to a life, too."

She thought of the piles of books stacked in closets that she had yet to get to, the gardening that she knew would be spiritually therapeutic, the Italian-language tapes unopened on her desk, the video catalog of movies Brent thought "childish drivel" that she yearned to watch, the cooking class on TV that she would like to try. The calligraphy set she'd purchased for herself on impulse and had yet to give adequate attention to. Her list of interests was as vast as some libraries' reference sections because her life had been . . . well, yes, *corseted* until recently. Yet she still denied herself her dreams to put her students first as much as possible.

But as soon as she saw Kristen's crestfallen expression, she knew she'd spoken too passionately. It was her flaw to throw all of herself into a conversation if her deepest emotions were roused.

"I guess I forgot." When she ducked her head, Kristen's bangs all but hid her eyes. "I assumed that with you being single..."

She could only imagine what revelation would come next. "Yes?"

"That you're lonely."

"Can the old-maid label be far off?"

"Oh, I would never say something like that! You're no-where near old. In fact, I think you're the best-looking teacher here! Even my uncle noticed."

Jordan promised herself to bite through her tongue be-fore succumbing to the temptation spawned by that com-ment. Her vow lasted about as long as the rest of her willpower had regarding Stone. "That's nice of both of you. How is your uncle? Your relationship, I mean. Getting along better these days?"

If her thoughts hadn't been wandering toward Stone again, the way it felt to be in his arms, the way her bed felt empty since they'd made love Saturday night, the way he'd told her that he wanted to come back, she would have caught her slip herself. Instead, she had to wonder why Kristen was looking at her so strangely.

"How do you know we don't get along?"

"Well...teachers share information. Ms. Flynn was singing your praises only last week, and she gave me a bit of help about your background." Thank goodness she had that to fall back on, although she had been avoiding Bess Flynn the way a dieting woman avoided the dessert table at a buf-fet. "So, are you? Getting along better?"

"We're trying to respect each other's space and not ar-gue as much as we did. And we did a couple of things around the house together, planting trees, that kind of thing. I suppose he feels if the exterior looks better maybe the in-terior is better, too. Who knows."

Jordan's heart ached for the girl. In some ways, she was a decade or more older than her years. "What is it that bothers you about your relationship most?" Jordan asked before she could stop herself.

Kristen averted her gaze again. "He never shows much emotion...unless he's chewing me out. I know his job is the pits, and he deals with a bunch of pain inside because of what happened to Aunt Tracy and the baby, but it's like...if he can't have them, the only thing he wants close to him is his grief. Do you know they call him the Stone Man behind his back?''

''I've heard that, yes.'' But Jordan knew that wasn't the man who'd announced he wanted to have a full-fledged affair with her the other night after the second time they'd made love. Granted, she continued to sense his inner conflict, but she was not one to criticize him for that. In bed, he was hot and passionate, and if he could be demanding, he was also breathtaking in his generosity.

''You're not interested. I don't know why I bother talking to you about this.''

Jordan realized she'd let her inner thoughts get the best of her again. ''Wait. I do care and I'm glad you stayed to talk to me. But this is a complicated situation.''

The girl hesitated. ''What are you going to do?''

''Go to Jack's house and speak to his parents.''

Kristen's soft lips tightened, and she shook her head. ''They won't listen. Mrs. Nolan's opinions always conform to what Mr. Nolan says, and Mr. Nolan sees himself and his family as the closest thing to royalty that Mount Liberty has. No one criticizes them. On top of that, Mrs. Nolan is pregnant with their third baby. She's so busy redoing the nursery from blue to pink because she's finally getting the girl she's wanted that she isn't going to like anything upsetting the perfect family picture she's drawn for herself.''

How interesting. ''If you're so disapproving of them, why on earth have you continued going with Jack all this time?''

She bowed her head again. ''Because they are the first family of Mount Liberty, and—oh, brother, this is embarrassing—I liked the status that came with that, the attention.''

Jordan didn't know many adults who could be so honest. ''It takes quite a person to admit that to oneself, let alone another person. Thank you for the confidence. But I still have to talk to the Nolans.'' Nevertheless, she thought Kristen deserved some gesture for the ground she'd gained today, and she reached into her open briefcase for the crumpled note. "Here," she said handing it over. "There's no reason why you shouldn't have this."

Perhaps only a sunrise could compete with the brightness that transformed the teenager's sweet face. "Ms. Mills! I'm sorry for what I said before. You really are...great! Bye!"

Kristen all but danced from the room. Jordan had to admit she enjoyed the feeling she got from seeing that. But she felt a twinge of wistfulness, as well.

When was the last time *she'd* looked so ebullient and full of hope?

The question didn't bear close scrutiny. The Reverend had seen any form of laughter, let alone dance, as the devil's idleness—and that was only the beginning of his list.

She glanced down and spotted the knife in the bottom of the case. No telling what he would have said if he'd been in the midst of that incident.

What was she thinking? No one would have dared pull a knife in the presence of the Reverend Charles Franklin Mills.

"Good choice of memories, Jordan," she muttered to herself as she collected her things. "Put yourself in a defeatist mode before you even get over there."

Kristen wasn't wrong about the Nolans; their house was the premier home in Mount Liberty, although it was located on the eastern boundary of town. It stood out among the modest farms and ranches that framed the rolling farm-to-market road, which became Main Street closer to the commercial center. It was meant to dominate, and not just because of its modern stone-and-cedar architecture. Mayor John Marshall Nolan, Sr., saw himself as the best ambassador Mount Liberty had, and to him that role came with responsibilities; as a result, he made sure he had the best-kept lawn, minus any of the nut grass or weeds that the wide-open Texas skies blew around without discrimination, and the best landscaping, thanks to the styling and weekly maintenance of a high-profile company from Tyler.

Every major holiday saw the Nolan property decorated to the nth. For Easter, there was a giant bunny and colored-egg display. For the Fourth of July, not just one flag would do—they lined the entire length of the football-field-long driveway, and floodlights illuminated a plywood-based rendition of the Declaration of Independence the size of a tank. This year, the lights had been so bright, a military helicopter experiencing trouble in bad weather had used the Nolans' lawn for an emergency landing. Jack Sr., a wealthy attorney with greater political aspirations, had loved it, and he'd used the opportunity to get his picture into the Tyler and Dallas papers, as well.

As Jordan turned onto the driveway, she noted that the Halloween decorations were already up. Ghosts and witches on broomsticks hung from the artfully placed magnolia and pine trees. The witches' attire looked suspiciously like silk, and the ghosts were stylishly made out of satin to add sheen both day and night. Pumpkins and stacks of dried cornstalks lined the driveway, and potted chrysanthemums framed the largest pumpkin at the entryway that she'd ever seen.

Megan Nolan answered the door looking very pregnant but fashionable in a dove gray tunic top over a darker gray skirt. Jordan had a hunch that ordinarily the platinum blonde wouldn't be caught dead without three-inch heels, but due to the advancing stage of her pregnancy, she was enduring gray tights and matching suede slippers.

"Ms. Mills? Megan Nolan. Do come in." Jack's mother nodded in lieu of offering her hand. Jordan didn't mind; she had an aversion to weak handshakes and knew this regal woman, when forced to touch a stranger, would provide nothing better.

"Thank you for seeing me on such short notice." Jordan entered the pristine foyer, where white marble gleamed on the floor and crystal and glass competed for brilliancy overhead.

"You said it was urgent, and that you wanted to discuss my son. What choice did I have?"

The subtle criticism convinced Jordan to avoid the invitation to sit down, if made. Clearly Mrs. Nolan had heard something from Jack Jr. and had already chosen to believe him.

"This belongs to your son," she said passing over Jack's knife. "Today he pulled it on another student. Fortunately I arrived before anything serious happened, but regardless, we're looking at a problematic situation."

Holding the knife in her hands as if it were the silver chalice, Megan Nolan responded with a serene smile. "If Jack Jr. pulled this knife as you say he did, Ms. Mills, then he must have felt a strong need to defend himself."

This statement came as no surprise, and yet Jordan gripped the strap on her black shoulder bag and slipped her fisted left hand into the pocket of her black blazer to keep from telling the woman how she felt about that. For the first time today, she wished she'd worn one of her more formal suits instead of this more casual jacket-and-skirt ensemble. Megan Nolan produced in her a need for all the professional credibility one could muster.

"While that must be what you'd hoped to hear, it's not what happened." Briefly Jordan explained her version of the story. She had no doubt it differed considerably from what Jack had told his mother.

Mrs. Nolan wrapped her arms around her belly, perfecting a pose of a woman who would protect life wherever she found it. "Ms. Mills, my son is the captain of the Mount Liberty Lions football team, senior-class vice president, a fine student and he's been voted Most Likely to Succeed by his fellow classmates. Ridge Biggs...well, he's always been civil enough when he's carried my groceries at the market, but let's just say that if he did lose his temper and provoke Jack Jr., he came by his moodiness through the blood."

Not at all pleased with the response, Jordan knew better than to try to reason with such unapologetic prejudice. There was no way Megan Nolan could know that her son's often troublesome grades could never compete with Ridge's exemplary record.

"I understand your position, Mrs. Nolan," she said instead. "Now understand mine. I have twenty-two other people to worry about in my class besides Jack, and I will not tolerate bullies or violence. There's a responsibility that comes with the positions Jack holds. You might remind him of that."

Megan Nolan twisted her platinum and diamond wedding rings. "Ms. Mills, I realize you're speaking as an only child, as well as a teacher." At Jordan's surprised look, she laughed, the sound melodious. "Small towns, Jordan, small towns. May I call you 'Jordan'? I do have to confess my big, strapping son is an energetic and passionate young man. Both of my boys are. However, I assure you that they fear God and their daddy equally. Having assured you that you won't see a repeat of this again, can we call the matter resolved?"

"It's not for me to say, Mrs. Nolan. Mr. Fields must decide that."

Megan Nolan's smile grew less natural. "My husband won't be pleased with that news."

"Meaning?"

"I don't see why something that turned out all right in the end can't be settled between the parents and their children. I even called Kristen before you arrived. She's a lovely girl, and we think she and Jack Jr. make the most darling couple. I'm sure after our little girl-to-girl talk, she understands that anything Jack Jr. did, he did because he was just head over heels about her."

It struck Jordan that no doubt many an emotionally or physically abused wife began her marriage with such assurances. "That's her decision to make, Mrs. Nolan, but I'm not sure Mr. Demarest will agree, and as her guardian, he'll have to be informed, as well."

That had her glancing at her watch. "I'll be sure to tell my husband, of course. Oh, dear... if that's all, Ms. Mills, I hate to cut this visit short, however, my younger son, Jeffrey, is waiting to be driven to his t'ai chi classes. I don't want him to get into trouble because of his mom's chatting. You do understand?"

Chapter Eight

"Thirty years old, and you haven't learned your lesson yet," Jordan chastised herself on the way home.

To think she'd spent the past dozen years weaving a mental coat of chain mail to protect herself from ever getting emotionally twisted into knots again, and here she was laying her neck on a chopping block for the sake of principle. Why was she shocked to find that, as usual, people weren't interested in principle, but were more concerned with protecting their own interests?

As if she needed reminding of how far back this lesson went, she passed Winifred Graves's house. The woman was checking her mailbox. When she spotted Jordan, Mrs. Graves intentionally maneuvered to present her back and avoid having to acknowledge her.

It was too much to resist.

Jordan braked and hit the button to lower the passenger window. "Why, hi there, Mrs. Graves! How about participating in a small survey I'm conducting? The question of the hour is—whose day did you manage to ruin?''

"*Well!*"

As the woman stalked off, Jordan rolled up the window and continued on her way. "Bad, Jordan. You're very bad." But she could feel a smile tugging at her lips, despite knowing she would hear about that little indulgence, along with the rest. At this point, however, she figured that if she was going to get into trouble, she might as well make it worthwhile.

She spent the rest of the drive home fuming, and took great pleasure in slamming doors once arriving there. Kicking off her shoes and tossing her jacket helped relieve a bit of stress, too. But before she could do more, Morris Fields telephoned.

"Jordan, what's this I hear about you threatening to suspend Jack Nolan?"

Plucking the hairpins out of her hair, she decided she needed to update her theory about how much faster venom spread than goodwill. "I did nothing of the kind, Mr. Fields. But I'll gather by that remark that you've heard from Jack's mother."

"Jack Sr. Needless to say, he's speechless, and frankly so am I, especially since you didn't see fit to inform me about the matter."

He had her there; she should have, but she'd been more concerned with whom Jack would first report to and try for immediate damage control. She knew better than to be that logical with Morris Fields and chose diplomacy instead. "I thought it would be wiser to call you at home this evening. I'd believed by then emotions and opinions would be more rational, sir."

"Ah. Good point. Er, even so...you know young Jack's record at Mount Liberty?"

"Are we speaking scholastically or athletically, sir?" She couldn't resist a touch of sarcasm with the question.

"Yes, well, both hold up well enough. The point is that if he and the Biggs boy got into a little tussle over the Thomas girl—"

"Whatever you're about to say, please don't reach for the 'boys will be boys' excuse."

He hesitated. "Isn't that what we're dealing with here?"

Jordan wouldn't dignify that with any sort of recognition. "I don't think you realize exactly what you may be dealing with here, sir." Sensing how close she was edging toward full-blown fury, she paused to collect herself. "I don't pretend to be an expert on the human psyche, Mr. Fields, but I do have to question how calm, not to mention protective, you would be of Jack if he'd succeeded in slicing Ridge open."

"All right, all right. I agree this was a particularly nasty incident, but thank goodness no blood was shed." He cleared his throat. "I just wanted you to know Jack Nolan's going to talk to his boy, and I'll have a talk with Mrs. Biggs tomorrow about Ridge."

"Why? He did nothing wrong."

"But the mayor brought up a point—and it was a good one—that it might look better if it appeared that both boys were given the 'elder statesman to young gun' speech."

"How democratic of the mayor."

"Now, Jordan, it's important to keep things looking orderly. I don't want to give the impression to the rest of our parents, as well as the school board, that we don't resolve these things quickly."

"But you haven't! What's more, you're not even going to try, that's what's clear in all of this. You're going to let the mayor wheedle you into protecting his son, and hang the injustice Ridge Biggs suffers as a result."

Morris Fields exhaled noisily. "Jordan, you've been gone quite a while from this town, and I'm going to assume you still have a few things to learn regarding the teaching profession. But you'll learn—if you plan to stay on at Mount

Liberty. Now, you have young Biggs in your homeroom, don't you? Send him to my office first thing. I'll—"

"I can't do that, sir."

"I beg your pardon?"

"It would embarrass him, and it would be unfair. He's not guilty of doing anything, except following his heart, and he has enough on his shoulders without you adding ridicule to his load."

"Aren't you the one who said she wasn't interested with involving herself in extracurricular activities or students' personal lives?" Morris Fields drawled. "If you've changed your mind, let me assure you that I can find plenty to keep you preoccupied. Until then, I'd suggest you leave policy and discipline to me."

He hung up without another word, but that was just as well, since Jordan was more than ready to slam down her receiver. "Damn and blast!" She glared at the white wall phone. "You pompous—"

The sound of a vehicle in her driveway cut her off. Now what? she wondered, heading for the front door.

It was Stone, and one look at his face told her that he'd heard, too.

"Kristen called me on my car phone," he told her as he entered. "I'm on my way home—that is, right after I hear the story from you and stop in town to give Jack Nolan a piece of my mind."

"Which one—father or son?"

"The father. Since I was out by Lake Fork, I had enough time to call him after Kristen and I talked. The snake told me he didn't blame his boy for protecting what was his. Can you believe it? *His!*"

Jordan didn't have to add her opinion to the comment; Stone was outraged enough for both of them.

"I've had it with that kid's temper," he continued, pacing several steps before heading back to her. "He's gotten away with too much for too long, and I've put both Nolans on notice. Jack Jr. better stay away from Kristen, or so help me, I'll show them what temper is." No sooner did he declare that than he pushed his hat back from his forehead and said more calmly, "I just wanted to check with you, see how you were doing and hear an impartial version of the story."

"Impartial! Stone, how can you say that? No one who'd been there could come away feeling that way. Not if they had an ounce of conscience. I went to the Nolan home myself."

"You did?" His look of surprise quickly turned to pleasure. "Thanks. From what Kristen said, I didn't think you were going to do anything. She says you reprimanded her somewhat, too."

"I warned her about playing dangerous games."

"What kind of games?"

"Holding on to one boy when she has a definite interest in another." Jordan could see by the way Stone raised both eyebrows that he'd had no idea about any of that.

"Isn't that shades of the pot calling the kettle metal?"

What the man could do with clichés. And what a rotten thing to say! "Excuse me, but if you're referring to that phone call the other night, may I remind you that I did tell Brent to leave me alone."

Stone acknowledged that—even though he took his time doing it. "I guess I just wanted to make sure you had your own mind clear on that."

"It's clearer than your logic."

"And has he called since?"

"No. What else do you want to know? That if he does, I'll hang up the same way I did then?"

"I'm not averse to some good news for a change."

They stood only an arm's length apart, and he wanted to kiss her. Jordan could see it warm his eyes and ease some of the grim lines around his mouth. "Consider it delivered," she said softly.

Slowly he reached out to touch her hair, but he resisted anything more. "Is that what's going on with Kristen? She's turning toward someone new?"

Men. "What on earth do you two discuss when you're together?"

"Not her love life, that's for damned sure. What did you and your father discuss?"

"We didn't. He lectured and I listened. Or he read and I listened. And then, of course, he preached and I listened." Jordan shrugged, knowing there was no way someone who hadn't lived the experience could understand how she'd meant very little to the Reverend. Even less than his congregation. "At any rate, you might as well know that your niece is falling hard for Ridge Biggs. They seem to have a great deal in common. They both like to read and write, they're sensitive and, despite what appearances might suggest, they're both on the introverted side. Most important, they share an acute knowledge of what it's like to live in a troubled home."

His gaze caressed her face. "Be careful, or you'll begin to sound as if you care."

"I'll blame it on hanging around you too much," she replied, although she allowed her smile to tease. Then she tilted her head toward the door. "Now, why don't you go pick on Junior and Senior? Me, I'm going to have a nice, long bath, maybe a cup or two of herbal tea, and for meditation I'm going to contemplate joining a cloister and mastering basket weaving or needlepoint."

Instead, he slid his hands up her arms. "In a minute. There's another reason I stopped by."

His hands felt good on her bare skin. "Do tell."

"Going to play hard-to-get?"

"Maybe even impossible."

"Then I'll develop a fetish for challenges. I just wish I had more time right now to prove it. Still...there is time for this."

Angling his head, he took her mouth with his, and within seconds had her forgetting that she'd promised to be more careful with how fast this relationship was moving. As he tugged her blouse from the waistband of her skirt, she went on tiptoe to get closer to his hungry kisses. When his callused hands swept under silk and over her back, she moaned into his mouth, and when those gifted hands moved around her to cover and mold her breasts, she felt the increasingly familiar melting deep inside that only he could spawn in her.

"You're walking trouble, Stone Demarest," she said, knowing full well she would need a cold bath, not a hot one, after he left.

"And you're delicious. Maybe once a week isn't going to be enough."

Sweet heaven, if she didn't stop him soon, they would be on the floor again.

"Ah . . . Jordan. You're the one sane thing left in this impossible world."

"You're going to be one miserable man if you don't stop and get out of here." For both of their sakes, she gently but firmly pushed at his chest.

He sighed. "I know. But first tell me you're not angry."

"It wouldn't do me any good. I've been thinking about you, too."

His hands tightened on her again. His expression held triumph. "So, you haven't changed your mind about our arrangement?"

They'd agreed to become lovers to satisfy each other's physical needs. It would be safe, harmless, because there would be no strings attached. Perfect, because they were two of a kind—loners who had no plans to ever risk their hearts again.

"Friday night, while the rest of the town is at the game, I'll be here." As he nuzzled her ear, she tried not to bury her hands in his hair and demand he kiss her again. "You'll remember to park in the back?"

He growled as he tasted the skin at the side of her neck. "You're worrying for nothing."

"You may thank me later. What if it got around that Kristen's uncle and her teacher were sleeping together?"

"Every man in town would envy me."

"You're hopeless. Go home, Mr. Game Warden. Your niece needs you."

"I'm going, I'm going." He did, however, indulge in one more thorough kiss. "Friday," he muttered, finally forcing himself toward the door.

"If you get a second, will you let me know how Kristen is?" Jordan asked, her lips tingling.

"I'll call. But that goes both ways. If you learn something, call me."

"Fair enough."

"Fair..." At the door, he hesitated and reached back to stroke her jaw. "I wonder if that's going to be possible, even between you and I."

By the next morning, Jordan knew she might never use the word *fair* again.

As promised, first thing upon their arrival, Morris Fields called Ridge and Jack on the intercom to come to his office. If she lived to see tourist travel to the moon, she would never forget the look Ridge gave her before rising and heading for the door. Ignoring the stares from the rest of the class, she followed him.

"Whatever happens, don't let them get to you, Ridge. Stay calm."

"This isn't right, Ms. Mills."

"I know." He had the clear, noble eyes of someone twice his age...and out of a different era when honor and respect meant life and death. She wanted to go to Morris Fields's office herself and give him another piece of her mind. "I did what I could, Ridge. Now you have to help. Don't lose control."

"Tell Kristen that I'm sorry for embarrassing her."

"Kristen's anything but embarrassed by your attention, Ridge. You're a fine, honorable person, and she knows it."

"Thank you, Ms. Mills."

That was the last time she saw Ridge that day. Rumors spread through the school like the most contagious of influenzas, and unable to last to seventh period, Jordan used her lunch break to go to the office herself, where she learned that the meeting hadn't lasted long at all. Morris Fields told her himself that he'd felt compelled to give Ridge two days' suspension because of his failure to respond to the simplest questions, while Jack had been respectful and responsive.

As unjust as that was, Jordan would have been grateful to see it left at that. But as the boys had walked out, Jack reportedly said something to Ridge. Ridge then hauled back and knocked him to the floor of the outer office. Not only did that earn Ridge a full week of suspension, but it had the ironic effect of turning Jack into the injured party. He spent the rest of the day strolling from class to class flaunting his cut lip and bruised jaw, and basking in the support of his teammates and the attention of every girl who'd ever envied Kristen's place at his side.

As for Kristen, with Ridge out of reach, that left her to reap the peer rejection he would have suffered. Because she was a cheerleader and quite popular, Jordan had hoped things would have gone better for her. But Kristen had not only turned her back on a school hero, she'd made the mistake of siding with a boy from the wrong side of the tracks, as it were. Those classmates who didn't treat her as if she were the female rendition of Benedict Arnold, did murmur among themselves that she "barely had the sense of a doughnut." Jordan heard enough to know that even her cheerleader friends had trouble trying to decide how to respond to her.

Regardless of the fact that she would have preferred to keep herself separate from it all, she couldn't deny the day's events took their toll on her already waning resolve. Especially when she saw Kristen opt to sit outside on a bench in the chilly wind during her fifth-period study hall, instead of indoors, where she would be subjected to stares and whispers. During the last five minutes of her own free period, Jordan made a point to go outside and sit down next to the girl.

"Every time I think I see something redeemable in the human race, someone disappoints me," she said, lifting the collar of her green cardigan against the chilly wind.

"If you mean me, Ms. Mills, I'm sorry. But I can't be in there."

It was all Jordan could do to resist hugging the girl. "Not you, dear. A few dozen other people, for sure, but not you. How are you holding up?"

"Debating if I care about how much trouble I would get into with my uncle if I cut the rest of the day."

"I know he would want you to try to hang on if you could. Not because you're in the honor society and don't need an unexcused absence, but because he understands how much tougher it would be to come back the day after, and the day after, until people find something new to gawk and gossip over."

"You think so?"

The funny look Kristen gave her reminded Jordan that she was speaking too much from the experience of having talked to Stone. "He strikes me as that kind of person."

"But earlier, as we were leaving the gym, one of the guys put a red *A* on my sweater, just like in *The Scarlet Letter*. I overheard that it was because Jack's telling everyone we were sleeping together. That I betrayed him by sleeping with Ridge!"

Jordan wouldn't want to start guessing who was still a virgin among these high-school students and who wasn't, but the boy's rudeness had her seeing red! "Tell me the boy's name who did that to you. I'd like a few words with him."

"No! Ms. Mills, you're making matters worse," she added as an underclassman passed them with unabashed curiosity. "Please don't say anything. Just leave me alone!"

The words shouldn't have stung as sharply as they did. Jordan had been rejected before. Often. Consequently she'd also done her share of rejecting. But having to walk away from Kristen cost a good deal. By the time seventh period rolled around and her senior English class began trailing into her room, she was as anxious to have the day behind her as anyone.

Jack strutted in as if he'd been on an all-day field trip. Kristen was one of the last to enter and looked pale and ready to burst into tears. She didn't take her usual seat, either—Jack invited a comely brunette with smoky green eyes to enjoy that honor—but even her choice of seats by the door put her too close to Jack's buddy Bo to give her any peace.

"Mr. Spradlin," Jordan said the second time she caught the big lummox leering at Stone's niece. "I think you've been holding up that wall long enough. Why don't you move into this seat?" she said, pointing to the unoccupied desk that faced hers.

"I kinda like it here, Ms. Mills."

"And I 'kinda' want you here, Mr. Spradlin. As the big, bad wolf said, 'The better to hear you, my dear.' Miss Thomas clearly isn't interested in anything you have to say, but you'll find I am all ears."

There was something about this scenario Kristen had been put in that reminded Jordan too much of when she was quite young and had witnessed one of the Reverend's most memorable "lessons." There'd been a young woman in his congregation who'd come to him quietly and had asked for counseling because of one brief marital indiscretion. Apparently the woman was living in torture over the brief liaison and wanted to know what she could do to make God forgive her.

The Reverend, after praying with the woman and sending her home, then decided to focus his next sermon on her situation and the needless fear she lived with because "God forgave all sinners." The poor, mortified soul had been called to the front of the congregation, and church members were encouraged to come forward and embrace her to "show their love." They'd done that, all right. And they'd snickered later when the woman had been cast out by her husband and separated from her children.

Memories and reality mixed badly for Jordan. Thus, it was also one of the longest hours she could remember, not made any easier by the students unwillingly taking turns reading from Shakespeare's sonnets. By the time the bell sounded, Jordan's head was throbbing and her stomach was in utter revolt. She could only imagine how Kristen felt. For her part, Kristen dashed from the room without waiting for dismissal, and it gave Jordan great pleasure to keep the rest of the class several moments longer, hoping that was enough to give the girl a head start for the parking lot and her car.

As soon as she could, Jordan made tracks for the faculty rest room, where she wet a paper towel to cool her feverish face and fight an inevitable wave of nausea.

"Are you okay?"

She would have groaned, except she didn't even have the energy to be rude. But she did wish Bess Flynn would have chosen any other moment to follow her in here.

"Fine. A long day, that's all."

Bess wandered closer to share the view of Jordan's mirror. "You look it. Definitely a bit yellowish green around the gills, even discounting this awful fluorescent lighting."

"That's nothing to how I feel inside."

"I heard about the trouble with your students. Tough break. For someone who doesn't invite conflict into her life, you sure found it."

Jordan tried not to notice how washed-out she appeared next to the other woman. "Believe it or not, it wasn't intentional."

"Well, there's one good thing to come of this. You don't have to wrestle over whether to take on a writers' group or not anymore. Morris Fields will be so upset with you for ruining the picture-perfect serenity of Mount Liberty, he won't let you hold so much as a wake for one of the biology class's frogs."

The reminder of the smells of formaldehyde she'd sniffed once too often passing that room had Jordan's stomach revolting again. She clutched her middle with one hand and grabbed at the sink with the other to keep herself steady.

"Hey, are you sure you're all right?"

"Just a nervous stomach. I skipped lunch and I guess that was a mistake after all."

"Positive?"

"Believe me. I worked thirty years to get this condition. I know what it is."

"Okay. I didn't mean to sound nosy." Taking another paper towel, Bess wet it and held it to Jordan's brow for her. "What happened to the kids was a tough break, but things have a way of working out in most cases. Though I am concerned for Ridge. I'm worried that he'll be defeated by this and not come back."

"You mean as in 'drop out'?"

"It's a possibility. Once his father learns about his suspension, things are going to be rougher at the Biggs homestead than usual. It might drive Ridge away once and for all."

Jordan squeezed her eyes shut, trying not to remember Ridge's pride when she'd presented him with an A+ for his last assignment. She'd added a suggestion that he submit the piece to the *Mount Liberty Journal* as a possible editorial. "He shouldn't have hit Jack."

"Depends what Jack said to him. Shoot, under the right circumstances, I could see myself taking a swing at some of the narrow-minded jerks in this town." With a sigh, Bess patted Jordan's back. "I think we could have made a difference working together. I'm sorry that circumstances have you more determined than ever to lock yourself away. Take care."

Even though Jordan opened her mouth to argue against that assumption, she didn't have the energy to follow through. What could she say anyway that wouldn't dig a deeper hole for her?

She wasn't feeling much better by the time she walked out to her car. Not even the first heavy drops of rain that began to splatter noisily, marking the end of their drought, could lift her spirits. All she wanted was to get home, curl up with a blanket and let the rain and the wind blowing lustily through the pines lull her to sleep. But when she saw a slope-shouldered woman walking along the road, she felt a sinking sensation inside her.

It was the white uniform sticking out beneath the ill-fitted all-weather coat that gave away Mrs. Biggs's identity. Jordan would probably have recognized her regardless, due to the coil of hair wrapped around her head. It was the same striking midnight black of Ridge's.

Her heart heavy, she stopped beside the woman and rolled down the passenger window. "Mrs. Biggs? I'm Jordan Mills, Ridge's English teacher. Let me give you a ride before you're soaked!"

Once the woman had been handsome, even pretty, but too many years of hard work and disappointment after disappointment had worn her down and stolen her ability to smile without effort. Who knew what other damage lay beyond the poor soul's opaque stare?

She tugged her jacket closer around her and peered at the plush leather passenger seat with nothing short of longing.

"I...thank you, but I'm sure my husband will be along. He must be running late."

He would be very late, unless that pickup truck that had rolled over down from her house had suffered less damage than she'd believed. It was Stone who'd told her that it belonged to Ridge's father. At the time, there hadn't been an opportunity to ask how that would affect the family. Now she couldn't focus on anything else.

"Why don't you get in anyway?" she said, leaning over to push open the door. "It's no trouble, and if we see Mr. Biggs along the way, we can wave at him to catch his attention." When the woman still hesitated, Jordan took a gamble. "Please, Mrs. Biggs, you'll catch an awful cold, and I know you must be worried about your son and be eager to get home."

Looking almost faint with relief, the woman got in. "Thank you. Thank you so much. His father will go crazy if he finds out about Ridge getting suspended."

"I'm very sorry, Mrs. Biggs." As Jordan accelerated again, she grimaced at how useless the words sounded.

"He came to tell me before he left the school. That's the kind of boy he is. Sensitive and strong. He doesn't let anything get to him. I taught him good. Taught him that all he can take from his youth is his education from that school and his freedom. Now he's on the brink of losing both. What's he going to do if he doesn't graduate from high school, Ms. Mills? You can't even join the army without a GED. And do you think they're going to keep him on at the market once it gets around that he beat up the mayor's son?"

Jordan gripped the steering wheel, feeling the woman's words like lashes from a whip. Her insides twisted themselves into yet another knot, and she had to blink often to keep the image of the road clear before her. "You'll have to tell me where you live, Mrs. Biggs. Do I go to the light? Turn before?"

"Left at the light, then the first left after the gas station. We're in the woods. You'll regret you offered the ride. It ain't just the roads, they're fair enough, unless there's flooding. But we don't— Well, I reckon you know we're poor, Ms. Mills."

The woman's abrupt conclusions disturbed her as much as anything else she'd heard today. "Do you think me that much of a snob, Mrs. Biggs? I live out here myself. I know what it means to live a frugal existence. My father was a minister at a local church. I never owned a new dress in my life until I was old enough to buy it myself."

"Excuse me." Ridge's mother turned to look out the passenger window. "You look so polished and assured."

"I'm a small-town girl who got lucky enough to locate a few scholarships, worked hard and scratched together an education."

"Ridge talks of you. He says you're a writer."

"Not a very successful one." And lately she'd been sacrificing writing time for too many other things because she was still trying to sort out too much inside her.

"Ridge says that you're the best teacher he's ever had."

The declaration left her feeling beyond humble. She didn't deserve the praise.

"I've barely been his teacher for two months, Mrs. Biggs."

"Long enough to know how he feels about you—and maybe how you feel about him?"

She cast the woman a sidelong glance and nearly got trapped by those dark, exhausted but wise eyes. Maybe in another life, Georgia Biggs had been a gypsy, and Jordan suspected there was still enough strength in her to cast a spell or two. "A ride is all I'm offering," she warned quietly. "I'm very fond of Ridge, but I'm in enough trouble without looking for more."

"I would never ask you to risk your own career."

And if Santa Claus could pick a chief counsel it would be Jack Nolan, Sr. Jordan's laugh held no humor. "You're trying to save your son's future."

"I have three children, Ms. Mills," Georgia Biggs said as Jordan turned into the designated county road and headed down into the woods. "Ridge is my oldest, and if something happens to me, I need to know he'll be able to take care of his younger brothers."

God. Would the shocks ever stop coming? "That's a terrible burden to put on a boy only in his teens."

"I know it. But when I had a chance to leave my husband, I didn't take it. Now I'm too scared. Too old."

"You're never too old to protect yourself and your family, Mrs. Biggs."

The woman didn't respond, but to Jordan's relief, soon afterward she gestured toward a nearly overgrown driveway. "That's ours. You can let me off here. There are enough trees to keep me from getting too wet."

Jordan couldn't deny she was relieved. Her father used to go calling on people all the time, and he would make her go, too. Accepting meals from people who barely had anything themselves, and lived in buildings that looked ready to fall down, had given her nightmares.

"You think me a selfish woman and a coward, don't you, Ms. Mills?"

"No, ma'am. I'm the last person to judge anyone, because I've made mistakes, too. But I do believe it's what you do with the lessons you learn that's important."

"Teach that to Ridge," the older woman said to her with a sudden intensity. "Help my son get what he needs, Ms. Mills. Fight for him the way I can't."

So that he would stay in Mount Liberty, under the roof with an alcoholic who Jordan suspected succumbed to streaks of violence when he drank? She had a feeling Ridge wouldn't thank her for that. But dear heaven, something had to be done.

"Be careful, Mrs. Biggs. And tell Ridge... tell him that I hope to see him in class next Wednesday."

Chapter Nine

"Bad news. I'm not going to be able to make it tonight. Kristen's no better."

Stone waited to hear Jordan's response, although he doubted she was surprised. He'd phoned her Thursday evening to tell her that his niece had come down with a bad cold, knowing she would wonder why the girl hadn't been in school and suspect the worst. Today the poor kid had almost no voice and a cough nearly bad enough to shake windows. It had been his idea to stay home with her instead of asking Mrs. Tucker to come over. Kristen hadn't seemed to care one way or another, which he told himself was testament to how bad she really felt.

"She must feel awful if she's missing the game tonight."

"Mmm...but I don't know that she's too sorry, under the circumstances. In any case, it's just as well, since it's still raining."

"Have you called a doctor?"

"I want to. But she's threatened to lock her door if I try it."

"I see. At least we know she has enough strength left to still wage war on you."

He could hear the smile in her voice and tucked the phone's receiver deeper into his shoulder, which was exactly where he would like to have her. "Do you have to sound so happy about it? You'll have me thinking you're relieved that I'm not coming over there."

"If you're fishing for sympathy, all mine is directed toward Kristen."

Stone had already figured that out, and as much as he loved his niece, the announcement made him jealous, too. Okay, not really jealous, but . . .

Oh, hell, Demarest, admit it. It's jealousy, and you don't like knowing it any better than you like hearing her take the news so cheerfully.

"Aren't you too big to sulk?"

Jordan's gently teasing remark was almost the same thing Tracy used to say to him when he didn't get a piece of her fresh-baked pie before company came over, or she wouldn't come back to bed on a Sunday morning. The memory brought a sharp ache under his ribs, sharper than he'd felt in a while, and drew his gaze to the photograph on his desk.

"Stone. I didn't mean to offend you."

He sighed, feeling tangled in knots from looking at the photo and wanting to listen to Jordan's sexy voice. "It's not you. It's . . . me. Forget it."

"No, it's me," she replied, her voice barely audible thanks to the rain pelting the windows of his office. "I guess I'm not yet used to the idea of . . . our arrangement. How to act, you know. And I was never any good at flirting."

She didn't need to learn; what she had was potent enough. Last night, for example, like the night before, he'd dreamed of her, and when he'd awakened, he'd been hard and miserable. If it wasn't for Kristen, he would have driven over to

Jordan's and convinced her to help him do something about it.

"Maybe we'll get better as we go along," he said, convinced things couldn't get worse.

"Maybe we'll wise up and quit while we're ahead."

Stone nearly snapped the phone in two from the verbal blow that struck somewhere around the solar plexus. "Is that what you want?"

"Do you?"

"You brought it up."

"Because you sounded so... indifferent."

He would have laughed if it had been physically possible at the moment. "Jordan. Trust me, I'm feeling anything but indifferent right now."

"Oh."

"Yeah. Oh."

She was silent for a second, then abruptly uttered a breathy laugh.

"What?" That provocative sound triggered sensors—all of them in the lower half of his anatomy.

"Maybe what you really need is one of those 1-900 numbers."

"What I need is you."

A microphone could have picked up a hair falling off a dog, she grew so quiet.

"That was nice, Demarest," she murmured at last.

Nice? He'd pulled those five words out of the deepest part of him, and all she could say was *nice?* "Are you sure you're an English teacher? I've met auto mechanics more expansive."

"Romantic. Provocative. Is that better?"

Much, but now something else intrigued him. "I think I embarrassed you."

"I'll plead the Fifth, if you don't mind. Suffice it to say, I've never been a great fan of telephones. I prefer to be able to see the person who's handing me a line."

"Is it a given that it was a line?"

"On the phone, I always suspect so."

"And what about your ex? Have you convinced him that that's what you think, too?"

"He's not my ex, and I don't know or care what he believes anymore."

"Ex-lover."

"Why are you doing this?"

"Because you've never told me about him, and in my book what a woman doesn't say means more than what she does."

"That's not what you said a moment ago."

"Don't change the subject."

After a low sound of frustration, she said, "He was one of my instructors in school. I was dazzled with his sophistication and his mind. Unfortunately I was too young and unsophisticated to see what else he was and wasn't. By the time I did, he'd done enough damage to my self-esteem to keep me nicely under his control. In other words, between the Reverend and Brent, I did the proverbial 'out of the frying pan into the fire' leap. Feel better now?"

Not much. It would do no good to wish for things to have been different. Back when she was falling prey to Slick's autocratic control, he was weaving fantasies of a long life with Tracy. But that didn't mean he didn't hurt for her, nor did it shut off an unusually strong rush of anger and possessiveness that came with the merest thought of her with someone else.

"I guess I'm realizing that I don't share well," he told her, trying to explain himself and yet not chase her away. "Just thought I'd pass that on for what it's worth."

"Stone, I've never been involved in more than one relationship at a time. I wouldn't do that to you, either."

"Thanks," he murmured gruffly, closing his eyes to savor the relief and pleasure. He needed to change the subject; otherwise, he would say something to scare her for sure. "Before I forget, Kristen did mention something about calling you in case there was some big homework project. Thought I'd warn you in case you're thinking about pulling the phone plugs again."

"As a matter of fact, there is a rather weighty assignment."

"Uh-oh. And I assured her that all she needed to worry about was getting better."

"True. On the other hand, this assignment might help get her mind off her troubles. I've directed the class to do a poem, a newspaper article, an essay and a short story all on the same theme. It will count as fifty percent of their final exam. I passed out the copies of the instructions today."

"Damn, Teach, you're one demanding lady."

Jordan chuckled. "Hey, they have until April to turn them in."

Nevertheless, Stone knew the news would throw Kristen into a panic. "I wish I could get hold of a copy of the instructions for her. At least she wouldn't spend the weekend biting her nails down to nubs as she's been doing all day. But I'm not about to leave here with her feeling as bad as she does."

"Well...if you thought it would help her, and you wouldn't mind...I could bring them over."

"You can't come out in this mess."

"I don't mind, and it's not as if traffic's heavy, since the diehard fans went to New Diana for this week's game. Of course, if you'd prefer I not—"

"What I'd *prefer* is not risking your health and safety."

"If it'll ease your conscience, I'll promise to wear my bulkiest weatherproof gear, drive slowly and only stay a few minutes."

"I'll set the timer on the oven," he drawled, smiling. "Besides taking a left at the light, do you know how to find us?"

He gave her instructions, and as soon as he hung up, he crossed the hall to tell Kristen. The girl had been lying listlessly in bed, watching TV but without much interest. The moment she heard the news, she croaked what was meant to be a shriek and sat up as if she'd been launched by NASA.

"She can't come here!"

"Why not? I thought you might be glad to have some company."

"Not her!"

"But you said you liked her."

"She's the best! How could you do this to me?"

Stone wasn't following this at all. "Help. What am I missing? You think the world of her—"

"She's smart and beautiful!" Kristen cried, her voice sounding even worse as a result of her increased anxiety. "And, oh jeez—she's *published*, Uncle Stone! We can't have a real writer come to this...cave and see me like this!"

"Whoa, whoa." Despite his shock, as the teen flung back her blanket and sheet and tried to scramble out of bed, Stone tucked her back in. "You're not going anywhere, young lady."

"I have to shower and do something with this hair!"

"Stop trying to scream at me, or you'll do permanent damage to your throat. What's more, there's nothing wrong with this house. You may not be able to eat off the floors, but you won't get carried off by pesky four-, eight- and hundred-legged critters, either. The important thing is that she'd called to see how you're doing, and—"

"I didn't hear the phone ring."

Damnation, he'd forgotten that he was the one who'd called Jordan! "It was one of those weird situations. I'd picked up the phone—and there she was."

"Really?"

The kid twisted his heart into a double pretzel with her waif face and hopeful, croaky voice. "Yeah, really. She may be cautious about getting close to people, but I think she has a particular soft spot for you. Why else would she want to come over in this kind of weather to drop off the assignment?"

"I wonder if Ridge knows yet?"

Stone smoothed her limp hair back from her pale face. "You can ask her."

Jordan arrived less than an hour later. Stone had used the time to try to qualify what he'd told his niece and raced around picking up the small mountain of newspapers spilling off the coffee table and spreading across the carpet, puffing couch pillows, swiping at suddenly obvious cobwebs under lamp shades and by air ducts. In the last second, he even changed shirts to something less wrinkled. By the time he remembered that his hair could probably use combing, too, the flash of headlights in the picture window told him that he was too late to worry about it.

"I'm going to create a new county lake in the middle of your living room," she said, dashing inside as he held open the door for her.

"Don't worry about it. We aren't doing the cover shoot for 'Texas Game Warden at Home and Play' until next week."

She'd been gingerly easing off the hood of her all-weather coat, but paused to give him a quizzical look. "That's a joke, right?"

"A lame attempt at one. Let me take that...published author."

After a slight hesitation, she set down a canvas tote and turned to allow him to help her off with the coat. "She told you."

"You're one surprise after another."

"What's that supposed to mean?"

"Nothing. It's just...I never pictured someone like me having an affair with a writer before."

"This is only a hunch, but I think you're setting yourself up for a big disappointment if you think that provides a greater afterglow."

The mouth on the woman. Stone came up behind her and wrapped his arms around her. "I'm impressed. Is that an acceptable comment?"

He watched her struggle for words. It happened so rarely, he had no trouble finding the patience to wait her out.

"It's a very personal thing, poetry. At least to me. It became more so when Brent read my work and categorized it as 'twentieth-century vapors.' I haven't been able to finish anything I've started since."

The faintest crack in her voice, easily missed if he hadn't been paying attention, had Stone turning her around. To his amazement, he saw tears in her eyes and a hurt that thrust a long sword into his heart.

He wrapped his arms around her again, and this time there was only compassion in the embrace. He might not understand her work, he might not even comprehend the psyche of what it took to be a writer, but he understood the soul under attack. It was that part of her that he ached for.

"The man isn't only a bastard, he's a fool."

"You know what? I think you're right."

They laughed briefly, and he allowed her self-conscious withdrawal, which let him note how young she looked again in her V-necked crimson sweater and jeans, how sweet with the rain lingering on her eyelashes and nose, and the finest strands of her hair that clung to her damp skin. Combined with the kick of sophistication and mystery of maturity in her eyes, as well as the coolness of the night clinging to her like cologne, the sum total created a wholly alluring enigma.

She was a complicated woman. What choice did he have but to reach out, frame her face with his hands and place a tender kiss on her lips? "Thanks for coming."

She smiled back at him. "How's she doing? Any change?"

"A considerable one. Now she's furious with me because her hair and the house aren't perfect."

Reaching for her tote, she nodded. "Let's see what we can do to get her mind redirected."

He simply could have told her that Kristen's room was the first on the right and left the two of them alone, but he was curious to see them together, to witness Jordan in the role of teacher, as well as that of woman, apart from the sexual persona he knew. Besides that, he'd also grown damned tired of his own company. Jordan, with her sharp mind, her elusive behavior and her physical allure, presented too much temptation even to a self-styled recluse like him.

"Kristen...?" Jordan said as she paused in the doorway of the room. "How's it going?"

"Hi, Ms. Mills. You'd better not get too close. I'm sure I'm awfully contagious."

If she wasn't, the kid did look and sound the part. But heedless of the warning, Jordan entered the room recently painted in a soft coral, and sat down on the edge of the full-size bed with its new Laura Ashley linens and comforter.

"I won't stay long. Poor thing, you do look as if you feel miserable. I only wanted you to know that I was concerned about you, and bring you what I passed out in class today."

Not everything she brought had to do with homework. Stone surmised she'd stopped on the way over to pick up a few things to pass the time in bed faster, too.

Besides the photocopied instruction sheets from class, she placed several fashion and beauty magazines in the girl's lap, a paperback romance novel and a small stuffed bear, whose fluffy pink fur just happened to match Kristen's nightshirt. The gesture was as thoughtful as it was generous, and Kristen gaped as if discovering Jordan was the real Santa.

"Ms. Mills... I don't know what to say. Thank you so much!"

Jordan shrugged away the compliment and indicated the magazines. "The book was the biggest guess. She tends to be one of my favorites."

"You read this kind of stuff?"

"I read everything. A great number of women do. Do you know surveys show that women are more diverse and well-rounded readers than men?"

That won a satisfied smile from his niece, who leaned back against the wall of frilly pillows and said to him, "Hear that, Uncle Stone?"

"Thanks for pointing out that I'm one of those who prove the statistics right," he grumbled, although he was enjoying himself.

Finally Jordan drew out a manila envelope and from it several pieces of paper stapled together. "This you may be less thrilled to look at."

As she explained the assignment to Kristen, Stone admired how she managed to make it sound adventurous and exciting. Even though she clearly didn't feel well, his niece's eyes soon brightened from more than fever.

"English tests are my favorite," Kristen said when Jordan was done. "But I have to admit that I'm looking forward to this project. What a learning experience."

Jordan nodded. "I'm glad you approve. I rather thought there might be a few of you who wouldn't cringe."

The mention of others inevitably triggered Kristen's sympathies. "What about Ridge, Ms. Mills? Have you heard anything from him? How's he going to get his copy of this?"

"I haven't heard from or about him," Jordan admitted quietly. "But I gave his mother a ride home the other day, and she seems a concerned and kind woman. I'm sure if I give a set to her on Monday, she'll see that Ridge gets them."

"But will he even come back to school? I have to tell you, Ms. Mills, if he doesn't, I don't know if I will, either."

This was quite a news flash to Stone, and he pushed away from his lazy post against the doorjamb. "Now, wait a minute, young lady...."

Jordan spun around to shoot him a look of appeal, then turned back to Kristen. "You don't have to worry about that right now. What you need to focus on is getting your voice and your health back." She rose. "I don't want to tire you any more than I already have."

"Oh, but you didn't! Please don't go."

"If I stay, you'll talk yourself into an even worse case of laryngitis." She stroked Kristen's hair. "Be well. And call me if you have any questions or concerns about the assignment."

"Or anything else?"

Stone had to give his niece high marks for tenacity, and Jordan for not freezing up as he expected. Instead, she considered the question and finally nodded.

"You have my number," she replied quietly.

Well, well, he thought, following her back down the hallway. When she would have turned right to head for her coat and escape, he took hold of her arm and tugged her left. In the kitchen, he took her near-empty tote from her, set it on the kitchen table and took hold of her shoulders again.

"You meant that? She can call you?"

"I don't make a habit of saying things I don't mean."

"Just checking my hearing." Knowing what that gesture had cost her, he added, "Can I get you a drink? Coffee?"

She touched a hand to her stomach. "Actually...do you have any milk?"

"Milk."

"Cold, hot, it doesn't matter. I happen to have this annoying condition."

Stone lifted an eyebrow, but he did open the refrigerator and reach for the carton. "How annoying?"

"Don't have a stroke, Stone Man. This is merely a pre-ulcerous stomach."

"Merely. Sheesh. You keep too much inside, that's what your problem is."

"Forgive me for pointing out the obvious, but aren't you the man who wants an affair with me because he knows I don't come with unwanted complications?"

Stone put down the container and all but swept Jordan into the dark cubbyhole that was the utility room. "That kid back there has sonar ears. And for the record," he added, boxing her in against the dryer, "you're definitely a complication."

He punctuated the remark with the kiss he'd wanted to give her the instant he'd opened the door to her. Immediately her lips yielded under the insistent pressure of his, and he took full advantage, driving his tongue deep into her mouth. She made a soft sound of pleasure and melted against him. It was all the invitation he needed. Wrapping his hand around her loose braid, he drew back her head and gave in to the craving that had been building inside him since she entered the house.

Her warmth, the intoxicating sweet taste of her, filled him, blocked out the pressures of the week, the future, every thought but her. The sweep of her hands gliding over his back, the sudden, surprising grasp at his hair, shot his desire into the next gear.

"I want to lift you onto this thing, rip your clothes off and take you right here," he said, inching toward her mouth again.

"If you kiss me like you just did, you might not have a choice."

"These walls are too damned thin."

Jordan pressed her face against his shoulder. "Groan. You should have let me go."

"The hell with that idea." The thought of having to deny himself the simplest contact with her for what appeared to be several more days had Stone yielding to impulse and, taking hold of her waist, setting her up on the appliance after all.

"Are you mad?" she whispered.

"Just for a minute." He pushed up her sweater and saw that, as he'd guessed, all she wore beneath was a red camisole. Nothing else.

He uttered a groan, covered and molded her with his hands and buried his face in the valley of her breasts. She was so soft, so alluring... he moved his head from side to side, nuzzling her with his nose and lips, breathing in her sexy, honest heat and the fragrance that was—Jordan.

"I want your mouth," she whispered, shifting to make it easy for him. In the process, the strap of her camisole slipped, causing lace and satin to cover a little less than before.

Stone's heart lifted to pound in his throat. No wonder artists endured poverty and whatnot to paint the female form over and over again. The combination of grace and strength, purity and the erotic were a narcotic intoxicating the eye and every sense at once.

He took her into his mouth, as much tormented as teased by the fine barrier that separated him from the already taut bud. When she wrapped her legs around his waist, suddenly a taste wasn't enough. He pulled her closer, deeper, desire growing needles like a thistle. All the while, her hands, slim and fluid, moved over his hair, his ears, his neck, easing the pangs, encouraging them.

"Maybe we could go out into the garage," he whispered against her damp skin.

"But your car's outside."

"I think I remember a sleeping bag out there. A lawn chair. Something."

Jordan's soft laughter teased his hair. "Let me down, Stone. Stone... what if Kristen—ah!"

He straightened but didn't release her completely. That would be asking too much. But to prepare himself for the inevitable releasing, he sipped at her lips and slid his hands to her bottom to rock her against his throbbing flesh. "You feel so good."

"I shouldn't have come. You're going to be miserable."

"And not you?"

"Me, too."

He finally backed away to rest against the washer. "We have to figure out a time," he said, raking his hands through his hair.

"Maybe Kristen will feel better in a day or two."

"But we're getting into my busiest time of the year. I could work around the clock and still have a backlog of work."

"I never realized. It is a seven-day-a-week job you have, isn't it?"

"Twenty-four hours a day."

"You'll make me feel guilty for taking you away even this long from Kristen."

He took her hand and lifted it to his lips. "I think I like you feeling sorry for me."

"And I think I'm going to get out of here while there's still time."

As she skirted by him and hurried through the kitchen to the living room, he followed. "What about your milk?"

"I have some at home."

When he began to protest, she touched her index finger to his mouth. "If I stay, we'll get into trouble, and I don't want Kristen to find out about us that way."

"Then I'll tell her, and—"

"No! Don't you see? The timing is terrible."

Everything was terrible, especially him. Stone paced half the night, or tossed and turned. Things weren't going much better for Kristen, only for a different reason. Every hour or so, he got up to feed her either cough syrup or aspirin. Then he went back to his own misery.

At 4:00 a.m., finally exhausted and her fever broken, she settled down into a deep sleep. He, on the other hand, remained as wide-awake as he'd ever been in his life.

"This is nuts," he muttered at nearly five. He tossed back his sheet and swung his legs to the floor.

In five minutes, he was easing his truck out of the driveway. In five more, he was knocking on Jordan's door.

"It's me!" he called when he heard her open the upstairs-bedroom window. Thank goodness her nearest neighbor was at least a mile away. Even so, he'd managed to annoy an owl in the woods that hooted in protest.

"What's wrong?" she called in that funny hushed voice people use in the dark. "Is it Kristen?"

"Let me in!" The heavy rain had stopped, but it was still drizzling. He hunkered deeper into his jacket's upturned collar to avoid its fine sting.

She came down, and he could tell by the way she tore at the dead bolt that she'd lost her sense of humor.

"If this is what I think it is, you're insane," she said in lieu of greeting, the instant she opened the door.

"Good. That's one less thing we have to discuss." Barely through the doorway, he hauled her into his arms and kissed her to make sure he didn't have to explain anything else. Then he reached back blindly to set the dead bolt and led her toward the stairs. "You can read me the riot act later."

Slow to recover, she didn't speak until he'd gotten her halfway up the stairs. "You left your sick niece alone to come here for sex?"

"Her fever broke. She's finally sleeping soundly for the first time in two days." In her bedroom, he stopped. Maybe it was the pristine whiteness of everything, the way it made him feel as if he were in the presence of an angel or goddess. Untouchable here in her own lair. Why had none of that struck him the last time?

Because you had a head full of stitches.

As if she'd read his mind, Jordan reached up to touch the bandage that covered the sutures, which wouldn't come out for a few more days.

"It's all right," she murmured. "I've been thinking about you, too."

Relieved, he reached for her. She brushed away his hands.

"No. Let me."

She eased his jacket off him and let it fall to the floor. Then she took hold of his T-shirt and started lifting it. As she did, she stooped to press openmouthed kisses on the skin she exposed. The featherlike caress of her lips, the way she nuzzled his chest hair, his ribs, his nipples...left him standing there like a fly in a spider's silken trap. By the time she dropped the shirt, searing-hot lava had replaced the blood racing through his veins.

He reached for the knot on her robe. Before he had it open, he knew she wore nothing beneath. Like before, the knowledge proved unbearably sexy to him, and even though she hadn't yet succeeded in completely unfastening his jeans, he slipped his hands inside the robe and drew her against him.

"God...that's so good. Heaven."

"Stone, let's get you undressed so we can both get under the blankets. It's chilly."

"I'll warm you."

He began by spreading kisses over her face—light, brief kisses that soon had her sighing in pleasure. When he got to her throat, he slipped his hand down her front, into the soft nest of curls between her thighs. He had no idea where his patience came from; his own body was stone hard and ached for release. Not the ideal condition for inspiring finesse. But touching her...somehow she made him draw something extra, something untapped within him.

He took her mouth again as he let his fingers venture deeper. She murmured or sighed, gripped his biceps, but pressed closer, closer. Her sleekness lured him, and her heat fed his, and he moved slower . . . slower . . . all the while directing them toward the bed, where the tangled sheets exclaimed in ghostly honesty that she hadn't been sleeping any better than him.

"Lie back."

She didn't sit—she flowed, arms and eyes wide open. He stripped off the rest of his things, watching her wait for him.

He almost forgot protection again. That's what the wanting did to him. But when he joined her on the bed, kneeling between her legs and running his hands, fingers splayed, he had control again. He drew his hands over her from her shoulders to her hips. When he heard her catch her breath, he knew her breasts were particularly sensitive tonight. He understood enough about women's cycles to know what that probably meant. He wondered if she suffered much during that time. Did she like to be held? He found himself wanting to know. Being a lover was different than having casual sex. It came with responsibilities, and that added something. He didn't mind at all.

"If this hurts . . ." he said, lowering himself and rubbing his cheek across her breast.

"No. Just sensitive. I must be getting close."

"A good sensitive?" he murmured, wetting her with his tongue. "Tell me what you want." He took her hand and closed it around his wrist. "Show me."

She wanted him everywhere, and she wasn't shy about showing him—nor was there an inch of her that wasn't as sensitive to his touch as she'd been those first times.

And then she proved again that she wasn't shy about exploring him.

They were both beyond ready when he finally reached for protection and entered her. She cried out, and the sound that rose in his throat was almost as piercing. Without a word, they sought each other's gaze and linked their hands. Then he began the deeper, harder thrusts.

If he could have had anything... anything at that point, it would be to live in this moment forever. But the instant he began feeling her spasm around him, his body followed her into a shuddering, breathless climax.

Chapter Ten

"We have to stop meeting like this."

Jordan lowered the damp paper towel from her face and dealt with the shifting-floor motions that came along with the feeling of déjà vu. Bess Flynn was entering the women's room again, and like the last time the woman couldn't have picked a more inopportune moment. Hoping to waylay at least a few of the questions she knew would be forthcoming, she dug into her purse for her supply of tissues and blew her sore nose.

"Now, that sounds bad. You should be home in bed."

"I agree," she told her fellow teacher, who didn't help her mood by looking fresh and radiant in a coral pantsuit. "But good old Morris is still angry with me for defending Ridge last week, and he made it clear that he didn't care if I contaminated everyone in Mount Liberty, he wanted me in class."

"Yes, indeedy. 'Revenge is mine,' sayeth Mayor Jack."

At least someone understood. Jordan tossed the tissue into the trash basket. "You can say that again. It didn't help that Jack Jr. scored fourteen points all by his lonesome self at last Friday's game in all that rain and mud." And now it was Wednesday afternoon, and she felt as if someone had driven over her with two eighteen-wheelers and backed up for a repeat performance. If she made it home, she promised herself an immediate hot-water bottle and bed.

"Did you catch this cold from Kristen? The poor thing sounds only a little better than you. Oh, don't roll your eyes like that. So what if she told me that you've been helping her and Ridge Biggs keep up with their schoolwork. If she hadn't, I would have heard the buzz from their other teachers that you approached. I think it's wonderful that you of all people are reaffirming the 'no man is an island' theory."

"So glad you're pleased," Jordan replied, fighting back another sneeze. Championing that, she dampened the paper towel again for her feverish brow. "Not everyone is, particularly where Ridge is concerned. A few think that a suspension cancels the student's right to make up any work. Charleton in the science department is going to give him a failing mark for the biology test he missed." She'd been furious. And people had called her remote?

"Mel Charleton's wife ran off with another man shortly before school began. In his current mood, he wouldn't save Kermit the Frog from a dissection knife. Tell Ridge to work real hard in class for a week or so, and then ask if he can do some extra credit project to offset the grade."

"Now you want me to coach him? Isn't that the guidance counselor's job? Why don't I offer to adopt him while I'm at it?" As a wave of nausea hit her, Jordan moaned and clung to the sink.

"Jordan, maybe you'd better sit down. Do you want me to call the office and insist they get someone to take your last class?"

"And leave Kristen and Ridge to the vultures circling to finish them off? I didn't break all of my own rules to see that happen."

Bess grimaced. "I do appreciate that, really I do, but I never meant for you to end up in a hospital in the process!"

It was a relief when some of the queasiness receded. "All I need to do is get through the next hour. Then I can go home and sleep until tomorrow."

"Sweetie, look in the mirror. You need more than sleep. You need a doctor."

Close inspections were one thing she'd been trying to avoid, too aware of what she would see. She'd been losing weight all week because the mere thought of food made her ill. What's more, her skin looked about as substantial as rice paper, and if her hair was a wig, it wouldn't bring fifty cents at a garage sale. Thank goodness she'd succeeded in keeping Stone away. After he'd heard she was coming down with what Kristen had, he'd wanted to bring her dinner from the local fast-food restaurant in between his hectic trips from one end of the county to another. Fortunately she'd convinced him that she had plenty of homemade soup in the freezer, which she did, but had no interest or energy to heat.

"I'll consider making an appointment if I'm not better by the weekend."

"By the weekend, you should be thinking of the color of satin you'd like in your coffin."

Groaning at the equally sick humor, Jordan tossed the paper towel into the wastebasket, as well. "For the record, I'd prefer cremation, thanks." The mere thought of someone thinking she might want to spend eternity next to the Reverend made her shudder.

Taking her arm, Bess turned her around and took hold of her upper arms. "Now, hear this, Corporal Mills. Field Marshall Flynn says that you're going to at least let me walk you to your room. Maybe this way, I won't have to deal with guilt over you fainting and breaking that perfect nose on the hallway tile."

Jordan didn't think to argue. She was too grateful to have the supportive arm.

Not only did Bess help her to her room, but she stayed until the first students began arriving. "Have someone come down the hall to get me if you need help."

"You're really being too nice."

"That's because I like you, and I want you around so we can become friends," Bess whispered in her ear.

"Are you that hard up for companionship?" Good grief, she'd never had a real *girl*friend in her life! How did you explain that to someone?

"Promise, Jordan."

Acquiescence was easier than arguing. Jordan promised.

After Bess left, Jordan knew she would have to summon everything inside her to appear, if not healthy, then strong enough to maintain control through this class. So, as her students arrived, she greeted them with nods and smiles.

She noted an electricity building in the air. It almost crackled when Kristen and Ridge entered. Then Jack arrived with Bo and several others, and the atmosphere grew explosive.

"Will you look who's here," Bo drawled. "Jailbait . . . and the teacher's pet."

Before anyone else could add to that, Jordan tapped a ruler on the metal surface of her desk. "That will be quite enough, Mr. Spradlin. Everyone sit down. We have a great deal of material to cover in this hour, and let me stress now that we either get to it now, or you inherit it as homework."

It troubled her that Kristen looked worse for wear as she neared the end of her first day back in school since taking ill. More than likely, that had a great deal to do with Ridge being back for the first day, too. When the two of them chose to sit side by side near the door, Jordan could only hope Ridge could restrain himself from doing anything if provoked. She wasn't sure she had the strength to stop things if the boys got physical.

"Let's get one thing straight," she continued once she saw everyone was present that would be. "There will be no outbursts or taunts. If anyone feels they can't get through the class without causing trouble, tell me now or forever hold your peace."

"I do," someone called in falsetto from the far side of the room.

Several giggles erupted at whoever had made the appropriate wedding-ceremony response. Although Jordan hadn't expected total compliance to her warning, she was still annoyed at the need for someone to test her. "Mr. Dodd," she said, glad to have spotted the person who'd spoken. "What seems to be your problem? Did you not hear me just say what I would not tolerate?"

Jack Nolan's favorite receiver blushed. "Sorry, Ms. Mills."

"Take care, Mr. Dodd. Mount Liberty may be undefeated so far this year, but if you end up with a week of detention, your absence from football practice might be sorely felt. Isn't that right, Mr. Nolan?"

Jack didn't look eager to be brought into the discussion. He shot his teammate a disgruntled look. "Sit on it, Mel."

After that brief exchange, things calmed down, and Jordan thought they might get through the hour without further incident. And to an extent, they did. The end-of-school bell sounded, and she excused the class without homework—mostly because, feeling the way she did, she dreaded the thought of having to look at a few dozen examples of horrific penmanship anytime soon. Cheered, most of the group raced for the door.

During that exodus, Jordan saw two girls stop before Kristen. Cassie McAndrews and Sheila Todd were the captain and cocaptain of the cheerleading squad. Because of the growing rigidity in Kristen's stance, along with Ridge's stunned, then furious expression, Jordan knew whatever was going on couldn't be good news. As a result, she drew out packing away her textbooks and notes for as long as she could. But once Kristen ripped a pin off her sweater and flung it at Cassie, she headed across the room. By the time she got there, however, the girls had collected the pin and left.

"Are you all right?" she asked Kristen, who'd sunk back into her chair and was staring at the floor. Ridge stood beside her, gently rubbing her back.

"No, she's not," Ridge said in her behalf. "They dropped her from the squad. Dropped her for missing the game! She was sick, for crying out loud! She couldn't help it!"

Kristen shook her head. "It's not because of that. It's because I broke off with Jack."

"That makes it even more unfair," Ridge countered, dark streaks of red appearing on his sharp cheekbones.

"You know what?" Kristen replied, lifting her chin. "I don't care. I don't want to be a part of any group that's so self-serving and snobbish that it doesn't care about the truth."

Ridge gave Jordan a pained, hunted look. "Is there anything you can do?"

What influence did he think she had? Hadn't she failed in her attempts to help him? Besides, if Kristen was right—and her hunch was to agree with the girl—she was better off separating herself from such a group.

"No, don't put Ms. Mills in a bind," Kristen said before Jordan could reply. "It's my decision whether to fight it or not, and as far as I'm concerned, they've done me a favor. It's time to focus on my future, not that childish sorority stuff."

But the smile she gave Jordan as she and Ridge left was more hurt than confident.

Youth, Jordan thought, driving home; as the saying went, they could be unkind. She wouldn't want to be Kristen or Ridge's age again for anything. Her own teen years had been her most difficult as she'd realized exactly how deep and vast the gulf was between her and the Reverend. It was then that she'd learned the true value of silence and keeping one's own counsel. Hopefully Ridge would, too. As for Kristen . . . she had Stone, who was on her side regardless of their occasional moments of miscommunication. He'd proved over the past few days that he had no personal agenda of his own for her, except that she fulfill her dreams and find happiness.

Thoughts of him eased her worry somewhat, but she was surprised when she pulled into her driveway and found him there waiting for her.

Her heart made an unignorable skip as he hurried over and opened her door for her. Since his surprise visit Saturday morning, he'd stayed on her mind almost to the point of distraction. She couldn't deny she was still coming to terms with the tenderness and caring he'd exhibited toward her in those wonderful few hours of stolen lovemaking.

"Let me guess," she said as he immediately took her briefcase from her and assisted her out of her vehicle. "Kristen called you on the car phone again."

"She told me you looked worse than she did the other day when I insisted she stay in bed, so I thought I'd come see for myself while things are a bit slow."

"Well, that's thoughtful, Stone, but all I really need—" She stopped only when he put his hand on her forehead.

"Little fool. You're burning up. Why on earth did you go in today in the first place?"

"To keep my job. I'm not the most popular English teacher at Mount Liberty, and if I start missing classes, Fields made it clear that I'll be out of work by next May, unless he can find someone sooner."

"If you don't start taking better care of yourself, it won't matter what happens next spring, because you won't be here." He exhaled loudly. "Damn it, Jordan, I listened to you about getting a doctor for Kristen. Will you listen to me about seeing yours?"

One thing was certain—being browbeaten like this certainly made her think a visit to a doctor would be a party in comparison. About to tell him so, she wasn't at all prepared for him—no, both hims—to start spinning as if she were watching him from a schoolyard ride. "Stone...?"

"Jordan!"

"Jordan? Come on, sugar. Work on getting those baby blues open."

What baby blues? Her eyes were brown.

It took enormous effort to open her eyes, but something told her she had better. When she finally succeeded, she didn't recognize any of her surroundings...especially not the woman in a white uniform who leaned over her and smiled.

"Ah—not blue. But it's good to have you back with us. That was quite a nap."

"I've been sleeping?"

"For the better part of three hours, I'd say. Since you were brought in."

"Who—what happened?"

"You fainted. You're in the hospital. Quitman. Stone Demarest brought you in, and let me tell you, he's about worn out the waiting-room floor worrying about you. Stay put and I'll tell the doctor that you're awake."

While the nurse went in search of the doctor, Jordan tried to adjust herself to being in the hospital. She didn't like the idea any better than when she'd been here during the Reverend's last days. Less, because she was now the patient.

Fainted...what was wrong with her? She ran her hands over her body, not sure what she was searching for. Maybe she'd hit her head and suffered a concussion. A broken arm? Leg? No, she was in one piece, and nothing was in a cast or even a bandage that she could tell. There was, however, an IV in her arm. That had her panicking a bit.

"Don't pull that out." The nurse came back into view. "You were severely dehydrated. Think of this glucose as getting your system rejuvenated. After you're done, unless the doctor says otherwise, you should be able to go home."

Before she could assure the nurse that she was ready now, the woman was replaced by a bearded man with bloodshot but kind eyes. Jordan decided by his stethoscope that he was the doctor who held her fate in his hands. The name on the pocket of his white jacket said Gray.

"Doctor... I want to go home."

"Why does everyone say that to us?" he replied with a bemused smile and shake of his near-bald head. "Well, in your case, I'm happy to be able to oblige that wish—if you promise to go straight to bed and get plenty of rest for the next few days. Will you do that?"

"Yes." Anything.

"Good girl. I'm going to give you a copy of the test results so you can give them to your own doctor, but I'm sure he or she will concur that the side effects of your cold shouldn't hurt your condition. Just remember, no medication, not even aspirin, until it's been cleared by your own physician."

"My... condition?"

Dramatic eyebrows lifted, and dark eyes grew warmer. "You mean you weren't aware of it?"

"I guess not."

"Ah. Well, then maybe it's a good thing you're already lying down. You're pregnant, Ms. Mills."

Stone almost wished he smoked. At least the bad habit would have given him something to do with his hands.

Once again, he checked his watch. It was almost seven o'clock, and as far as he knew, Jordan was still out of it. How could the doctor say she was all right if she wouldn't wake up? Maybe he'd been wrong and she had hit her head before he caught her. Maybe she'd slipped into a coma. Why didn't the doctors have more to tell him?

He tried to swallow away the metallic taste that kept filling his mouth. It brought back too many memories of the night Tracy and Billie Ann had died. Surely God wouldn't take Jordan from him, too?

"Mr. Demarest?"

He sprang to his feet the moment he saw her—them, actually, because it had been the matronly nurse who'd spoken and was assisting her. But it was Jordan he focused on. She looked as white as the nurse's uniform, and she walked as if unsure of her legs. That was, however, good enough for him.

"Hey, look at you!" He forced a grin, although his throat felt as raw as the rest of his insides. "I was beginning to think you were trying to avoid me and snuck out the back door."

"She's fine," the nurse replied, relinquishing her charge to him. "You just make sure she gets home safely and goes straight to bed."

"Consider it done." He hoped Jordan didn't feel how hard his heart was pounding as he put his arm around her and used his body to help support her. To his relief, though, she looked too dazed to follow much of anything. He planted a kiss on her left temple. "How do you feel?"

She waited until the nurse was out of hearing distance. "Awful. Get me out of here anyway."

The plea came out as barely a whisper, but that was good enough for him. "You bet. Easy does it. The exit's this way. Can you walk, or do you want me to carry you?"

"Why don't we simply hire a blimp to announce we're here together?"

He didn't mind who knew what anymore; however, too grateful to make a fuss, he settled for letting her use him as a brace.

They exited the hospital to find that night had fallen, settling a bone-permeating chill that promised winter was coming—something easily forgotten during the day when the warm sun evoked the glory of Indian summer. Fortunately, since this was a small community hospital, Stone had been able to park only yards away.

He had her settled inside his truck with a minimum of fuss. "So, what did the doctor say?" he asked once he climbed in on the driver's side.

"Um, no one told you?"

"Nope. Other than you needing some rest, and that they wanted to give you the IV. Remember, I'm not family. They weren't about to breach your right to privacy—not that it mattered in this case, right?"

She drew in a deep breath and exhaled with equal care. To Stone, it sounded close to relief, although he assured himself it was probably effects of the cold.

"There's no big mystery," she said at last. "I'm run-down more than I thought. Guess I'd better find myself some good multivitamins."

Stone felt guilty for previous statements when he'd been upset with her for not jumping at his request for her to help with Kristen. He was only beginning to learn how she filled her days, but he should have known that being someone with her innate curiosity and hunger for knowledge, for life, she had been doing too much. Add to that her internal battles over the people who'd disappointed, abused and hurt her, and it was probably a testament to her own willpower that this hadn't happened sooner.

She was more fragile than he'd let himself acknowledge because he'd had his own needs and trouble. It was time to be honest with himself and face up to the truth: Jordan meant a great deal to him, and he had no intention of losing her.

He reached over and stroked her cheek. "I'm sorry."

She jerked back as if startled out of her own mental ruminations. "What for?"

"Sitting all that time waiting for some news about you, facing the possibility that the news could be bad, I realized how... special you are to me. It's still difficult for me to think about being in a relationship, but... I am grateful you're in my life."

She closed her eyes. "Your timing, Stone Man."

Her voice was about gone, and he had to strain to hear. "Pardon?"

"I don't mean to sound ungracious, but I'm afraid if you don't get me home soon, I may pass out on you again."

Kissing her the way he wanted would have to wait. He settled for a light kiss on the tip of her nose, then concentrated on keying the engine and setting the heater to keep her warm. "You're right. Besides, Kristen probably won't get any real rest until I get home and report on—"

"Kristen! Oh, Lord! Did you hear about what happened at school today? How's she doing?"

Stone nodded, his mood growing grim again. "I heard and I've been checking in with her every hour. She's depressed but more concerned with how you're doing. And I phoned Morris Fields to let him know what happened and that he damned well better let you have some time off."

"You didn't!"

"Damned right I did. What's wrong with that?"

"We weren't going to advertise our affair. Now he'll know that we're at least *seeing* each other!"

"Is that so bad?" Stone didn't like the anxiety he heard in her voice.

"Stone, your niece is in my class! She's dealing with enough right now, does she have to be taunted by speculation about us?"

After watching the way Kristen responded to her, he thought the kid would like knowing that he cared for her teacher. He'd believed that she might see it as an opportunity to get closer to Jordan herself. The kid needed a positive female influence in her life. But he'd forgotten about gossip. Oh, he was aware of it in local politics, but it tended not to play a big role in his day-to-day life.

"I guess I owe you another apology," he said, rubbing the back of his neck.

"An apology isn't going to stop what's going to happen, Stone. Damn it all! I am so sick and tired of other people always making my decisions for me."

He shot her a quick look. "Other people?"

"All right—men! You should have at least asked my permission before you threw away my privacy!"

Although he knew she was referring to more, much more than what he'd done, the words cut deep. Consequently the reminder that she was physically wiped out and emotionally drained hardly eased the hurt. "My intentions were good."

"Ah, well . . . that makes it all right, doesn't it? Even the Reverend used the quote about the road to hell being paved with good intentions. But that didn't keep him from turning right around and doing whatever he wanted in the name of his version of religion, and hang people's feelings or the consequences. Oh, the hypocrisy of it all!"

Stone gripped the steering wheel to keep from slamming on the brakes and giving her a good shake. "I am not your father," he growled between clenched teeth, "or your ex-lover."

"No, you're not," she said with more weariness than anger. "But you are another man who does what he wants to do because you think your opinion is the only one that's valid." She sighed and dropped her head back against the seat. "What were you thinking, Stone? It wasn't just about me. I don't have any illusions about us, but what were you really thinking?''

He had to admit the truth, although she was underrating herself and them. Big time. "Kristen."

"I see. What did you have planned for me, some kind of big sister, aunt and mentor all in one neat package if only I became indebted enough to you?" Her laugh was more of a sob. "Oh, Stone...as I said, you couldn't have had worse timing. She's *not* going to thank you for this."

She turned her face toward the passenger window, and Stone didn't try to reason with her again. He didn't dare trust his own temper.

When they arrived at her house, she wanted him to let her go inside alone, but he insisted on helping her. "Call me a meddling, intrusive male," he muttered, sweeping her off her feet, "but I'm not leaving until I know you're all right."

He'd carried plywood less rigid than she held herself. It made him all the more stubborn, so that he didn't put her down once they were inside, either. He carried her all the way upstairs.

"This is ridiculous!"

"I agree."

"Stone, put me down or so help me—!"

"Go ahead and make yourself ill again, and then you'll never get rid of me. Or better yet, I'll take you back to the hospital."

Seething, she glared at him. But he saw the tears burning in her eyes and felt as much disgust with himself as satisfaction for making her back down.

In her room, he set her on the bed and kept her there by blocking her in with his hands. "I'm going to say this one more time—I'm sorry for creating a potential problem for you. If there's anything I can do to undo it or repair the damage, I will. Not because of Kristen, because it would make *me* sick to know you were that upset with me."

She tried to avert her gaze. "It's no use, Stone. This isn't going to work. I can't expect you to change who you are any more than you can wish me into being more like—"

Although she didn't finish the sentence, Stone had a good idea what she'd been about to say. He sat down and took hold of her chin, forcing her to meet his gaze.

"What do you know about Tracy?"

"Nothing," she admitted, her eyes overbright. "You can barely bring yourself to mention her because she was everything you'd ever wanted."

"Listen to me," he said, wondering if she could feel his anguish as easily as he could feel hers. "Tracy is dead, and for a long time after she and my baby died, I wanted to be dead, too. But try as I might, somehow I avoided joining them in the grave. It finally struck me why.

"It's because I like being alive. You want to know who made the difference?"

"No."

"Fine," he murmured, lowering his head to hers. "Then I'll show you."

He was careful, so careful, but insistent, too. This was the one way he knew how to reach her, and by heaven, she could chant for her independence until rattlers grew long horns, he would make her admit one thing. When they touched . . . there was magic.

The instant he felt her lips soften beneath his, his heart swelled. She was too drained for what he wanted to share with her, but he gave her a great deal to dream about. Then he took some of her sweetness and spice for himself.

Finally he raised his head just enough to rub his nose against hers. The tears that had filled her eyes before were back, but not the anger.

"That wasn't fair, Stone Man."

"Give us some time, Jordan. We'll work it out."

"Some things—"

He touched his finger to her lips. "No more tonight. Get some rest. I'll check on you tomorrow. But call me if you need anything. Promise?"

The stubborn woman refused to do that, but when he kissed her one last time, she couldn't keep from responding. That, at least, made him feel less hesitant about leaving.

Tired but feeling a good deal better about things, Stone drove home looking forward to a hot shower, a beer and bed. What he found was Kristen, dressed for bed, pacing in the kitchen.

"How's Ms. Mills?" she demanded from the doorway even before he finished setting the dead bolt.

"Exhausted, but she'll be fine, hon."

"Great. In that case, would you mind telling me what's going on between you two?"

Chapter Eleven

He had hoped he would have until morning to think of a gentle way to prepare Kristen for what she might hear at school tomorrow. But as Stone watched his niece drag out a handful of tissues from the pocket of her robe and sneeze before scowling at him again, he accepted that the shower and sleep were still some time away.

"You should be in bed, too, young lady." He drew off his jacket and hung it in the coat closet. "Or are you trying to have a relapse?"

"Don't try to change the subject." The teenager pocketed the clump of tissues in the fluffy lavender robe that made her look about twelve. "After you called me from the hospital to let me know you'd be late, I thought about how vague you'd been when I asked you about Ms. Mills. Remember? When I questioned why you'd been at her house in the first place? You gave me this lame excuse about feeling guilty that she'd caught my cold."

"That wasn't lame—I did feel badly. And it's a good thing I was there." Stone had left his hat in the truck and smoothed back his wind-mussed hair before giving his niece a kiss on the cheek. Then he continued into the kitchen. "If I hadn't, who would have gotten her to the hospital?"

"Michelle and her mother were driving to Tyler after school, and they passed Ms. Mills's house. You'll be interested to know they saw you with your arms around her."

That little salvo had Stone glad he had his back to the teen. Grimacing, he reached for a beer from the bottom shelf of the refrigerator.

"Michelle who?" he asked, double-checking the can to make sure he hadn't reached for one of Kristen's diet soft drinks.

"My friend from the squad, which I am no longer a member of."

He'd flipped open the tab, but the can didn't make it to Stone's mouth. In all the upheaval, he'd forgotten about Kristen's heartbreak. "Jeez, Kris. Hon, I'm sorry about what happened. You must be—"

"Never mind, Uncle Stone. As usual, I'm well aware of coming in a far second to anything else on your mind. Just tell me if Michelle was right about what she saw. Were you and Ms. Mills . . . you know?"

Stone could feel any progress that he and Kristen had been making begin slipping away. But he was somewhat peeved by her condescending tone, too. "Of course I was holding her. She'd fainted. It happened right as she got out of her car. She'd barely had time to confirm what happened to you at school today, and . . ." Gesturing with the can to indicate he'd told her the rest on the phone, Stone then took a long, grateful drink.

Kristen leaned back against the doorjamb, her expression growing smug. "Terry's sister-in-law works at the hospital in Quitman."

Now Stone understood. He'd been set up. "Terry...
Terry... She's your other cheerleader friend?"

"You got it, although I know you're just guessing. You
don't pay attention to any of my friends, either, except to
criticize who I date."

"You're right. I'm a miserable failure as a human being—and boy, was I wrong about Jack, wasn't I?"

Despite her blush, Kristen's scowl deepened. "Terry's
sister-in-law says that you paced around in the waiting
room."

"Guilty. I paced."

"She says if you'd been there much longer, they would
have had to replace the linoleum floor."

"Are we having a good time yet?" Stone drawled,
matching her stance but using the counter as a brace.

His niece's triumphant smile reminded him of a TV
prosecutor about to deliver the final blow to a prime defense witness. "Terry's sister-in-law said that you were pacing as anxiously as an expectant father awaiting news from
a delivery room."

Now, that wasn't amusing in the least. "Tell Terry's sister-in-law she should moonlight for the tabloids in her free
time. Or better yet, tell her to mind her own business!"

"Answer the question, Uncle Stone."

"Yes, all right? So we know each other."

"How dare you!" Kristin's cry broke, due to her still-
weak voice. She pushed away from the doorway, her hands
fisted at her sides. "You could have picked anyone, why my
teacher?"

"Believe me, Jordan has been even more sensitive to that
than I have. And not that this will impress you, but we've
done our best to keep out of the public eye."

"To the point of lying to me."

"We prefer to see it as protecting you."

"How convenient when you're the one defining things. You were sneaking around behind my back because you were ashamed," Kristen shot back with disdain.

Stone set the can onto the counter with extreme care. "Hold it right there. Whatever you think of me is one thing. It's obvious I can't do one thing right in your eyes, but don't you dare treat Jordan with anything less than the respect she deserves."

The kid did not appear impressed. She crossed her arms. "Just tell me one thing. Are you having sex?"

It was a good thing he didn't have a mouth full of beer or it would be all over the kitchen. "Pardon me, young lady, but if we were in a *relationship,* it wouldn't be any of your business!"

"That's it!" Kristen threw up her hands and stormed from the room. "I'm dropping out of school."

"You are not!" Stone yelled back, following her.

"I'm already the laughingstock of the senior class. When this gets around, I'll be totally humiliated! I'll never be able to show my face in Mount Liberty again!"

She slammed her door and locked it before he could stop her. Frustrated, Stone gave the plywood one hard wallop with his palm. It wasn't as satisfying as putting his fist through the Sheetrock wall, but it was less painful.

How in heaven's name did this keep happening? he wondered, raking both hands through his hair. It was beyond him what a person had to do to find a little peace of mind, more than ten minutes of happiness in this world. Wasn't he entitled to either?

He strode back to the kitchen and snatched up his beer, which he finished in two angry gulps. Then he reached for another. He thought of Jordan and how lucky she was; at least she would get a good night's sleep before she had to face the uproar.

* * *

As soon as she felt she could stand without keeling over, Jordan rose from the bed and went to the bathroom, where she turned on the light and stood before the mirror. She stared at her abdomen. Of course, there was nothing to see, especially since she was still wearing her suit; nevertheless, she remained transfixed.

Pregnant.

It couldn't be. She'd been on the pill for years and hadn't been off for that long. What's more, they'd only been careless once. This had to be a mistake.

Numb, she slipped off the navy jacket and let it fall to the floor. Like the rest of what she had on, it was wrinkled and would need to go to the cleaners. Her white silk blouse had a large handprint at the waist, no doubt from where Stone had grabbed her when she'd fainted. She vaguely recalled thinking he must have come straight from some wrestling match with an alligator, he'd been that grimy. But whatever he'd been doing, she bet he'd won the tussle.

She put her unsteady hand over the print. As expected, she could still see a good deal of the stain around her fingers and beyond her palm. Small wonder that Stone made her feel possessed when they made love . . . and had left her feeling haunted tonight.

She stripped off the blouse and the slim skirt, her camisole and slip. Far more clothes than she usually wore, although she liked feminine underthings. But lately she'd taken to wearing all she could to hide her weight loss. With a sigh, she conceded it wasn't fooling anyone, and she took off the lingerie, too.

Her pantyhose had a run from the knee up, and her knee was bruised. She stripped off the hose and flung them into the wastebasket. Left in her bra and panties, she dared to look once again at her reflection.

The doctor had asked her if she knew how far along she was. She hadn't admitted that she knew because she hadn't wanted to accept that his conclusion could be true. But she knew.

Over three weeks. Nearly a month.

What did that mean? She didn't begin to have a clue, since not only did she have no close female friendships, but she'd been extra careful to steer clear of expectant mothers. Why not, when she had nothing in common with them. She certainly never planned to have children of her own.

Had never planned. Past tense.

"Oh, dear God," she whispered, touching her belly.

It wasn't showing...was it? Was her imagination playing tricks, or did she feel a slight bulge?

She clapped her hands to her mouth to keep back a cry, but new tears spilled freely. "I can't be," she sobbed, sliding to the floor. "I can't...I can't!"

The next morning, Stone was as good as his word. Although he couldn't get Kristen to open her door, let alone go to school—which delayed him considerably—as soon as he went next door to ask Mrs. Tucker to keep an eye on his niece, he headed straight for Jordan's house to check on her. Discovering her car missing caused him considerable concern.

Surely she hadn't tried to go to work, after all?

He drove to the school. But a thorough inspection of the parking lot didn't bring any greater success.

Although wholly perplexed and concerned, he decided he had no choice but to get to his office at the Quitman courthouse and check on phone messages and the mail. Yesterday's detour to the hospital had set him back considerably; although dove season was ending this week for their north zone, bow season for white-tailed deer was in full swing, and the general deer season would be gearing up in a few weeks. From now into the new year, he would be lucky to get six hours of sleep a night, and as for a personal life... Well, maybe this was as good a time as any for him and Jordan to see how things went with her tolerating his schedule.

At the square in Quitman, he circled the courthouse and parked in the back by the old jail. Ralph Spradlin's car was already there, and he knew if anyone could keep his mind off his personal worries, the sheriff could.

"Hey, what are you starting to do, keep banker's hours?" the older man said as he came down the courtroom stairs. "I need to talk to you."

"Well, let's grab a couple of coffees, and you can have all of my time you want—until the phones and our pagers make us deaf."

A few minutes later, they settled in a pair of creaky chairs in Stone's musty office, and eyed each other across a desk that stayed littered with paperwork no matter what Stone did to try to keep up. As he shoved some of the mess aside to make room for his cup, Ralph shook his head at him.

"You shouldn't shove it, you should shovel it...right into the nearest burning barrel."

"Hey, I'm proud of this," Stone replied, nodding to his messy but accurate filing system. "There's nothing here that's more than a week old."

The sheriff eyed him dourly. "Now I know it's getting time for me to consider retirement—I'm beginning to believe you."

He was, indeed, less than a year from retirement, but Stone knew that wasn't what had the veteran lawman looking so defeated. "All right, out with it. What's up?"

"Remember a couple weeks ago when you stopped to help at that wreck outside of Mount Liberty?"

Because it had involved the father of the guy Kristen now seemed sweet on, Stone grew more alert than he might have. "Riley Biggs. Suffered a few cracked ribs and lacerations, but he wasn't as badly hurt as you first thought. What about him?"

"His wife, Georgia, filed a missing-person report on him this morning."

"Jeez." Maybe bad news did come in groups of three...or the old-timers were right about the full moon bringing out the erratic in everyone. Whatever the case, Stone took in that revelation and found no place to file it. "Let's catch the next plane for Aruba. Anywhere."

"It's a thought. But as the saying goes—and I can back this up by experience—bad news has a way of catching up with you, no matter where you run."

Saluting that wisdom with his foam coffee cup, Stone thought about Riley Biggs. "When was the last time his wife saw him?" He quickly filled Ralph in about Kristen and Riley's son Ridge. "I'm wondering that my niece didn't say anything."

"Understandable. Supposedly the guy takes off so often, his wife isn't sure when to worry or when he's holed up somewhere sleeping off another drunk."

Stone winced and slouched deeper into his chair. "Sounds like a model family. Keep talking and I'm going to ship Kristen off to college before she even graduates from high school just to get her away from them."

The sheriff scratched at the silvery stubble his craggy chin had denied this morning's razor. "Can't say as I blame you. I don't know why the woman didn't throw the bum out years ago. But I'm no psychiatrist. It does seem a shame, though, that folks don't pay more attention to how their choices affects their kids' lives."

"Any idea where Riley may be?" Stone knew that however his friend answered it would inevitably add to both of their workloads.

"Well, you're the one who said he liked to fish. Could be he went out on a lake somewhere and fell in one way or another."

"Are you suspicious of foul play?"

"With a guy like Riley? Who knows what he's into to pay for his next drunk."

"That johnboat he was in when I caught him would do the trick if he was looking for trouble. The thing had enough holes to have been used for target practice. When I came upon him, he'd been filling the holes below the waterline with bits of his shirt and cementing it in with chewing tobacco."

"Guess he isn't much of a mason."

"But he's one helluva fisherman. He had almost three times his limit flapping around in the bottom of the boat."

Ralph rubbed at his furrowed brow. "That's what makes tragedies . . . a cold-blooded killer can paint you a picture that'll take your breath away...a child abuser can be a gifted orator and beloved public servant in the community...a burglar who's ripped off countless residences might rival the best engineering talents in the country. I'll never figure out what it is that makes people turn their backs on their natural gifts and cross forbidden lines."

Stone used his thumbnail to cut a design into his cup. "You may not be a psychiatrist, but you're a damned fine philosopher, Ralph."

The bespectacled man lifted both silvery eyebrows in a subtle shrug and finished off his coffee. "Will you keep an eye out, especially when you're following up on those alligator sightings?"

"And the big-cat sightings."

Although both of them were serious, it was an ongoing joke, too. The alligators were a result of too many mild winters and the critters' long-protected status, which had allowed the boldest to wander north from the Gulf along East Texas's numerous waterway systems. Ironically it was only when people weren't swimming, water-skiing or racing their Jet Skis that they worried what the Texas Parks and Wildlife Department was doing about "the problem." Only last month, Stone had gotten yet another phone call from an elderly woman who'd sworn that she'd heard her neighbors' kids talking about flushing "one of them critters" down the commode. She'd felt it her civic duty to let him know he should be on the lookout for "Chopper."

In the southern half of Wood County, a cougar, or mountain lion, as some preferred to call them—although you'd have to shovel a good deal of dirt to raise the area's location much above five hundred feet—had been spotted and blamed for attacking ranchers' stock. Several calves, sheep and goats had been lost, and after Stone viewed some of the carcasses, he hoped the animal or animals' success didn't extend itself to some child or isolated resident before it was found.

What annoyed him was that he suspected the big cat had escaped from one of the wealthier ranches, where it was rumored that exotic game were brought in for friends and clients to hunt. Naturally the rumors couldn't be substantiated, and so far, whenever he'd gone for a "friendly" visit to those locations, he'd found nothing except polite, tight-lipped staff.

"Kinda makes you wish you'd taken up carpentry or something, huh?" Ralph said with an irreverent grin.

"Look who's talking. Did you ever believe you'd have to chase timber rustlers in our time?" Stone countered, referring to the unscrupulous cutters who were taking trees illegally off private land because of attractive pulp prices.

"Ain't life grand?" Ralph used the chair's worn arms to push himself to his feet. "You let me know if you see any sign of our friend . . . and be careful out there, Stone Man."

"You do the same." Stone gave a final salute to the departing lawman, but even before Ralph shut the door behind himself, his thoughts were on Kristen. How was she going to take this latest piece of bad news? Damn...she did choose her friends. And how he wished he didn't have to be the one to tell her.

* * *

Jordan poured herself a mug of warmed milk before she sat down on the couch to look at all the brochures her doctor had given her. There were so many, she knew she could read through the weekend and not absorb all the information included in them. She needed time to deal with the shock of what she'd learned during her visit, too.

After a near-sleepless night, she'd telephoned the school to report that there was no way she could be in. Fortunately she'd sounded as congested as she felt. Then she'd phoned her general practitioner to explain her dilemma. Dr. Colby had told her to come in first thing, and within an hour had confirmed Dr. Gray's findings. Thereafter, the visit had centered around options, expectations and reality.

"The good news is that you're young. Thirty is nothing these days, even if this is your first child," Evelyn Colby said in her breezy way that still held authority. "You're strong, although I am concerned that your blood count is low at the moment. And as you explained yourself, you're going through a prolonged stressful period. With a few minor adjustments in your life-style, and some preventive care, there's no reason to assume you won't deliver a healthy baby come June.

"On the other hand," the doctor had added with the utmost sensitivity, "if you feel this pregnancy is...impossible, there's still time."

At first Jordan hadn't grasped what the other woman was suggesting. Completely overwhelmed by the thought that she'd gotten pregnant in the first place, she'd been slow to determine the next school break when she would be guaranteed a few days off to recuperate. However, once she had realized that meant Thanksgiving and had focused on the posters on the wall, she'd been appalled.

Jordan opened one of the brochures that outlined what the poster had. She studied the sketch of what an embryo looked like now and how much more developed it would be by Thanksgiving. In other words, her baby already showed a human form. To imagine such a wonder was difficult enough; how could she possibly contemplate doing anything to harm it at this stage let alone later? *It?* Him. Her.

Goose bumps rose on her arm beneath her wool dress. But sheer terror gripped her, too. She knew nothing about being a parent. And once Morris Fields and the rest of the community learned she was going to be an unwed mother, exactly how long would she keep her teaching position at Mount Liberty?

She was reaching for a booklet on good eating habits for the expectant mother when she heard a not-so-welcome sound outside. "Oh, no," she whispered, closing her hand around her throat. In the next instant, she was gathering up all the brochures and pamphlets and dumping them into her briefcase by her desk. Snatching up another tissue from the box there, she hurried to the door.

"Woman, you're going to give me your ulcers. Do you know I've been calling you all day? Don't you check your machine?"

As he brushed by her, Jordan glanced over to her answering machine on her desk, where indeed the message light was flashing. "Sorry. I haven't had a chance yet—"

"When I saw your car wasn't in the driveway or at the school this morning, I didn't know what to think." He spun around and faced her, hands on his hips. "Do you realize how ill you were yesterday?"

"That's why I went to my doctor today. She's in Tyler."

He looked at her as if she'd just given away the punch line to his joke, only to exhale in a rush and draw her into his arms. "Ignore me. It's been a full day."

Jordan didn't doubt it, but thought that was about the biggest understatement she'd ever heard.

"How do you feel now?" Stone asked. "What did the doctor say?"

She thought of all she could tell him. He had a right to know. Eventually. At the moment, however, she needed a bit more time. Good grief, she still hadn't sorted things out for herself yet; she didn't need a bulldozer pushing her along.

"Stone, your concern is sweet, but you shouldn't be hugging me, you should be concerned about catching this bug yourself." She tried not to be swayed by his strong heartbeat pounding against hers, tried not to remember how it literally thrummed after they made love.

"Considering that Kristen has it, too, it may be too late to warn me. Anyway, since it's the only way I'd get any time off right now, it might be welcome." He stroked her hair, which she'd worn loose today. "You look feverish. Good enough to take a bite of, but nowhere near ready to be on your feet. Did the doctor give you something to kick this thing?"

There wasn't much Evelyn could prescribe without jeopardizing the baby. Especially not until they got the results of the blood work her physician had ordered. The only things she'd recommended were old standbys—a vaporizer to help breathing and peppermint tea for her sore throat. Besides that, there was a small arsenal of vitamins to help her help the baby develop properly. With a jolt, Jordan realized they were still on the kitchen counter.

"Um, I'm allergic to quite a few things, so I've begged off on all the fancy stuff. Can I get you something?"

"How about twenty-four hours with nothing to do but crash on that couch with you as a blanket?" He sighed. "See what you do to my imagination? But you're in no shape for that, and I can't turn my back on my responsibilities."

She was embarrassed that she could experience such a tidal wave of relief at his bad news. "How's Kristen?" she asked, wanting to change the subject. "Is she feeling any better? Did she go to school?"

"No. She locked her door last night, and Mrs. Tucker— that's the neighbor who keeps an eye on her for me—says she hasn't budged all day."

"She's angry because you were late getting home last night, isn't she? She needed your support after being kicked off the squad, and your not being there made her feel even more rejected."

"I imagine that had something to do with it. But there's more. She knows about us."

Jordan grasped her throat. "Oh, no!" she cried hoarsely. "You didn't go ahead and tell her the truth, did you? Not everything!"

"Easy, now." Frowning as his gaze skimmed her features, Stone led her to the couch. "You're looking shaky again. Come sit down." When they were seated face-to-face, he took her hands in his. "It wasn't a secret we would have been able to keep, regardless of whether Morris Fields talked or not. Friends of hers saw us together. All she needed was confirmation from me, which she demanded as soon as I walked through the front door."

"Stone...poor you." Jordan touched his cheek. "No wonder she locked her door. How am I going to be able to face her tomorrow?"

"You may not have to. There's a second kick to this bomb."

"What do you mean?"

"She doesn't want to go back to school."

Jordan's mouth dropped open. "She can't drop out!"

"You say it. I say it. But that's the line she's touting at the moment. And now there's more bad news to add to that. Ridge Biggs's father is missing. His wife filed a report this morning. If Kristen doesn't already know—but there's every reason to assume she does—she's going to turn all her attention and energy to the Biggs kid. Any thought of school, let alone college, will go straight out of her mind."

"Don't exaggerate. She cares for Ridge, and I think he's a fine boy." Jordan moistened her lips, wanting to choose her words carefully. "If you...knew of a friend who needed considerable and special understanding, wouldn't you do all you could to help that person?"

"I would...and I have." His smile reminded her of yesterday, and he picked up her milk and handed it to her. "Go on, drink it before it gets cold."

She tried, but the intense, aware look in his eyes made it impossible to swallow more than a sip. "What happens with Ridge's father?" she asked, putting down her cup. "Will there be a search of any kind?"

"The report goes out on the computers, but to answer your question, no, not unless something substantial comes up. Men like Riley Biggs...they don't inspire the same kind of search that, say, a child would."

"Or a well-known, beloved citizen?"

"As unfair as that may seem, it's true." Stone took her hand again. "I wanted you to know because I'm hoping Kristen will come to you for comfort regardless of how angry she is with me. If she does, will you be there for her?"

Life was getting more complicated by the minute. "I'll do the best I can." She couldn't hold back a rueful smile. "The kid knows how to grow under your skin."

"Like her uncle?"

Very much like her uncle, but she had no business feeling what she did under the circumstances. And when he leaned back against the couch and took her with him, she tried to protest.

"Stone...you said you had to leave."

"I do and I will. Soon enough. I only want to hold you for a minute. You don't know what it does for me when I feel the walls lower that you keep around yourself, and you open up toward me...agree to take another risk." He sighed when she let him take her weight and stroke her hair. "I'm not trying to barge into your life. Hell, I made Tracy's life an ordeal always being gone, always letting work, responsibility to the state come before her and Billie Ann. I've learned my lesson about thinking I can do what others have failed at—trying for a normal relationship. And whatever time I do have, I owe a good chunk to Kristen until she's on her feet and off to college. But these moments with you," he added, his voice growing thicker, "Jordan . . . they make me feel—"

"Don't say it, Stone."

"Why not if it's true?" he demanded, angling his head to align his mouth to hers. "They make me feel as if I haven't run out of dreams after all."

She didn't have the willpower to resist his kiss as she knew she should, especially when he kissed her as if he did indeed carry the weight of the world on his shoulders and she was his sole source of nourishment, his place of peace. He made tears burn behind her closed lids, and she stroked his whisker-rough cheek with the backs of her fingers, aching for the true love that she sensed was so close but fated by circumstances to always evade her.

Stone shifted. "What am I sitting on? Shoot, I'm crushing some of your work," he murmured, squirming and reaching behind him.

To Jordan's horror, he brought out one of her pamphlets! It must have slipped from her grasp and gotten caught between the cushions. Worse yet, it was the most explicit one of the bunch!

She sat up and held her breath, awaiting the inevitable.

"'Preparing for your baby...'" he read, sitting up, too. His expression was one of slow revelation, then shock, then dread. Finally he looked up at her. "Tell me this isn't true."

Chapter Twelve

It might have been easier if he'd yelled at her, but his quiet statement ripped at her heart. In sheer reflex, those walls he'd talked of sprang up inside her so fast, she could almost feel the shudder of mortar striking mortar. Even as one corner of her mind argued that he might not *know*, let alone mean, what he was saying, she knew she couldn't take any chances. Because sooner or later—once he recovered from the shock—he would mean it.

"I'm afraid I can't do that." She was barely aware of clasping her hands in her lap in that odd, fisted way that was a nervous holdover from her childhood when she would pretend to be in prayer, while at the same time hoping that the Reverend would stop berating, criticizing, or—dear God, would she ever get that voice out of her mind?—condemning. "As...as a matter of fact, you might as well know that's the real reason I went to the doctor today."

"You mean you knew?"

"No. There w-were signs, I realize now, but I thought I was simply run-down. Dr. Gray informed me otherwise last night."

The mask that had earned him his nickname slipped back on his face. Masculine but hard granite lines cut deeper with every second. "Last night! And you didn't think I deserved to know then?"

Her cupped hand cramped from the tight fist she made. "Would you have been any happier with the n-news than you are now?"

So disgusted with herself that the stuttering was back, she hardly cared that the question was almost an accusation. She'd spoken a truth.

He didn't bother answering. She could tell he'd already moved on and was trying to remember the when and how of it all.

"It was the night after you spoke to my seventh-period class," she said, speaking more carefully, slowly, in order to avoid the embarrassing condition.

"I know. Now. I guess I've always wondered... worried." He hung his head and shook it over and over again. "This will sound terrible to you, but...I'd promised myself."

"I d-don't really need to hear this."

"I promised myself that I would never be responsible for bringing another child into this world." The words were slow to come, like an oath themselves, as if saying them caused unbearable pain. "I couldn't bear to live with the idea that what happened to Tracy and Billie Ann could happen again."

"You don't have to." Jordan was amazed at the unexpected anger seething inside her, even as her heart ached for him. "I'm not asking anything from you, Stone."

"I'm fifty percent responsible."

"But I'm the one who's pregnant! And correct me if I'm wrong, but you don't hear me s-sputtering about how my condition is destroying my life, do you? Yet *I'm* the one this affects most. I don't have a choice!''

He grimaced. "Well, you have a choice, although they're not any I'd want you to have to endure."

She shot off the couch and charged for her briefcase, turned the thing upside down and, from the mess that spilled onto the floor, snatched up the pamphlet she'd been looking at prior to his arrival. "See this?" she snapped, holding the diagram under his nose. "That's my baby. They still call it an embryo, but this is what he or she would look like by the time I could schedule that 'choice' you mentioned. It has a suspiciously close resemblance to a human being to me. Does it to you?''

"Jordan, I—"

"And you have the unm-mitigated gall to talk about *e-enduring?*" She covered her belly with both hands. Funny how until today she'd always been alone and it hadn't mattered. But now the prospect terrified her. At the same time, she had the strongest, indefinable sense of protectiveness toward what nestled inside her. "Exactly what do you think this child would have to endure if I—?''

He grabbed her hands. "That's enough! I wouldn't let you—" His beeper went off. He swore and jerked it off his belt, muttered, "I have to borrow your phone," and strode to the kitchen.

Jordan sank to the couch and hugged her middle. She knew if she'd tried to continue standing, she would have crumpled like a falling building, and the last thing she wanted was any more charity from anyone or gestures from him.

"A boat's capsized on Lake Fork," he said, returning to the living room. "One of the people who were on board hasn't been accounted for. I have to go."

She nodded.

He continued to stand there looking at her. "Jordan . . . I hate leaving like this. But I do have to go."

"I know it." And she did understand. His news brought terrible images to mind, and she couldn't begin to comprehend what the other person or persons on the boat were going through—or those waiting at home. "Go."

"I'll be back as soon as I can."

"No, don't bother."

"Jordan—damn it! What I said before—"

"Will you please get going!"

He was at the door in only two steps. He shot her one last look, and then he was gone.

As soon as Jordan saw the door close behind him, she curled up onto the couch into a tight ball. The tears that poured from her eyes were for him. They were for all of them.

She didn't see Stone again that day, nor did she hear from him, but then that was a given, since she pulled the phones again to give herself a decent night's rest. By the time she turned on the TV the next morning, the news out of Tyler was carrying the incident at Lake Fork, and she saw him with the other Wood County game warden and deputies from the sheriff's department. The cameras were too far away to catch the men's expressions, but she knew Stone well enough to recognize the tension and fatigue in his body, as well as the determination he brought to the search.

Knowing she couldn't possibly go in again, she plugged in the phone at her desk and called the school. Morris Fields's secretary, Ruby, took the message but warned her that he might be calling her later.

"I'll be here," she told the polite but distant woman, her voice barely a rasp.

After she hung up, she made herself a pot of the peppermint tea and mixed in honey for her throat, knowing she might need it when she called Kristen—and then if she could get the Biggses' home.

Preoccupied, she jumped when she heard the knocking at her front door, and tea spilled into the saucer. Who on earth—? She'd never heard a vehicle pull in!

Dreading the thought that it might be Stone, especially when she looked a wreck and still wore her robe, she went to the door.

"Kristen! Ridge!" She stared at the somber-faced teens holding hands before her. "Come in...come in!"

The autumn chill was intensified by a heavy fog. Jordan shivered as she shut the door behind them and tugged her collar higher around her neck. While she was pleased to see that Kristen's coloring looked better, she thought the two teens appeared as nervous as they did remote. For good reason, she decided, thinking there was any number of reasons for them to be here.

"We know we're early, and that you're very sick. If you'd prefer we come back later..." Kristen shot a beseeching gaze at Ridge.

"We won't stay long," he assured her.

"Don't be silly." Jordan swept her hair back from her face and motioned them to sit down. "I'm glad to see you both. Kristen, how are you feeling? Ridge, I heard about your father and I'm so sorry."

When Kristen failed to answer, Ridge swallowed and nodded. "Thanks, Ms. Mills. Mom's holding up well, all things considered. She's just worried about keeping a roof over our heads. It's my kid brothers who are having a tougher time. They don't understand why the police keep coming and going. We only want to know what happened to him so we can move on."

How tragic to hear a son be so damaged by a father that those could be his only comments upon the parent's disappearance. And how well she understood. Jordan felt her usual instinct to back away yield to something far more compassionate and maternal. "When was the last time you two ate? Let me get you something to drink to warm you, too. I have a fresh pot of peppermint tea, but I could make coffee. Juice?''

Ridge asked for coffee, and Kristen declined everything without looking at her. Jordan brooded about that as she went to the kitchen to choose a sturdy mug for Ridge instead of the delicate china she'd used for her tea. Despite the soft stereo music playing in the background—a melancholy piece by Bach played on cello—she could hear the two teens whispering. Wondering what she was in for, she quickly put together a tray of imported cookies and, as soon as the coffee water boiled, carried the whole thing to the coffee table.

''How do you take it?'' she asked, hoping Kristen remarked about the glass of orange juice she'd added for her just in case. She thought it might feel good on her throat, but the girl simply sat watching Ridge reach for his mug.

''Black's fine, thank you,'' he murmured.

Jordan wondered if they knew how adorable they looked sitting so close their ski jackets whispered as the slightest movement had their arms rubbing together. She herself collected her cup and saucer and settled in the high-backed chair across from them.

''How's your cold, Kristen?'' She decided she might as well find out sooner or later how the girl felt toward her.

The teen's hair was smoothed back in a ponytail at her nape, and the only makeup she wore this morning was mascara and a faint touch of lip gloss, making her appear younger and wholly vulnerable.

''Fine. And I know you think I should be in school, but—''

''I don't think anything of the kind. If you're not feeling physically or emotionally ready, there's no reason to put yourself through that.''

Startled blue gray eyes settled on Jordan. ''You do?'' When Jordan nodded, the girl gnawed at her lower lip. ''You don't feel very well, do you?''

"It's been a rocky night. I just hope my germs don't give you a relapse or contaminate Ridge."

Both teens murmured a brief dismissal of any concern. Since Jordan still didn't have a clue as to what was on their minds, she decided to let them direct the conversation where they would.

"Ms. Mills..." Kristen hesitated, rubbing her hands on the knees of her jeans. "I don't know how to ask this without embarrassing myself..."

Wanting to make it easier for her, Jordan smiled. "It's all right. Your uncle told me that you know he and I have been seeing each other."

The girl bowed her head. "It's not just that."

Jordan thought it wiser to set down her cup before she had a real accident. Once she did, she couldn't help but place her hands against her stomach, which was exactly where Kristen's gaze settled.

"Is it true? Are you going to have his baby?"

A cardinal flew into a tree outside the living-room window and peered in at them. Jordan figured its glorious red coloring was nothing compared to what flamed in her face. With a shake of her head, she forced herself to meet Kristen's unblinking gaze. "We don't make good examples, do we? So he told you."

"No. He hasn't been home all night. He's still out helping in the search for that fisherman. I found out about... um, through friends. Friends who have family at the Quitman hospital."

What did one say after such a bombshell? The two teenagers looked as embarrassed as she felt, and yet she had to give Kristen credit for not being immediately accusatory. "I suppose I could say that the administrators there wouldn't be pleased to hear that their staff is so indiscreet, but that's hardly relevant at this point, is it? And truth be known, I'm somewhat relieved. This isn't the easiest news to break no matter how you try to look at it."

"How do you feel about it?"

Jordan lifted her hands. "I don't know. I'm still in a state of shock."

"Are you going to keep it?"

"There's no doubt about that. Yes."

"Is Uncle Stone going to marry you?"

An inevitable tingling sensation ran through her. "You know what your uncle has been through, Kristen. He's not in a position to think about a serious relationship, let alone marriage. And definitely not a baby. No, to answer your question, I don't foresee that happening."

"Then what will happen at school? Will they let you stay on at Mount Liberty?"

"I don't know. Legally they have no right to fire me. But they could always accuse me of being incompetent—"

"They wouldn't dare!" Kristen cried. She exchanged looks with Ridge, who appeared equally upset about that.

"And I could take them to court," Jordan replied with a smile. "But I wouldn't do that, either."

"Ms. Mills, you can't leave! You're the best teacher we've ever had. We both think so, don't we, Ridge?"

He nodded, his handsome, dark face appearing almost shy. "School has always been a trial for me. You've seen how I don't exactly fit in with the superjock crowd. But your class... It's not so much what you're teaching, it's all you bring to each class. Your experience and your faith in the human spirit. You don't merely make us read stories, you challenge us to find all the potential meanings and to make decisions for ourselves."

Jordan had to take a sip of her tea because she was sure her voice would quake with emotion if she spoke. "I'm...without words," she said at last. "Thank you. Thank you both." She had to add an incredulous laugh. "Good grief—I expected you to be furious about all this!"

Once again, Kristen exchanged glances with Ridge. "I was," she admitted sheepishly. "But then when I talked to Ridge, he made me see what a nitwit I was being."

"You were reacting with your heart," he said, touching her hair. "But you also needed to think about how this could turn into something good, too."

Bemused, Jordan could only sit back and listen.

"Ms. Mills . . . oh, this is ridiculous!" Kristen cried with a laugh. "You're going to have my cousin! Can I call you Jordan?"

"Well, I . . . I don't see why not. Outside of school, of course."

"Of course. Jordan." The teen beamed. "So this is my idea. I want to come stay with you."

Jordan broke into a coughing fit. It took her a few tissues and several sips of tea before she recovered. "Just like that?" she asked, wiping residual tears from the corners of her eyes. "We haven't known each other long enough to become, er, roommates."

"But you're going to be my aunt—or as good as that. I want to be there for you when the baby starts to grow and you need help and support."

"That's sweet and thoughtful of you, dear, but—"

"And you know the gossips will have you for breakfast, lunch and dinner, so you won't want to go through that by yourself. And what about childbirth classes? I could be your partner!"

Her enthusiasm was endearing, and Jordan was flattered that the girl wanted this, but somehow she wondered if she were being told everything on the teen's mind. "What about college?"

"That's a whole year away."

"Okay, then let me put it this way. Regardless of what I said, you must know that your uncle would never approve."

"You're carrying his baby, Jordan. How pigheaded is he going to get?"

There was something about her excitement and her logic that nagged at Jordan. She narrowed her eyes. "You *do* want us to get married. This is all machinations to get to that final end. Why? I thought you two are constantly at odds?"

Kristen made a face and shot Ridge another embarrassed look. "We could do better if I gave him half a chance. I guess I've been angry that I've lost so much. I didn't want to understand that Uncle Stone has an incredible responsibility with a job he had long before I entered the picture."

"That wouldn't change if anything came of our relationship. His work is always going to be demanding."

"That's different than saying you don't like him."

"Of course I like him! That's not the issue."

"He's had a tough time dealing with Aunt Tracy and Billie Ann's deaths," the girl said, sobering. "He blames himself because he'd been out on a call. He never says it, but I think he believes if he'd been home, he could have saved them."

Jordan had suspected something like that, but Stone's wife and daughter had always felt like an untouchable topic for her. To be fair, she hadn't wanted to deal that intimately with Stone's pain when she had plenty of her own.

"You could change him," Kristen said to her. "I saw the way he looked at you when you came to see me that evening."

Jordan could feel another blush rising to heat her cheeks. No telling how aggressively the girl would be campaigning if she'd seen the rest.

"And think of all the wonderful time we'd have to talk about writing and books. Then Ridge could come over..."

Now she understood. "I think you just want a live-in tutor," she said with a rueful smile.

Although Kristen smiled in return, she replied calmly, "We want the life you're creating for yourself. Jordan, you're a Transcendentalist just like Emerson and Thoreau, and you're doing what Jo said in *Little Women*. You're pursuing a course of excellence and self-discovery. Listen to that music, for goodness' sake!'' she cried, pointing to the stereo. "Do you know what Ridge would have to endure at home from his father—if he could even afford a CD, never mind the stereo to play it on?"

"It took me thirty years to get here," Jordan said, seeing a need to point that out.

"But you had a mentor to guide you, didn't you? Someone?"

Yes, she had someone. Brent had been a huge influence in expanding her horizons, though not in molding her tastes. The man might have been domineering and deceitful, but she could give him credit for the good he brought into her life.

"Uh-oh. Your uncle must have spotted your car." Ridge nodded out the window to where Stone pulled up beside Kristen's car.

"Maybe he has news about your father, Ridge," Kristen said.

Jordan thought it possible, but more than likely he was here to finish what they'd started yesterday, only she didn't think she was up to it. She definitely didn't want a scene in front of his niece and Ridge.

Trying to control her inner jitters, she rose and went to the front door, wishing yet again that she'd done more than washed her face and brushed her hair this morning. Even to have put on the pretty jeweled house slippers would have made her feel better, but she'd put on thick crew socks instead because they were warmer.

He opened the door before she could reach it. Jordan froze, lifting both eyebrows at his boldness.

"Are you all right?"

How could she be angry with him when he looked beyond exhausted and as haunted as she'd ever seen him?

Jordan eased her hands into her pockets to keep from reaching out to brush the hair off his forehead and touch the new skin where his stitches had been.

"Yes," she replied for his ears only. "You?"

"We found the other fisherman. He hadn't been wearing a flotation vest."

"Oh, Stone. That's so sad."

He nodded and glanced at his niece. "What are you doing here when you and Jordan are both supposed to be in bed?"

"I'm feeling better, Uncle Stone."

Stone shoved his hat farther back on his head and placed his hands on his hips. "If that's so, then you should be in school."

"I'm not going back without Ridge and Jordan."

"'Jordan'?"

"She said I could call her that."

Jordan watched Stone pinch the bridge of his nose for several seconds before casting her a "what else did I miss?" look. She gave him a shrug and signaled for his jacket.

"Did you hear anything about my father, sir?" Ridge asked in the ensuing silence.

"No, son. I'm sorry. I rechecked everywhere I could before leaving Quitman."

Ridge appeared more bitter than upset about the news. "He always did say that one day he was going to catch a ride to the Gulf and never come back. Maybe he actually did it this time." He shrugged. "For all our sakes, but mostly Mom's, I hope so."

Jordan and Stone exchanged glances, and she gestured him to take a seat. "You might as well join the party."

"You're in no shape to be entertaining."

"It's a euphemism. Besides, I need to sit down and I'm not likely to do that while you're standing there glowering at everyone."

Although his expression told her that he didn't think he was glowering, he did sit. He was painstakingly polite in turning down anything to eat or drink, and at the first opportunity he said to his niece, "You seem more upbeat than the last time we talked."

"I asked Jordan if I can move in with her."

To his credit, he didn't expose any physical reaction. "You already have a home."

"I have a house. I want a family. A real family, not just a semblance of one. With Jordan pregnant with my cousin—"

This time he did a double take. "You know?"

"I had nothing but time to put it all together, Uncle Stone. And you know the sources I had."

"Don't remind me." He turned to Jordan. "And what was your response to that?"

"I'm ill. I refuse to make any decisions until I'm germ free and in control of all my faculties again."

Stone turned back to his niece. "I'm grateful that you're not angry, but—"

"I didn't say that. I'm very upset that you didn't think I was mature and fair-minded enough to understand."

"Next time when you slam and lock your bedroom door, I'll remind you of that."

With a fleeting smile, Ridge cleared his throat and touched Kristen's hand. "I have to get home. I left my youngest brother with a neighbor, but I promised to be back soon. Besides, I think your uncle and Ms. Mills need to talk without us around to make things more awkward. Ms. Mills—" he gave her a shy smile "—thank you. For everything."

Jordan rose and never thought twice about giving him a hug. "I hope things work out, Ridge. We'll be in touch. In the meantime, if you need something, my number's in the new book."

She gave Kristen the same warm embrace, but then tapped her on the nose. "Behave."

"Can I call, too?"

The girl was a charmer and would take a mile if given any leeway at all. "Provided you go home, take your medicine and get back to school tomorrow. Both of you," she added to Ridge.

They made all the expected groaning noises, but the affection in their eyes gave her a unique thrill.

Stone watched the little scene play out and thought it very domestic. Waves of amusement, affection and annoyance all jockeyed for position in his mind and heart.

He'd had every intention of coming here this morning, even if he hadn't seen Kristen's car. He owed Jordan an apology for his behavior yesterday. But as he watched her close up after the kids, he realized how much further and deeper his motivation went. Then she turned, and he saw that he might not get the chance to explain any of it.

"You don't have to stay, you know."

"You're throwing me out?"

"If that were physically possible, I'd consider it. Under the circumstances, I'm resigned to plead for amicability."

He took hope in the realization that she could still be witty. Surely that meant she didn't despise him completely?

"We do need to talk, Jordan."

"Haven't we hurt each other enough?"

"Come sit down."

She frowned at his reply, but edged closer. Closer. When she was within a few feet, he extended his hand.

She halted and eyed it. Him.

"Come on. I won't bite."

The regal look he admired so transformed her face. "There's a deliciously morbid poem by Vachel Lindsay called 'The Spider and the Ghost of a Fly' that's quite clear about listening to such nonsense. The spider did more than bite the fly... and Mr. Lindsay's end wasn't any happier."

"If anyone can believe a person can change, you can."

He kept his hand extended. Just when fatigue and disappointment almost won out, she sighed and gave him her hand. When she did, he only had to tug a little to get her off balance and draw her onto his lap.

She protested, of course, but he touched a finger to her lips and then tucked her head against his shoulder. Once she quieted, he eased his hold and closed his eyes to savor the moment.

"This is what I kept coming back to," he murmured after he felt that silence had become a more comfortable thing between them.

"When?" she murmured, the question warm against his throat.

"While I was driving away from here yesterday. When we were dragging the lake and freezing our butts off half the night. When I saw the guy who survived see his pregnant wife arrive in a police car, and he crushed her in his arms and broke into sobs."

"In theater, it's easy to see principles and understand values in the big moments. It's the day-to-day stuff that clouds our vision."

He lifted her chin. "There's been nothing day-to-day since the moment I met you, Jordan, and I swear on all I've ever held dear... I never wanted to hurt you."

"I know. That's the silly part of it. You're a good man, Stone. But you're still imprisoned by your pain."

"And you're not?" He reached for one of her hands and inspected her graceful, unpainted fingers. "One thing about searches, especially at night. There's an incredible amount of time to think... and remember. You know what flashed in my mind? How you sat on that couch as I... lost it. How these hands were like watching sapling roots exposed to the most brutal elements, cold, heat, drought... until they've withered and gnarled into lifeless knots. And then I remembered how when you tried to speak, you couldn't get the words out. Which one of them did I make you remember, Jordan? Which one took your voice and told you what you had to say was so worthless, so useless, that you developed a speech impediment?''

"The Reverend."

"Holy mother," Stone whispered, and folded her closer.

"But I'm better."

"I'll say. To think my first impression was that you were born with the proverbial silver spoon and all that.''

"You are funny."

He kissed the top of her head because, although she was trying to stay lighthearted, he could hear the sadness in her voice. "Do you think my sense of humor is a good enough lure to convince you to marry me?''

She tried to sit up. He tightened his arms, unwilling to break their physical contact. Crazy as she might think it, things seemed clearer, saner, when he kept her close like this.

"Stone, you don't want to get married."

"I believe I just brought it up."

"Okay, then I don't want to get married."

"And I don't want our child to come into this world without my name."

"Fine. How about if I promise you that I'll make sure it's on the birth certificate?''

He decided to ignore that. "As you said, I come with a great deal of baggage, but I'll never lie to you. I'll do my damnedest never to hurt you again, and I won't hide from my financial responsibility to the baby."

"But will you love it?''

The soft challenge shut him up. He should have guessed she would know the one question he was afraid to answer.

"Stone, let me up. Let me up!''

He let her go, more concerned that she might hurt her voice worse than it already was. And there were benefits to having her where he could see her. She was slightly disheveled, so he got to enjoy an expanse of shapely leg and the hint of breast as she paced before him.

"We have to be logical about this. You already have a house, and I don't want to give up mine," she began, gesturing to make up for her weak delivery.

"We could move in here and sell Kristen's. That would guarantee her a nice nest egg to start off her life once she gets out of college."

"Stone, this place only has two bedrooms. Where do we put the baby?"

"We'll build on. I'm not coming to this situation penniless."

He had indeed been giving the idea considerable thought, and as he saw Jordan realize that, she grew more agitated. "Will you look around you? I'm only beginning to get the place set up the way I like it."

"You're doing a wonderful job."

"Everything is *white!* And look at your clothes. Add an energetic, accident-prone teenager running rampant in here—maybe two, from the way those two are acting—not to mention a baby who then becomes a drooling toddler with sticky hands and more."

He tugged at his ear. "That you're going to have with or without me."

"Are you listening to me? For the first time in my life, I'm getting to live on my own terms. I'm totally independent and self-reliant, and I love it. Maybe that sounds selfish, but it's new and enervating, not to mention enlightening, and—What are you doing?"

He was getting up because he'd heard all he needed to hear. "You don't have to change," he said, following her as she backed away from him. When she bumped into the wall, he cupped his hands around her face. "Say yes," he murmured before kissing her.

He loved the way she trembled yet shifted closer to his touch. In this way, he knew they were unbelievably attuned. Everything she'd said was true, and more. She might not be able to stand the demands of his job; he might take one look at their baby and run like Ridge's father had. Who was to say that they even had that much time? But she possessed a vibrancy and integrity of spirit that awed and inspired him. He couldn't leave her exposed to small-town gossip and venom. No matter what memories haunted him or emotionally crippled him, how could she expect him to turn his back on this? Her?

"Why?" she moaned when he let her breathe again.

"Because I want you. Because maybe we were born to save each other's sanity. Marry me."

"Oh, Stone...what if you're wrong? What if we were born to break each other's heart?"

"No one who's come as far as you have could believe that. Say yes, Jordan."

Chapter Thirteen

" Yes ... I will."

Although her reply promised yet another nest of headaches for her, Jordan walked out of the school office and returned to her class with her head high. She would be darned if she would let Morris Fields or anyone else get to her.

Only days before her wedding, and the biggest upheaval of her life, Jordan had just been informed that she would be supervising detention this week. Again. It was by no means fair—in fact, she knew full well that it was punishment for taking a few days off as a result of her cold—but nevertheless, Morris Fields had the right to choose whichever of the faculty for whatever jobs he wished. As a result, she'd been careful to keep her temper and refrain from burning bridges not easily mended. Not that it was her job she worried about; somehow or other, she would find a position near to home. Good teachers were as fine a commodity as they ever were. But Kristen and especially Ridge relied on her protection. She refused to abandon them to a feeding frenzy by the sharks, no matter what inconvenience it cost her.

Gossip was running rampant throughout the school and around town, too, from everything the kids told her. Since she continued to avoid most of the local stores as much as possible, at least she missed the latter episodes. But sometimes the others weren't so lucky—as when Kristen was cornered by the librarian, who recommended several pamphlets on birth control and the medical dangers teens face with intimacy because, as the old prune had put it, "I've heard you aren't getting good advice at home."

Poor Kristen had been mortified. "Everyone thinks Ridge and I are sleeping together," she snapped late one afternoon. They'd gone to Tyler to shop for some new curtains and linens for Kristen's new bedroom, which Jordan hadn't yet gotten around to redoing. "If I was still going with Jack, no one would say a thing. It would be as if he was entitled to me!"

"If you chisel things down to the basics, maybe people did believe that," Jordan replied, thinking back on her courses and particularly her readings in mythology. "When we get home, I'll give you some material that might help explain it better. But very generally speaking, your situation is no different than if Jack had been a favorite gladiator in old Roman times. To pay him homage, the poor town that has nothing else to offer him, lets him have one of their vestal virgins. You."

Kristen had laughed with embarrassment, but her eyes had lit with interest and understanding of the metaphors, too. "And who's Ridge in all this?"

"Maybe he's the one who knows, or at least recognizes, the other half of you."

"What other half?"

"What some call the inner half, the wild half, the secret half. She has many names depending on the culture, but she's there in you and you know it."

"Do you think Uncle Stone knows your other half?" the girl ventured slyly.

Jordan smiled. "Knows? No. But he's extremely acute about catching glimpses. Woman is the more complex creature," she said quietly, making sure the younger girl drew close and paid attention. "Once I was almost crushed by rage and cruelty. Then I naively trusted what looked sweet but was bitter. If I can give you any gift, Kristen, it's this. Never sell yourself short."

The girls eyes had filled, and she'd hugged her right there in the store. "I've been waiting my whole life for you, Jordan," she whispered. "I don't care what else happens. I know we're going to be happy."

What else happened was that Ridge was let go at the grocery store due to several churchwomen from the Reverend's old congregation, including Mrs. Graves, suddenly refusing to let him carry their groceries to the car. Although frustrated, and even sympathetic, the store manager had explained to him, "If you can't do the work I need you to do, I can't afford to keep you on."

Since there was still no word on his father, and Ridge needed the income more than ever to help his mother make ends meet, Jordan spoke to Stone, who suggested a wise and timely resolution.

He'd heard the *Mount Liberty Journal,* the local weekly newspaper that was always phoning him for arrest reports and confirmation of facts, was about to lose their general clerk and apprentice to a larger paper. The publisher was Saul Houston, an indomitable, crusty presence in the community, and Saul had been about to phone the school to ask for suitable and interested student candidates. Jordan had driven over, presented a folder of Ridge's work and insisted Saul could save himself the search. It turned out he agreed with her.

And so from Monday through Friday, Ridge reported to the *Journal,* which luckily was only the equivalent of a city block from the school. On weekends, Ridge and Kristen helped Jordan prepare for the move that would bring Stone and his niece wholly into her life. Stone helped in the evenings and with the heavy things, but by and large, it was just Jordan and her two helpers, which inevitably kept them discussing writing.

If people would have told Jordan that she would have become a mentor, as well as a wife and step-aunt in the course of a few weeks, she would have told them they had her confused with someone on a TV sitcom or soap opera. Unfortunately there were enough sobering moments to keep her feet planted firmly on the ground.

On Monday, just five days before the wedding, she entered her seventh-period class and knew she'd come upon one of those moments. Jack Nolan's group was surrounding Ridge and Kristen's desks, provoking the young couple.

"C'mon, teacher's pets, tell us when they're getting married. What's wrong with that? It's not as if we asked if they were going on a honeymoon or anything."

"That's what I want to know," Bo Spradlin countered.

"Why?" another taunted, sticking out his belly. "Everything that could happen already has."

Deciding she couldn't have been given a better cue, Jordan cleared her throat loud enough to cause a small panic. "If we're through with the improvisational theater, people, maybe we can get to work?"

The group disbanded willingly enough, but not without some borderline comments and much giggling. Jordan refused to be baited. She knew she held a trump card for the whole issue and planned to use it if necessary.

"Ms. Mills? I have to leave early for a doctor's appointment," Bo Spradlin called from his seat.

"All right, Mr. Spradlin." Jordan eyed the wall clock at the back of the room. "What time?"

"Me too, Ms. Mills," Kenny Hillcrest said before Bo could reply.

"I have an appointment also, Ms. Mills," Jerry Sawyer announced beside Jack Nolan.

Sensing a setup, Jordan crossed her arms. "And what seems to be the ailment, gentlemen?"

"Morning sickness!" they all declared in unison.

Expecting nothing less than this, Jordan found it easy to keep a straight face during the guffaws that followed. It cost her more to ignore Kristen and Ridge, who spun around furious and ready to protect her.

"I hope you didn't stay up all night working on that joke, gentlemen. Although the good news is that if you don't succeed in getting athletic scholarships, you'll certainly be able to get work writing for one of the late-night talk shows. The question is," she added with an amicable smile, "will you be able to graduate from Mount Liberty?"

The room grew silent. "Are you threatening us, Ms. Mills?" Jack Nolan said, looking surprisingly eager for a fight.

"No, I'll leave posturing to you, Mr. Nolan. I explained what I expected from you people the day you entered this class. Nothing has changed. Neither my responsibility to you, nor my expectations for the energy I expend here. If you have a problem with that, we can discuss it during detention. And, yes, folks, your worst nightmare has come true. I'm supervising detention again."

The rest of the class went rather smoothly, all things considered. Jack did make a remark about how a teacher shouldn't be able to teach family, but Jordan and Morris Fields had already discussed that.

"Not that this is any of your business," she said to the class after the remark, "but because of the size of Mount Liberty, there is only one teacher per grade subject. Principal Fields advises me that he will gladly monitor the grades being given in this class, so if there are any doubts or suspicions about validity or favoritism, please feel free to take the matter up with him."

Once school was out, Kristen and Ridge waited only long enough for the rest of the class to leave before rushing to her side.

"They're jerks," Kristen said, giving her a hug.

"They're young," Jordan replied.

"But how are we ever going to get ready Friday!" They already knew Stone had scheduled for a justice of the peace he knew to perform the civil ceremony at five o'clock in the afternoon. "If you have detention, we'll have to kick things back an hour."

"No, we won't," Jordan assured her quietly. "I've talked to Bess Flynn. She's more than willing to take my place. But to ensure that nothing goes wrong, be careful where you talk about this. Not a word to anyone."

"How can I order you a bouquet!" Kristen whispered.

"I can forgo the flowers if it means getting through this without a nervous breakdown."

"How romantic," Kristen grumbled, leaving to accompany Ridge to the *Journal*.

He hadn't said a word to anyone, except to the captain in the Tyler office. But on Friday afternoon, Stone stood outside of Jordan's house and felt sweat pour down his back, despite the mild temperature that was already beginning to slip from the low sixties. There was no sign of the others, and it was a few minutes after three!

What if Jordan had changed her mind about getting married and decided to run after all? He wouldn't blame her if she did. He'd hardly been any help in the past two weeks as they'd prepared for this. There'd been one thing after another taking him away. She might as well be marrying the kids!

Then the white car and the red one sped into the driveway, and he allowed himself to breathe again.

They all looked excited as they raced from the cars, but he had to admit he only had eyes for Jordan. She came to his side, and he immediately angled his head because of his hat to get the kiss she offered.

"Thought you'd stood me up," he murmured.

"Glad to know you were worried."

"I was worried."

She grinned. "Give me two minutes to put my briefcase inside and check my makeup, and I'll be right with you."

She was as good as her word. No sooner did she and Kristen rush inside the house than they came out laughing like kids. Taking her keys, Stone held the passenger door of her car open for her, and the kids slipped into the back seat. Despite the undeniable euphoria of the group, they all looked as if they were better dressed for an arraignment than a wedding, he thought with some glumness. He still wore his cool-weather uniform, the long-sleeved khaki outfit with tie, his badge and gun that he was required to carry at all times. Even the felt hat. Although Kristen wore a preppy blazer over her outfit, both kids were in their school uniform— jeans. Only Jordan looked somewhat festive for the event, although her double-breasted silk suit in a beguiling teal was modest by any standards.

"Anyone besides me nervous as a rookie sky jumper?" he asked.

"You'll do great, Uncle Stone," Kristen declared from behind. Since the three of them had decided they would move into Jordan's house after the wedding, she'd been a wholly new person. "Besides, we memorized your lines, in case you need coaching."

What coaching did he need besides to pray that fate not kick him in the teeth again? To let them do this, have this small corner of happiness they'd carved out for themselves. Jordan looked happy, didn't she? Heaven knew Kristen was.

"There's still time," Jordan said cryptically as the kids got involved in their own conversation.

So she'd been watching him and, as usual, drawing the worst conclusions. He reached across the seat and took hold of her hand. The words would have to wait for when they were alone.

Less than an hour later, they stood before the justice of the peace at the Smith County courthouse. He was a cheerful little man Stone couldn't remember having seen before, but Stone was just grateful that the ladies at the Texas Department of Parks and Wildlife had arranged for someone to be here to marry them. The man deserved a tip for keeping the ceremony short, and apparently Jordan agreed, for when it came time to place his ring on her finger—the slenderest band Jordan could have chosen—he felt her trembling so much, he wondered her knees weren't starting a brushfire.

"... by the power vested in me by the state of Texas, I pronounce you man and wife."

Oblivious of their audience, Stone turned to Jordan and slipped his arms around her. Finally something felt familiar and oh, so right. Apparently she thought so, too, because her lips grew pliant against his, welcoming. He would happily have deepened the kiss into more, but the justice of the peace coughed discreetly, forcing him to abandon desire for responsibility.

Nodding to Ridge, he had the boy—who'd served as his witness—give the man the envelope he'd been holding. Then he watched with a quiet pride as Kristen teased, "Aunt Jordan!" and gave her an enthusiastic hug, almost striking her with the bouquet of white roses she'd been holding for her—the bouquet he'd had waiting here as a surprise.

After the small group had either embraced or shaken hands, Stone gestured them out. "Let's go get something to eat." He could use a drink.

"Can we have champagne, Uncle Stone?" Kristen asked, more cheerful than his sedate bride.

"Nice try, but Jordan can't drink, and you two are underage."

Despite the little groan of disappointment that followed, they had a surprisingly enjoyable dinner, and it was dark by the time they returned to the house. More than ready to be alone with his bride, Stone heard Jordan seeking excuses not to be alone with him.

"Kristen, you've already brought your things over, it's silly not to stay here."

"No, Mrs. Tucker's expecting me, and you two need the time alone. I'll be over sometime tomorrow. Not too early," she drawled. "And then we can help Ridge get his family into our old place."

That was the other revelation. Kristen had vetoed the idea of selling her inheritance once she knew Mrs. Biggs had filed for a divorce on the grounds of desertion. She'd made her uncle agree to rent to the Biggs family for a modest fee that would provide her as good an income as if they'd put her money into an interest-bearing account, but be fair to Mrs. Biggs. As proud as he was of his niece, and as satisfied as he'd been after his talk with Georgia Biggs, who'd seemed a nice lady, he was still concerned that she was linking herself to Ridge too quickly. But there would be time to worry about that later.

After they said a final goodbye, Stone watched Jordan close the door behind the kids. Still holding her flowers, she was lifting them to catch their fragrance once more as she turned to face him. Their gazes met over the ivory blossoms.

"I do adore these," she murmured. "And I was so surprised."

"I'm glad."

"Who chose them?"

He wanted to tease her. They'd been upbeat and cheerful for the kids, and he would have liked nothing better than to see her laugh again for just him. But there was nothing funny about the flowers.

"I did. I thought, 'White for her perfect skin. White for the way the moon looks in her hair. White for those too-brief, flashing smiles. White for the sheets I first laid you across.'"

Her eyes grew wide and bright.

Stone crossed to her. It was dark outside, and with only the kitchen light on, the room had a romantic, seductive feel. Expectation was all but humming around them like a stereo left on and forgotten.

"I'm sure my poetry can't compete with what you've heard before," he said, convinced it was true.

"It's the most wonderful tribute I've ever heard. And you don't have to compete with anyone, Stone Man."

The sound of his nickname allowed him to smile. "Nervous?"

"More like overwhelmed. I feel as if a tornado just set me down. I'm trying to get my bearings. It seems as if I'm fated to play some kind of musical role-model game."

"We are nothing if not a modern family."

"So cynical."

"Maybe a bit worried."

She looked at her flowers again. "I'll try not to disappoint you."

Remarks like that left him with no choice but to touch her, slip his arms around her and draw her close, so that she understood *she* worried for nothing. "Not you. I'm concerned with me disappointing you. Can this come off?" he added, unfastening the clip at her nape. A moment later, her hair fanned out and down her back.

He slipped the adornment into her pocket and combed his hands through the lush silk. "Why don't we go upstairs?" he said, kissing one corner of her mouth and then the other.

"We don't have to do anything, but I have to admit I have been focusing a great deal about spending a whole night with you."

"You have?"

"Mmm-hmm." He added brushing kisses to her earlobes beside the delicate gold loops that were as fine as her wedding band. "Sometimes in my fantasies, we don't get up until seven or even eight and then we make breakfast together."

"Do we get around to eating it?" she asked, looping her arms around his neck.

"Eventually. But it's pretty cold. Not that we notice." He led her toward the stairs.

In her room, *their* room, Stone left the lights off, sat on the bed, placed her bouquet on the nightstand and drew her onto his lap. Taking her mouth with his, he began tasting her the way she and Kristen had patiently and carefully sought all of the delights of their Napoleon pastry during dessert. He'd barely begun to satisfy himself when Jordan gently pushed him back . . . and got up.

"What are you doing?" he demanded.

"Undressing." Sinking to her knees between his legs, she took off his boots and socks, then began unbuckling his belt. His gun was locked away in his truck. He'd done it for her sake, although he'd felt naked from the moment he took it off. But he quickly forgot that as cool air touched his bare skin . . . then she did. Her slightest caress had his abdominal muscles clenching. When he felt her breath on him, he swore.

"Jordan, you little . . ." He swept her up and beside him on the bed. "You've already had dessert, Mrs. Demarest. Now it's my turn."

Chapter Fourteen

Marriage, Jordan decided, could almost be described as heavenly—if not for the intrusion of life.

She discovered she adored the idea of coming home to hugs, kisses and laughter. She found raucous music occasionally interesting, a thousand and one questions stimulating and decision making for a family of three challenging. So did Stone, it seemed. He did everything he could to be there as much as possible—which was virtually *im*possible—or at least make it home at a reasonable hour. For the most part, if they couldn't eat together as a family, he usually got in at an hour where she could keep him company and have a cup of tea while he ate. When he didn't manage that, she would sleep fitfully until she felt his weight sink the mattress and his strong arms slip around her to draw her into the hard, welcoming curve of his body.

If they had been flowers, they would be the hearty summer butterfly weed that lifted its bright orange face to the sun and welcomed whatever the day brought. Much of

Jordan's happiness was for Kristen, who, once she saw how *she* threw herself wholly and completely into her marriage, grew closer to Stone, as well. He, in turn, relaxed with her, because he now had another female's input to guide him. But to Kristen's credit, she was evolving and changing as fast as any of them were, which made her a double pleasure to be around.

Ridge came over whenever his work at the newspaper permitted and he wasn't needed at his new home. Not surprisingly there had yet to be any news of his father. Jordan and Stone had helped Georgia Biggs with her divorce and the move to the Demarest house, as well as with filing for temporary aid from social services for the two younger boys. That didn't begin to make things easy for them, but between the two of them, Georgia and her son had found a serviceable used car, and their lives were gaining a new and marked dignity. And Mrs. Tucker next door, who'd been so distraught that she would have nothing to do when Stone and Kristen moved out, took an instant shine to Brian and Billy, Georgia's nine- and seven-year-olds, leaving Ridge with the first real free time he'd ever known.

When Ridge joined them at the house, Stone teased them that it was a good time to be out checking for hunting licenses because the place became like a salon. The remark startled Jordan, but he was right; the arts were the primary focus of conversation, and books, music and conversation flowed then, which only made the house that much more lively and warm.

Of course, nothing could compare to the nights when she and Stone made love. Afterward they would lie in each other's arms, share the news about their days. She didn't know which one of them started it, but they always tried to pass on something personal, too. A memory from their childhood, although she tried not to speak of hers much because she saw it upset him. But there were treasures uncovered during those nights.

It was then that she learned how wonderful his parents had been. He'd inherited his love of nature from them, and it had been their strong encouragement that had convinced him to try out for the Texas Game Warden Academy after college, and to endure the competitive and grueling training and background investigation that followed. And he'd first discovered how devastating the loss of love could be when his beloved parents and Janine, Kristen's mother, were struck and instantly killed in their vehicle by a drunk driver.

His tragedies had come in groups and violently, first his parents and sister, then his wife and baby. That explained much to Jordan about how he'd earned his nickname and his fear of opening his heart—more than any words could. And if those magic words stayed unspoken between them, Jordan tried not to notice. She was certain that love had its own way of developing for everyone, and that the best and strongest kind came from patience, understanding and a deep and abiding respect. Once the baby arrived, she often dreamed while lying in bed waiting for Stone, the intricate tie that had bound them all together would be complete. And then there would be no more fear of the words. At least that helped with her own fears of all they'd taken on.

What they were attempting wasn't easy by any means. Their schedule remained crazy at best, and sleep was often a compromise. Yet somehow they managed. If outsiders didn't keep interfering, their world would have been . . . just about everything they could have asked for.

But day after day, from one week to the next, there were new tests. There was a local consensus that regardless of whether "the teacher" and "the Stone Man" had "done the right thing" by marrying, they were still too "uppity" and "holier than thou" not to have everything they did or said put under a microscope or philosophically challenged. Consequently, Jordan's contests of wills continued at school, and they were compounded with every inconvenient schedule switch and dreaded supervisory responsibility that Morris Fields could find for her. Fully expecting not to be rehired next year, she began sending out her résumé to other area schools. The promise of an end to this nonsense made classes bearable, and allowed her to face her most challenging students no matter how irreverent they became.

But what hurt her most was that Stone suffered because he was a favorite son who'd chosen the wrong side. Her. As deer season opened, he received several crank calls that led him on wild-goose chases, and another time someone even let the air out of one of his tires in the school parking lot as a prank. However, it was when he got a fake call to investigate a poaching incident and found instead an openly disgruntled parent complaining about the failing grade his son received in Jordan's class that Stone declared he'd reached the end of his patience.

Furious with the stupidity of the man, who didn't even realize that he was a certified police officer, Stone arrested the man for endangering the community by falsifying an emergency. Although he let the horrified man go after a drive to the county jail, he also called Ralph Spradlin to the house. However, even asking for the sheriff's help to put the fear of the law into everyone proved useless.

"I have been warning them," he said with a pained look. "But they aren't listening. Don't be surprised if this doesn't accelerate as the football season reaches its climax. I'm telling you, you'll wake up one morning and your mailbox will be bashed in, yours and the kids' cars will be vandalized and you won't have any witnesses to anything. Jordan, if you could just ease up a bit. Stop pushing so hard."

"Those big lummoxes are one step away from being thugs," she declared. "All I've ever asked them to do is keep their butts in their chairs, their mouths shut and to do their assignments. I will not compromise on their education."

By Thanksgiving week, Jordan had seven members of the football team in detention, and three in danger of failing her class. One of the three was Ralph's own nephew, Bo. One of the seven was Jack Nolan, Jr. Neither Ralph nor Jack Sr. was amused, according to Stone, who had been cornered by Ralph at his courthouse office.

"You know it's not me, Stone," the sheriff said. "It's my brother. Mount Liberty is a small town, and a person's humiliation shows up more here than in other places. Now my sister-in-law has this big shindig planned for after the big Thanksgiving game. What'll they do if your wife keeps Bo from playing?"

"Freeze the leftovers," Stone had replied.

"You're gonna get a bunch of citizens very upset about this," Ralph warned. "There are people coming, do you understand? Important people who will be guests of Jack Sr. to come look at Jack Jr. They may see a place for Bo in their organization. Now, I don't want to put you in a bind—"

"That's exactly what you're trying to do," Stone told him, "and I've stopped listening."

When he got home that night, Jordan had her own stressful story to tell. She'd experienced an equally difficult run-in with Jack Sr. and was still shaken by it.

"He actually cornered me and began yelling at me as I was getting gas. I accidentally dropped the nozzle, and something happened, it malfunctioned. Stone, there was fuel spilling all over the place. Can you imagine what could have happened?" she cried, her arms wrapped protectively over her slightly rounded middle.

Stone was so infuriated, he bolted out of his seat to go have it out with Jack Sr. there and then. Only Jordan and Kristen physically grabbing him stopped him from finding a violent outlet for his fury. Kristen's tears stopped him, too. She was devastated that her long liaison with Jack Jr. was helping to create this mess for the family. It then took both Jordan and Stone to reassure her that none of this was her fault, and that she couldn't take on guilt for something that would have occurred anyway.

* * *

Two nights before Thanksgiving, the weather went ber-
serk as a blue norther blew down from Canada and brought
with it the kind of snow-and-ice storm that Texans liked to
take roll after roll of pictures of, and drove in like ele-
phants on ice skates. Early the next morning, school was
canceled, and though Jordan wasn't sorry to hear that on
the early TV news, she dreaded the mere thought of Stone
being on the road in such conditions.

"I have to go," he told her when he came downstairs and
accepted the mug of hot coffee she handed him. But with his
free hand, he drew her against him and planted a kiss on top
of her head to let her know how much he liked her worrying about him. "In weather like this, the police and sher-
iffs' departments everywhere could be twice their normal
size and still be overwhelmed with calls and emergencies."
Their own phones had rung throughout the night, and no
one had gotten much sleep. Stone had even put the chains
on his truck before going to bed, and weighed down the vehicle with bags of sand, plus added shovels, an ax and a saw
for fallen trees he might come across on the roads.

"And don't think that just because most businesses and
schools are closed throughout the north and east part of the
state that there won't be a few fools out getting themselves
frostbit in some loony attempt to bag a prize buck."

"Idiots," Jordan grumbled, and began inspecting his
clothes. "At least you seem to be wearing enough layers of
warm clothing."

He chuckled as she slid fingers between buttonholes and
beyond waistbands. "Mmm...now I know what expert to
call on when I come home and need help to get all this off."

"You can count on me," she replied, lifting her mouth to
his because she wanted a real kiss.

Within seconds, Stone groaned and set his mug down.
"Mercy, woman...you are one temptation after another."

Then he wrapped both arms around her and kissed her with the same unbridled passion they'd shared last night.

"Wow!" Kristen whistled as she froze in the middle of the living room. "I guess I'd better wear my earphones to bed again."

Stone swore under his breath, and Jordan muffled her laughter by pressing her face into his chest.

"Kids," he muttered. But before he released her, he whispered into her ear, "To be continued."

"I'll hold you to that," she replied in kind. Collecting her pleasantly scattered wits, she concentrated on finishing packing him several sausages and biscuits that he could eat whenever he got hungry throughout the morning, plus the large thermos of steaming coffee.

After giving them both a good-morning kiss and playfully rubbing Jordan's belly to "see if she grew during the night," as the teen always teased, Kristen peered out the window. "It's still coming down."

"My niece the meteorologist," Stone drawled. But his gaze was tender.

Kristen wrinkled her nose at him good-naturedly, and poured herself a cup of coffee in one of the porcelain cup-and-saucer sets, the way Jordan liked to drink hers. It was one of many habits she'd taken on from her, and Jordan was as touched as she was flattered by what that meant.

"Do you think they'll cancel the game?" Kristen asked, adding the milk and sugar Jordan skipped in her tea or coffee.

"Wouldn't that be poetic justice," Jordan murmured, casting Stone an amused, wry glance.

He nodded. "Less expensive, too. The temperatures are supposed to stay below freezing through the weekend, so you know how many wrecks there'll be even if the county and state road departments get sand on all the highways and farm-to-market roads leading to the stadium. Then that football field will need to be resodded because it won't stay frozen long with all that testosterone burning through the snow and ice."

"That's how I want my tax dollars spent," Jordan said, zipping shut the thermal luncheon sack she'd bought for him.

With a sigh, Stone finished the last gulp of his coffee and headed toward the front closet for his down jacket and hat. Jordan followed with the thermal sack.

"Do you think there's a chance you'll be home for lunch?"

"It's a wonderful thought, but I can't promise."

"We'll be in the kitchen all day preparing for tomorrow, so I'll start a pot of vegetable soup, too, just in case."

"I can smell it already," he said with a smile as he put on his hat.

He looked so handsome, so dear, that Jordan's eyes filled unexpectedly. He saw it before she could blink away the tears.

"Hey, what's this?" he murmured, stroking her hair.

She tried to joke it away. "What can I say, I'm pregnant." But she hugged him tight because an awful sense of foreboding had suddenly overwhelmed her. "Promise me you'll be extra, extracareful?"

"Only if you'll promise me not to wear yourself out," he replied quietly, placing a hand on her abdomen.

His touch was far different than Kristen's had been, and like the look he gave her before kissing her goodbye spoke of all the things he never voiced about the baby.

"I wouldn't think of it," she said, trying to put all the messages she could into her smile. "I have a hot date tonight."

"And don't you forget it."

But when he was gone and she and Kristen waved from the side window, the foreboding returned. Even Kristen picked up on it.

"Are you feeling okay?"

Not wanting to worry her, she'd forced herself to beam. "Just trying to reorganize tomorrow's menu in my mind."

"Well, since you promised Uncle Stone that soup, you'd better start with that, and I'll peel and peel and peel apples for your pie Uncle Stone loves so much."

The joking helped redirect her attention. They did have a great deal to do, since their ambitious decision to throw their first party. Tomorrow Ridge and his family were coming to Thanksgiving dinner. They'd also invited the widow, Mrs. Tucker, as well as Saul Houston, who was a lifelong bachelor and had shown great support and kindness to Ridge.

"But how's everyone going to get here?" Kristen said, voicing a worry that Jordan had, too.

"If it's too bad for Ridge to manage the roads, I'm sure your uncle can get through in the truck. We'll deal with that challenge when the time comes."

Apparently it wasn't all that bad yet, because Ridge surprised them a few hours later by pulling into their driveway bearing a freshly made carrot cake from Mrs. Tucker, and his mother's sweet-potato pie. After taking a break to listen to his news about the road conditions and the power lines he'd seen down due to the buildup of ice, Jordan urged them back to work.

"We'd better get as much done as possible in case we lose ours, too. Somehow I don't think anyone's going to find a half-baked anything too tasty. Ridge, you're drafted. You start chopping all those pecans for the tassies, and that will give Kristen the time to roll out the pastry dough for the shells and get them browned."

"You'll wish you stayed home," Kristen teased. "We can be awful slave drivers."

"I don't mind a bit."

Jordan couldn't help but notice the secret look the two teenagers shared. So, when Stone did arrive home shortly after noon, she sent the teens for a walk up the long driveway to put the mail in the box that she'd forgotten earlier.

She knew exactly how special that time alone could be in a young romance.

It was special in a more mature romance, too, she mused as Stone joined her at the stove and nuzzled her ear. "How's it been so far?" she asked, barely able to focus on giving the soup one last stirring.

"Dangerous enough to get stubborn people into some real trouble, but not so bad if you take it slow and don't panic." He told her about the pickup he'd watched go off the road near Lake Hawkins and slide into the lake. "Fortunately I was right behind him and could throw the guy a line before the truck went under."

Jordan shut off the stove and spun around to hug Stone. This was exactly the kind of thing she had been worried about. But she knew better than to voice her fears to him. This was his job, and she'd married him fully aware of what she was getting into.

"Okay?" he murmured against her hair.

"Mmm. Just terribly proud of you."

"Jordan . . ."

He was going to kiss her. No, not only that, she thought, seeing the stark emotion on his face. Her heart began pounding as she saw some deeper intent in him.

But even as he began to speak, they heard the screams from outside. Then the front door burst open, and a gasping Kristen stumbled inside.

"Uncle Stone! Come quick! A car's crashed on the curve, and we think it's Mrs. Nolan!"

Chapter Fifteen

Jordan reached for the phone even as her gaze locked with Stone's. "I'm calling 911. You go on ahead."

He lingered only a second, his eyes sending her an intimate message. Then he ran to snatch up his heavy jacket and hurry out the door after Kristen.

Before the door finished closing, Jordan had spun back to the phone because the connection was made and the Emergency operator had begun to ask for information. As soon as she reported the incident, its location and the fact that Stone was already on the scene, Jordan hung up and hurried for her own jacket.

Precipitation was still falling—now it was more ice than anything else, and that wasn't good news. Why on earth people would be driving in this stuff when they should be home with loved ones readying for the holiday was beyond her. If it was Megan Nolan...she didn't want to think about that. Good Lord, the woman was due to have her baby any day now.

Doubting she would get her car up the driveway, let alone to the accident site, without getting stuck, and not wanting to create her own traffic jam for when emergency vehicles arrived, Jordan decided against taking her car. Instead, she cut a diagonal path across her property and then climbed the rise to the road. Her jogging shoes and thick socks were soaked by the time she made it to the top, and she was breathless. The latter made her reaction all the more difficult to control when she spotted the accident site.

Megan Nolan's car had done more than slide off the road. It had gone airborne off the highest point of the hill, and shot straight into the dense woods only yards from the road. Now it sat like a large blue bird on a precarious nest of pines and hardwood limbs.

"Dear heaven . . ." she gasped as she joined Stone, Kristen and Ridge.

The four of them stood looking up at the stranded car. Stone had been studying the situation, trying to figure out a way to reach its occupants.

"The good news is that the engine stalled," he said after circling the site. "The bad news is that those very pine tree branches which buffeted her fall aren't going to hold a car that size. Especially if the occupant or occupants start moving around in there."

Jordan felt sick to her stomach at the mere thought of witnessing that. "Is it Megan?"

"Look at the license plate."

It did indeed read NOLAN2.

"I can see her blond hair," he added, "but what's disturbing is that she isn't moving."

Jordan laid a hand on Stone's sleeve. "Oh, God. Stone, her baby's due any day. What if she's in labor? What if she's not breathing?"

Before he could respond, they heard a young voice cry out for help.

"That's Jeffrey!" Kristen gasped, clutching her throat.

The boy's shout was followed by the car shifting slightly and limbs cracking. Inside, the boy screamed louder.

"Kristen, run over to the far side of the car and call to him to keep still!" Stone snapped. He then motioned to Ridge, and they ran to his truck.

"We can't wait for the emergency vehicles," he said to the boy. "In this weather, there's no telling where they are and how long it'll take for them to get here."

Ridge nodded. "I'll help any way you need me to, sir."

When Jordan saw them bring out heavy ropes, her heart began pounding with renewed fear. "What are you going to do?"

"Get up there and get them out."

She couldn't seem to get air into her lungs fast enough. "You can't! You're too heavy!"

As she grabbed the sleeve of his jacket, he wheeled around and grabbed her in return. "Jordan, think! I either go up or that car comes down. It's my job!"

She knew he was right, and she didn't want him *not* to help. But... "I'm sorry. I'm just frightened," she whispered, praying he wouldn't hate her for confessing that.

He slipped off one glove and touched her cheek. "I'll be fine if you give me something to hang on to." When she looked dazed at him, he said more quietly, "Will you tell me you love me? I know you do."

What she saw in his eyes filled her with so much emotion, she could have sworn that there was only air beneath her feet. "Stone... you love me?"

"Finally figured it out, huh?"

Although he tried to make light of it, there was a catch in his voice. "When?"

"A good while. Maybe that first night. I don't know. But when I get down from there," he said, nodding to the car above them, "I'd like nothing better than to hear you say the same thing back to me."

"I do love you," she whispered back at him. "I don't want to wait. I love you."

She would have said it again, but he kissed her hard and fast. Before she recovered, he was heading for the nearest sturdy tree to the car.

"Ridge! What are you—?"

At Kristen's cry, Jordan turned to see the young man climbing a tree on the other side of the car.

"Good idea. Thanks!" Stone called to him, seeing the boy had another rope over his shoulder. But before he or Ridge got any farther up the tree, the back door of the car opened and Jeffrey Nolan cried out.

"Help! Help me!"

His frantic impulse had a violent reaction on the car's position in the tree. The child yelled in terror.

"Talk to him!" Stone called to Ridge. "Tell him he has to stay absolutely still, damn it!"

Ridge nodded and began to speak with quiet assurance as he climbed closer. For his part, Stone had gotten high enough to see inside the car from the driver's side. He glanced below to Jordan.

"She's bleeding from her forehead, but she seems more dazed than unconscious."

Jordan watched with growing dread as Stone then looped his rope over a higher branch and tied it around his waist. Then he threw the other end down to her and Kristen. "Wind it around the trunk of a tree, and get ready to pull in case I slip. Wind, not tie! You'll have to let us down if I get hold of her."

Were they strong enough to do that? Jordan could read Kristen's worried look and saw her glance toward her stomach.

"We have to," she whispered to the frightened girl.

Above them, the driver's door opened. "Stone? Help me! My baby's coming!"

"Stay still, Mrs. Nolan. Any abrupt movement is going to endanger you and your boy. We're going to get Jeffrey out first. It'll only be a minute."

Ridge had the better, sturdier branches on his side of the car. Nevertheless, it was far more than a minute before he could reach the boy and get young Jeffrey to trust him enough to reach beyond the car for his hand, then to step out onto the branch.

"Have him get onto your back!" Stone shouted.

There were some terrifying moments as Jeffrey panicked at the sound of sirens. Hoping it might be a fire engine with a ladder, they were admittedly disappointed to see only Sheriff Ralph Spradlin with Mount Liberty's police, as well as Jack Nolan, Sr. One look at Jack Nolan's face, and Jordan could see his shock and terror. Despite their personal conflicts, she felt an inevitable compassion for him.

"I'll take over from here, Mrs. Demarest," the sheriff said, the first to slip and slide over to where she and Kristen held Ridge's rope. He quickly took the pressure off both her and Kristen by grasping the rope himself.

"Thank you, Sheriff. But is there anyone else coming? We're worried the limbs under the car aren't going to hold much longer."

"They have more than weight working against them," Ralph said, narrowing his eyes as he quickly glanced at the darkening sky. "The temperature's dropping again, and if it gets any colder, those pine limbs will start snapping with or without anyone on them. As for your question ... Ah! That's the volunteer fire department," he said as another siren could be heard in the distance. But he shook his head as he looked around him. "No way we'll be able to get it down into this draw without sinking it beyond the axles, though."

Jack Nolan grabbed at his sleeve. "You think I care about a truck getting stuck? You do what you have to do to save my family, Spradlin!"

The older man looked from the hand on his jacket to the mayor. "Let go, Jack. And back off. Looks to me as if we have half the problem solved," he said, easing on the rope as Ridge began climbing down. "I might add . . . you might pay . . . attention . . . to who's risking their own safety . . . for your family's. Interesting, no?"

Although there was a look of chagrin on the mayor's face, he didn't respond. As soon as Ridge was far enough down, Jack Sr. ran to the tree and lifted his son off Ridge's back.

Kristen ran, too, barely beating the volunteers from the volunteer fire department, who surrounded the boy and clapped him on the back.

As happy as Jordan was for them, her attention turned to Stone, and she hurried to the driver's side again, along with several others. Because they heard another series of cracks, alternate methods of getting Megan Nolan down were abandoned for Stone's directives. He tied the rope under her arms and signaled the firemen on the other end to let her down. Just as they were about to start, there was a horrible crystalline sound, and then the luxury sedan crashed through the remaining branches. The force of the fall jerked Megan from the car, and screaming, she swung like a pendulum. At the same time, Stone was yanked off balance.

Jordan watched in horror as he tried desperately to catch at any branch, but one after the other they splintered, dropping him, dropping him. . . .

"No!"

Jordan began running before the sedan hit the ground, which was probably why someone snatched her back. But she fought blindly to break free. Succeeding, she passed the firemen who caught hold of Megan and lowered her to a waiting stretcher, and tumbled past the downed car into a ravine where she saw Stone lying on his back.

"Stone! Oh, God . . . oh, God, please . . ."

She crawled on all fours the last few feet and thrust away broken branches and pine cones to get at him. She never saw a more wondrous sight than when he opened his eyes and swore.

"Faulty trap door," he muttered.

She burst into laughter or tears—she wasn't sure which. After insisting he stay still a moment to make sure he hadn't broken anything, she helped him sit up and brushed the rest of the woods off him.

"Oh, Stone, your poor face," she whispered, wincing at the blood already streaking down his forehead, across his cheek and down his chin.

He touched the worst—close to his last wound—and inspected his fingers. "If I don't start being more careful, sweetheart, you're going to be married to Frankenstein's monster."

Jordan wrapped her arms around his neck. "I'm so proud of you," she whispered, kissing him with all of her heart.

"Me? You! What were you trying to do, take the shortcut under that car to reach me before I hit?" He hugged her fiercely. "It was like a slow-motion nightmare. Medic! Come check my wife!"

"Hush! You're the one who needs medical attention."

The two volunteers who came down the slope helped them both to their feet and assisted them up the hill. By the time they reached the top, they saw an emergency medical vehicle had arrived along with a few other law-enforcement vehicles, and Megan Nolan was being lifted into the ambulance.

Leaving his son for a moment, Jack Nolan approached them. He looked pale and not quite in control. "You have no reason to bother speaking to me, but I wanted to say thank you. Thank you for what you did for my wife and son."

"We were glad to be here when they needed us," Stone replied matter-of-factly.

"Please pass on my gratitude to the Biggs boy, as well."

"His name is Ridge . . . and he's right beside you."

The mayor turned as Ridge and Kristen joined them. Quietly, humbly the shaken man extended his hand. "Thank you. For everything."

Ridge eyed the well-manicured hand before giving him his filthy one. "You're welcome, sir."

As the senior Nolan ran to scoop up his son and follow the ambulance, Jordan stood with her family and watched. "Dare we hope things will change?" she murmured.

"It's close enough to Christmas to be a viable wish," Stone replied. He hugged her closer. "How about we go find someone with a needle and some thread so we can get home and warm up?"

Stone earned nine stitches for his bravery. By the time they returned home, Saul Houston telephoned with the news that Megan Nolan had given birth to a seven-pound-seven-ounce girl, whom it appeared Megan insisted they call Jordana Kristen Nolan. Saul informed them that he would be having Ridge write the article on the accident and rescue.

Thanksgiving was a frantic blur, not only due to the weather, but the company that invaded their house. Due to his injuries, Stone's fellow game warden for the county, Hap Conroe, took over his responsibilities for the day. That allowed Stone to share the entire day's celebrations with their guests. And what a group they had. The Biggses, Saul, Mrs. Tucker, a florist who delivered an exquisite centerpiece from the Jack Nolan family. Ralph Spradlin dropped off one of his wife's pies, a bottle of Stone's favorite Scotch and proceeded to apologize to excess, until Stone opened the bottle, poured him a drink and ordered him not to say another word until it was gone.

But it was Saul who delivered the day's nicest surprise. After reading only the first draft of Ridge's article, he announced to Georgia that he finally knew what to do with his life savings. He was going to finance her son's education.

It seemed that nothing could top that, but on Monday when Jordan entered the school building only steps behind Kristen and Ridge, she was startled by thunderous applause. A salute to the football team because they'd won their game? she mused, still preoccupied with her memories of the weekend. Then she saw that the students who were lining the hallway were applauding Ridge as he and Kristen walked to their homeroom. Suddenly Jack Nolan, Jr., stepped out and offered his hand, and the applause became a roar.

"All right, all right," Morris Fields finally declared, although he was flushed and looking very pleased himself. "We still have a few weeks before Christmas break, and plenty of work to do. Let's move on to class now."

"And would you believe," Jordan said later that night while in Stone's arms, "old Mrs. Graves—remember the grouchy old lady next to the school that I told you about?— she even stopped me as I was leaving this afternoon to pass on a box of her homemade canned fruits and vegetables for Mrs. Biggs and a loaf of her homemade multigrain bread. She'd read Saul's article and said she'd been moved to tears by the family's hardship. Talk about having heard everything. She knew perfectly well about the Biggs family because she was one of those who wanted Ridge fired from the market!"

"Now, now..." Stone kissed her on her forehead. "As long as people come around, what's the big deal if they take a shortcut or two?"

"Or three or ten?" Jordan mimicked, less willing to let the crafty old crocodile off the hook so easily. But Stone's tender strokes on her back and his equally tender kisses had their usual effect, and before long he had her all but purring.

"Better?"

"You should let me enjoy my occasional growl," she sighed, teasing the crinkly hair at the base of his throat. I've heard pregnant women are supposed to acquire at least a few eccentric indulgences."

"I'll let you eat cold spaghetti for breakfast, how's that?"

"You already have a niece who does that. Yuck."

"She learned it from me. Comes from late nights working and not having the energy to make anything decent."

"Poor darling," Jordan crooned, tilting her head to kiss his bandaged chin. "I promise I'll always get up no matter the hour and make you something if you'll promise to tolerate that I'm never going to be quite the sweet-natured thing you'd like me to be."

"I love you because you're you," Stone replied, running his hands all the way to her hips and drawing her closer there, too.

"I like the sound of *that*." Jordan sighed. "I like the *feel* of that."

Stone gently eased her beneath him. "I was rather hoping you would." Then he kissed her the way he always did when he got this close. "Ah, love...don't you know by now that everything's going to be fine...just— Just fine."

"Uh-uh...perfect."

Raising himself on his elbows, Stone angled his head to nuzzle her already taut nipple. "I think being pregnant with my son is making you more sensitive than ever."

"Your son!" She pushed at him to see his face. "What makes you think we're going to have a boy?"

"I dreamed it last night. And I never dream. At least, not that I can remember."

Not sure if he was teasing or what, Jordan stretched to turn on the lamp. "You're serious," she whispered, scanning each feature.

He smiled, looking unashamed of the moisture that seeped from the corners of his eyes. "Yup. He's going to be as big as me and as blond and gorgeous as you. Want to know what his name is?"

"He *told* you his name?"

"Blue."

Jordan winced. "What! Stone, I think you got a concussion falling out of that tree. I would never name a child of mine something so ridiculous as—"

"Did I forget to mention that he's going to have my eyes?"

As quickly as they'd come, gone were her fleeting thoughts of a more noble literary appellation. Just as quickly, she found herself hypnotized by the love and desire in Stone's wonderful eyes, haunted no more, and overwhelmed by the power and masculinity of the body possessing hers. She licked her lips. "Well...I guess I'll love him no matter what."

Stone lowered his head. "And me?"

"Without a doubt. And with all my heart."

"Then Blue's gonna be one lucky boy."

Their soft chuckles mellowed into sighs of pleasure and whispers of encouragement, and neither one of them bothered turning off the light for a long, long time.

* * * * *

FORTUNE'S *Children™*

Bestselling Author
LINDA TURNER

Continues the twelve-book series—FORTUNE'S CHILDREN—
in November 1996 with Book Five

THE WOLF AND THE DOVE

Adventurous pilot Rachel Fortune and traditional Native American
doctor Luke Greywolf set sparks off each other the minute they met.
But widower Luke was tormented by guilt and vowed never to love
again. Could tempting Rachel heal Luke's wounded heart so they
could share a future of happily ever after?

MEET THE FORTUNES—a family whose legacy is greater than riches.
Because where there's a will...there's a *wedding!*

*A CASTING CALL TO
ALL FORTUNE'S CHILDREN FANS!*
If you are truly fortunate,
you may win a trip to
Los Angeles to audition for
Wheel of Fortune®. Look for
details in all retail Fortune's Children titles!

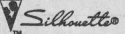

As seen on TV!
Free Gift Offer

With a Free Gift proof-of-purchase from any Silhouette® book,
you can receive a beautiful cubic zirconia pendant.

This gorgeous marquise-shaped stone is a genuine cubic
zirconia—accented by an 18" gold tone necklace.
(Approximate retail value $19.95)

Send for yours today...
compliments of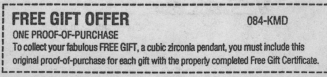

To receive your free gift, a cubic zirconia pendant, send us one original proof-of-purchase, photocopies not accepted, from the back of any Silhouette Romance™, Silhouette Desire®, Silhouette Special Edition®, Silhouette Intimate Moments® or Silhouette Yours Truly™ title available in August, September, October, November and December at your favorite retail outlet, together with the Free Gift Certificate, plus a check or money order for $1.65 U.S./$2.15 CAN. (do not send cash) to cover postage and handling, payable to Silhouette Free Gift Offer. We will send you the specified gift. Allow 6 to 8 weeks for delivery. Offer good until December 31, 1996 or while quantities last. Offer valid in the U.S. and Canada only.

Free Gift Certificate

Name: _____

Address: _____

City: _____ State/Province: _____ Zip/Postal Code: _____

Mail this certificate, one proof-of-purchase and a check or money order for postage and handling to: SILHOUETTE FREE GIFT OFFER 1996. In the U.S.: 3010 Walden Avenue, P.O. Box 9077, Buffalo NY 14269-9077. In Canada: P.O. Box 613, Fort Erie, Ontario L2Z 5X3.

FREE GIFT OFFER   084-KMD
ONE PROOF-OF-PURCHASE
To collect your fabulous FREE GIFT, a cubic zirconia pendant, you must include this
original proof-of-purchase for each gift with the properly completed Free Gift Certificate.

084-KMD-R

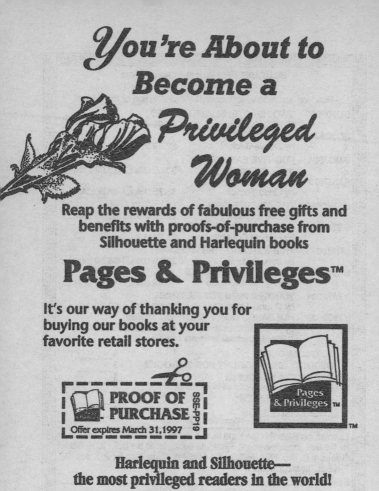